Storm Path

Storm Path

Hadley Hoover

Writers Club Press
San Jose New York Lincoln Shanghai

Storm Path

Writers Club Press
an imprint of iUniverse, Inc.

For information address:
iUniverse, Inc.
5220 S. 16th St., Suite 200
Lincoln, NE 68512
www.iuniverse.com

Cover photo by Kendall Web Graphics.

ISBN: 0-595-24977-9

Printed in the United States of America

To my one-and-only Love—thanks for the ready, steady hand to hold in every storm we face.

Annie-Ran: you write the music that first-graders sing! Thanks.

To friends who've survived storms as harsh as what Helen faces in this novel: This story isn't *about* you, it's *for* you. I salute how you've never lost sight of *North*.

Chapter 1

With his nose brushing against the door's window, Bob Marshall peered into Joy Jenkins' first-grade classroom and murmured, "Hmmm." Throughout his career as school principal, *hmmm* had proven to be a useful word. When a child spun a tall tale of innocence in a schoolyard tussle, an abrupt *hmmm* meant *Yeah, right!* If parents fussed about a teacher's grading system, a drawn-out *hmmm* and slow nod said *I hear you*—yet made no promises. Repeated *hmmms* accompanied by eye contact in the school cafeteria allowed him to communicate—and still eat lunch.

Standing in the hallway, he employed the *Well, whaddya know?* sliding-scale version of *hmmm*. What he saw inside mystified him. A crazy quilt of mismatched bed sheets covered the entire mid-section of the sunlit room. Spring-type clothespins connected the expanse of fabric and books stacked on desktops anchored it in place. The billowing canopy rose and fell in random motions like a volcano churning below the earth's surface.

"That was quick!" Janeen Woods, the school secretary, said when Bob returned to the office.

"Whatever is going on in Room 112 is exactly why Fred Becker wants a last-day-of-school article on Joy for the *Prairie Rose Chronicle*."

"What's happening?" Janeen spun away from her computer.

"Not sure; desks are pushed against the walls and there's a whooshing sound beneath some tent-thing."

"That's their hot-air balloon! I loaned Joy a couple of bed sheets for it."

Bob's eyebrows arched. "Hmmm?"

Having worked with Bob Marshall for over a decade, Janeen was no stranger to the *hmmm* lexicon. "The first graders have studied what Prairie Rose looks like from the ground and the sky. So their last-day-of-school activity is a hot-air balloon trip!"

Bob nodded thoughtfully. "Joy has been a marvelous teacher for twenty-two years. She leaves mighty big shoes for Amy Carter to fill. Give me a buzz when Fred gets here, okay?"

In Room 112, Joy sat cross-legged on a mat beneath the makeshift canopy. Several fans set at high speed created the requisite ballooning appearance Bob had observed. Appropriate sound effects from a cassette player provided a realistic experience for fifteen bright-eyed children.

Joy glanced around the circle and felt a pang of something between regret and relief. For nearly two decades, she had welcomed children to this room in the PRAIRIE ROSE PUBLIC SCHOOL. The crucial kindergarten year gave them a nudge past their initial fears; but first grade was the launching pad, the foundation, the linchpin.

The awesomeness of her responsibility to each incoming class always weighed heavily on her mind. For years, that realization had provided restless nights during the final weeks of summer. But once the bell rang on the first day of school, she was *home* and fully confident in her work.

Now it was ending. At the end of the day, Joy Jenkins would join the segment of humanity for whom the term *new year* meant January 1, not a floating day in early autumn.

"Missus Jenkins?" A familiar voice broke through her brief reverie.

"Yes, Sally?"

"I think we should sing *My Little Compass.*"

"That's a good idea!" Joy smiled at the raven-haired girl.

"Missus Jenkins, will you tell your class next year that we wrote that song?" Todd blurted out.

"Todd, did you forget?" Sandy gasped. "Missus Jenkins is done teaching. We're the last class she'll ever have!" She turned to Joy. "That makes us special, doesn't it, Missus Jenkins?"

"Every class is special in some way, Sandy, but you're right, Todd—I'll always remember this class wrote the compass song."

Todd scowled at Sandy. "I know you aren't going to be *our* teacher, Missus Jenkins, but who will be my little brother's first-grade teacher?" His glower changed to confusion.

"Missus Carter will teach in this room, starting in September. She and her husband are moving here this summer. She has taught first-grade for several years in Rochester, Minnesota. Remember when we found Rochester on the map and wrote her a letter?"

"I thought she was going to be a substitute teacher," Todd said morosely.

The door opened. From her place on the floor, Joy saw two sets of men's shoes. To prevent the children's distraction, she quickly said, "Sally had a good idea—let's sing!" She pulled her pitch pipe out of her pocket and blew a note. Fifteen index fingers shot up in readiness to act out the song, and a chorus of young voices joined together in a simple melody:

I use my little compass to help me find my way.
If I get lost, I pull it out any time of day.
When I see where the needle goes,
That is where I'll point my nose.
Remember, north never moves!

Bob whispered to Fred, "If you were a TV reporter instead of a newspaperman, you'd have a good sound-bite! I don't want to interrupt them, so I'll catch you later."

Fred adjusted his camera to the classroom light. The newshound in him twitched his nose at the scent of a marvelous front-page shot for the next weekly issue of the local newspaper.

The song ended and Joy said, "Look, children, someone is floating up on the south side of our balloon. Hello, Mister Becker! Did you just parachute out of an airplane?"

Fred quickly got into the spirit. His knees cracked, but he gamely crawled in beside Todd. "Where am I? I'm all discombobulated!"

"Who can figure out what 'discombobulated' means?" Joy asked. Several attempted answers:

"Goofed up?"

"Lost?"

"Good job figuring out a new word! Petey, what could we tell Mister Becker to help him feel less dis-com-bob-u-la-ted?" The children carefully processed the dissected syllables.

Petey promptly replied, "You're in a hot-air balloon basket flying over Prairie Rose. That's in the northwest corner of North Dakota."

"Thanks, Petey," Fred said. "Back on earth, I'm a newspaperman. This seems like a good place to get a story. So, enjoy your trip and I'll ride along and do my job."

Todd studied him solemnly. "You could write about how Missus Jenkins won't ever be a teacher again."

"That's a good idea," Fred replied with matching somberness. "Tell me, did the whole class help build this?" He pointed at the sheet overhead.

The question stymied Todd, but Ellen leaned forward and said firmly, "No; it comes from the World-Famous Jenkins' Hot-Air Balloon Factory."

That's when Fred realized that for the children seated on mats, it wasn't merely bed sheets pinned together. They truly *were* in a basket floating in the clouds. When Joy ignited her students' imaginations, they blazed like any flame beneath an actual hot-air balloon.

The next hour kept Fred's pen and camera busy capturing how a gifted teacher incorporated the full range of lessons into one activity and yet gave it all the sizzle an end-of-the-year party deserved. Fred found himself caught up in the adventure.

When the children landed back in the classroom, Joy called the office on the intercom. As prearranged, Janeen escorted the group outside for recess. In their absence, Fred helped Joy dismantle the balloon and shift the desks back into place.

Returning with much teasing and giggling, the children began the last-day rituals of cleaning out desks, stacking books on shelves, and filling garbage cans with the scraps and accumulation of a year in Room 112. Conversation flowed freely:

"Missus Jenkins, here's my missing story about rabbits! It was on the last page of my tablet. Will you please grade it?"

"Hannah, you've *still* got all your valentines in your desk? Valentine's Day was *years* ago!"

"Ned, you give me back my compass! I earned it from Missus Jenkins' prize bucket."

"I'm going to leave this sucker for the kid who sits here next year. I only licked it on one side."

Joy's egg timer rang, signaling the end of the day. She raised a familiar basket high in the air and the children cheered. Room 112's traditional Friday dismissal pattern provided a fair way for each child to have a special moment with the teacher, rather than jostling to leave. The children squeezed their eyes closed and each removed a laminated numbered card before passing the basket along. "Who has number one today?" Joy asked.

That child picked up a backpack and made his way to the classroom door where Joy waited. "You'll have fun this summer with your new puppy, won't you, Joey? Come show me when he knows how to walk on a leash!" She gave the boy a quick hug and helped shift the straps on his backpack.

"Who drew number two?" Ellen picked up her bag and walked slowly to the door. Joy said, "In just a few days, I'll have a piano at my house so come play your piano piece for me before your recital, okay?"

Ellen's face lit up. *Even though Missus Jenkins won't be my teacher anymore, I'll still see her!* Relieved, the child flung her arms around her teacher and received a loving embrace in return.

Each successive student soaked up Joy's personal words of encouragement or praise and comments about taking swimming lessons or visits to cousins or grandparents or upcoming fishing trips. The twelfth child received a slip of paper from Joy. "Here's how to spell 'discombobulated,' Jillie. I could tell you liked that big word!"

"That does it!" Joy's eyes were suspiciously bright in the vacated room. "Did you get enough for an article, Fred? There's not much teaching on the last day."

"More than enough for a good article. And I beg to differ with your assessment of today. I saw plenty of education in action, and evidence much occurred over the past nine months. Any second thoughts about retiring?" he asked nonchalantly.

Joy shook her head even before her words began. "No, I sense it's time for me to leave the classroom, even though I'm only fifty. I'm not sure what lies ahead, but I am delighted to turn the keys to this room over to someone of Amy Carter's caliber."

"What are you going to do, Joy? In the fall, I mean. You're used to summers out of the classroom, but when the first day of school rolls around, what will you do then?"

"Be Al's wife and Dave's mom?" Joy suggested impishly. "Though after putting up with me in that role all summer and realizing it will now go on *forever*, they may beg me to return to teaching when summer ends!"

Fred laughed, but quickly turned serious again. "Seeing you in action today made me realize what a significant role teachers play. That's what I hope to communicate in this article. You've touched a lot of lives, Joy."

Joy shifted a half-packed box from a bookcase to her desktop. "Whatever a person's occupation is, they owe it to themselves to do the best they can. It's true of every job, but if teachers don't live by that principle, kids suffer."

After a few posed shots, Fred packed up his gear and left Joy to conduct her final tasks. She never liked the way a classroom looked on the last day of school. It always reminded her of Emily Dickinson's poetic lines:...*the sweeping up the heart and putting love away...*

"Hey, teacher!" A deep masculine voice rumbled through the room. Al Jenkins lounged against the doorframe and snapped a picture, resting the camera against his broad chest as the flash faded.

"Hey, yourself, postmaster! I'm not sure how that picture will turn out. I'm a bit gloomy."

"Tough day?"

"Emotional. I didn't cry...yet...but I surely could have, several times."

"Second thoughts?"

She tipped her head. "That's what Fred asked. It's always hard to say goodbye to the kids. Okay, I'm ready. I'm glad we took a load home earlier this week; we can easily carry what's left." Crosshatching the box flaps, she slid it across the desktop toward Al. "This is full of bed sheets, so it may be heavy; sorry. The two on top are Janeen's; I'll drop them off in the office when I turn in my keys."

"Do you want any more pictures of your classroom?"

"Not looking so desolate—I have plenty from when it looked real."

She picked up two canvas bags, the wicker basket holding the numbered cards, egg timer, and her purse. Scanning the room with a practiced glance, she flicked off the light with her elbow and smiled tremulously at Al. He shifted the box to his hip and leaned down to kiss the lips he knew so well after three decades of loving one woman. "Hold it, Missus Jenkins! My number from the Goodbye Basket was sixteen. Does it earn me a smooch with the teacher?" He waggled his eyebrows and puckered up in readiness for more.

Joy laughed. "Well, there's smooching, and there's *smooching*. Put that box down and I'll teach you the difference, ol' Number Sixteen!"

Ten minutes later, they walked down the echoing hallway bumping hips to the beat of Al whistling the Stylistics' hit, *Let's Put It All Together.* When they mentally reached the words *my lips are meant to kiss you*, tradition demanded a kiss. Despite being loaded to the gills, Al leaned in for a loud and lusty smacker.

From behind the office counter, Janeen noted lipstick on Al's ear and what looked like a whisker burn on Joy's chin, but accepted Joy's ring of school keys and the return of the bed sheets without comment on these intimate details. "I'll bet I don't need to tell you to enjoy retirement, huh, Joy?" she teased as she checked Room 112 off the list. "But remember, just because you don't teach anymore doesn't mean you can't drop in—you *know* you'll miss the teachers' lounge coffee!"

Joy laughed. "Oh, yeah, especially the days Bob makes it! If we ever need tar for our driveway, I'll give you a buzz!"

The door to the schoolhouse closed behind them with a distinct *click*. Al intoned with seriousness befitting a world event, "This just in: at 4:30 PM on May 17, Joy Jenkins leaped over a giant hurdle in life. Tell us, what is behind your early retirement?"

Faking a wide-eyed and smiley expression, Joy drawled, "Ah *am* getting a *pee-yan-o* and *Ah* just *don't* think it's *right* to assume responsibility for something of *that* magnitude and then just *leave* it home all alone." She batted her eyelashes furiously. "Ah plan to spend the *rest* of maw life giving maw sweet lil ol' *pee-yan-o*—oh, and maw *handsome* husband and our *wonderful* son—all the *luuuv* and attention they deserve."

"Whew, I'm glad Dave and I made it onto your list! About this piano…remember, it's older than dirt and most likely not in tune."

"The age is part of the charm—and I already have the phone number of Amber Larson's piano tuner."

Al revived his announcer persona. "There you have it, world! Stand back: Joy Jenkins is officially beginning retirement!"

CHAPTER 2

"Hey, Joy-Bells, your Piano Man's home!" Al's shout rolled up the driveway and into the house.

"Good, because I'm in the mood for a melody!" Joy called back, wiping her hands and tossing the towel over the oven door handle on her way to the garage. "I was getting worried when it took you so..." The looming contents of the pickup truck backed into the driveway immediately diverted her attention. "Good grief! Are we positive that thing will even fit in our living room?"

"It better," Al said ominously, "And if we ever sell this house, the lucky new owner gets a piano thrown in with the deal. No way am I ever going to move this thing again." His sputtering reverted to whistling and soon the melody of *Piano Man* spun a web around them. He unwrapped the piano bench and jumped off the tailgate to lift it off the truck and place it carefully on the lawn.

Joy lifted the lid to the bench and exclaimed, "Look—there's still sheet music in here!"

Al nodded, but his mind was stuck on his troubles. "Three muscular guys in Bismarck gave up a precious hour of Memorial Day weekend to help me load it, but if two small boys and an elephant would have walked by Aunt Lorene's house at the right time, I would have drafted them, too. You can't believe how heavy and awkward an upright piano can be."

"But nothing keeps my favorite postman from delivering!" Joy teased, closing the bench's lid carefully. She began to refold the blankets as Al discarded them.

"We removed the two pieces covering the soundboard to lighten it as much as we could," Al nodded toward two long, flat sections still wrapped and tied against the truck's sideboards, "but this is just one honking-big piece of furniture."

"You'll need more help than Dave and Frank to get it down, then," Joy said practically.

"Two steps ahead of you, m'lady! I stopped by the grocery store, so Dave knows to come home and help. I also rounded up Hal and Fred and Rusty who were just shooting the breeze on Main Street, anyway. But where's Frank?" Al arched back to unkink his muscles before climbing into the truck. Untying the ropes that secured the piano, he whistled his way through the song again, belting out words each time he reached...*I'm the piano man...*

"Haven't seen hide nor hair of him. Want me to call THE CLIP AND CURL? They're closing at noon for the holiday weekend, so maybe it got busy at the last minute. Helen could tell me if he's on his way, at least."

"Sure, give 'em a jingle. Hey, would you grab a screwdriver off my workbench? The bumpy ride home made these knots all the tighter and I need something to get them loosened. Once I get this thing off here and in place, I'm going to soak in the tub and not come out until every muscle in my body has forgiven me."

"Poor baby!" Joy dodged the roll of rope Al lobbed at her, then picked it up and headed to the garage. She found a screwdriver and delivered it to Al who hunkered down in the truck bed. Reaching over the sidewall to tousle his hair, she said softly, "Thanks for all your hard work, Big Guy. I'm going to love having a piano!"

"Shucks, Missus Jenkins; it weren't nuttin' at all." He aimed a noisy air-kiss at her that she caught and blew back to him across her opened palm.

She returned to the kitchen to make the call, tossing several sections of rope on Al's worktable as she passed by. His space was as neat as a pin. She knew that on his first trip to the garage, Al would stop and put the rope in its proper place. That was Al—a man who ranked neatness right up there with honesty, bravery, and diligence.

Leaning against the kitchen counter with the phone wedged between her ear and shoulder, she hummed along with Al's sporadic whistling and looked around the sunny room. In 1974, as newlyweds moving into a house already fifty years old, she and Al had peeled ancient ugly wallpaper off the walls and made a trip straight to the dump with four sets of droopy Venetian blinds. Summer weekends that year had disappeared like smoke in the wind as they stripped, scraped, puttied, painted and varnished—all the while listening endlessly to the Hit Parade. To this day, every time she heard *The Way We Were* she could swear she smelled paint.

A smile flitted across her face. The music of that decade was part of the fabric of their marriage, as evidenced by Al's *Piano Man* remark. No one was banging down their door begging the Jenkins to perform, but they both knew all the words to a hefty collection of songs that wove their way through daily conversations and dominated the Jenkins' music collection.

Twenty-eight years after that refurbishing marathon, here Joy stood with nearly every mixing bowl she owned either dripping in the drainer or soaking in the sink or still on the counter with dabs of batter drying to the edges. The kitchen had been her oasis all these years after hectic days as a first-grade teacher.

Except for updated appliances and the addition of a dishwasher and microwave, the room hadn't changed over the years. It was as comfortable as her marriage to that lovable guy in the driveway who was now booming "...play us a song..." Opposites in some ways, Al and Joy were compatible in all the right ones. She would no more change her husband's personality than she would her kitchen's decor.

Joy knew Al would roll his eyes when he set foot in the kitchen. They shared kitchen duties, but not cooking styles. Whereas Al cooked and cleaned as he went along, Joy's preferred method was to line up all the utensils and equipment and work her way down the line, leaving mayhem in her wake until the end of a recipe. They had agreed long ago to live-and-let-live; spats over neatness just weren't worth it to either of them.

Finally, it registered that she was listening to an unanswered phone ringing in her ear. "That's odd." She stared at the phone as if expecting to find an answer inscribed on its surface. "Nobody's picking up," she called out to Al from the doorway. "I'll bet they closed up early and are on their way over."

"Try Frank's cell phone, just to be sure," Al suggested, coming into the garage.

Within a minute, Joy said, "It clicked over to voice-mail so I left the message that you're waiting for him. You're probably just one of many people asking for his time!"

Al chuckled. Incorporating words from old songs into everyday conversation was part of their special love language and he knew the rules—one person picked a song, the other responded from the same song—so he followed through with "But he's an old friend of mine!" as he stuck his head into the kitchen and inhaled dramatically. "Hey, whatever you're baking smells great."

"It's the reward for the piano movers, and if I don't keep my eye on the brownies, all I'll have to offer is a pan of soot." She heard voices in the driveway at the same time the oven timer buzzed. Setting the pan on a rack to cool, she went outside. Doing a quick head-count, she said, "Frank's still not here? And where's Dave?"

Hal stared at the pickup's ominous load and joked, "Frank probably saw Al hauling this monster through town and decided he had better things to do than spend Memorial Day weekend nursing a backache!"

"Yeah," Fred said, "he's the smart one of the bunch! I did see Dave, though; he was talking to Helen outside THE CLIP AND CURL."

"Good; if he ever gets here, my son can give us the story on Frank," Al said.

The piano was rolled into launch-position on the edge of the pickup bed, and the neighbors were treated to a rowdy rendition of *Chopsticks*. Still, neither Frank nor Dave arrived. The men carried the piano pieces and bench into the living room. Still no new help on board.

"I've already done this job once today with only four guys, and it's no picnic," Al warned, "but I sure hate to have you standing around wasting time. Are you game to try it with just the four of us?"

Rusty joshed, "We're a lot tougher than those Bismarck dudes! We can do it." The others agreed.

"Okay," Al said skeptically. "But when you're moaning and groaning later, remember, I *had* lined up two more guys."

The men took their positions and managed to unload the upright piano without mishap. Once it was on the ground, Rusty hooted, "Told you so! We can take on Bismarck any time."

"We're going to have to carry it in," Fred said. "The ground's pretty rough. So, once we get it off the ground and moving, we keep moving. If we lose our momentum, we're sunk. Ready, set, hoist!"

Joy raced ahead to open the front door and pinned herself between the screen door and the porch wall to give the men maximum access. Grunting and straining, they called out directions to each other:

"Easy now!"

"Okay, watch it on the left, Hal,"

"Got it, Fred?"

"Almost there, guys!"

Once inside, Joy watched them navigate the path she had cleared earlier. With the piano rolled into position and the sections back in place over the soundboard, they joked about being able to haul the hefty piece this far, only now to struggle to lift each corner high enough to wedge a furniture caster under the wheels.

Mission accomplished, Al sighed and rotated his shoulders in their sockets. "Since you missed out on coffee and treats at the café today, come out to the picnic table for some of Joy's good stuff, hot from the oven."

It didn't take long until the plate of sweets was half empty. Joy was refilling the men's glasses and cups when Dave rounded the side of the house. "Hey, son!" Al called out. "We really needed your help with the piano. Where'd you disappear to?" He had to ask the question, but Al managed to keep anger out of his voice. Anger confused Dave.

Twenty-six years old and a handsome merging of two ordinary gene pools, Dave was Al and Joy's only child. Physically an adult, his mind was locked in early adolescence. Dave was proud of his job at LARSON'S GROCERY. In hiring him, Luke had enraged several families whose sons were denied the employment given Prairie Rose's only mentally challenged citizen. But the uproar was short-lived, and Luke's actions had won him the town's respect and the Jenkins' unending appreciation.

Dave's face lit up. Leaning over Joy's shoulder to grab a fistful of treats, he paused long enough to peck her on the cheek. "Hi, Mom. Peanut butter cookies—my favorite!"

"Hey, those are for the guys who actually helped!" Al teased, his flash of irritation already past. "Fred says he saw you talking to Helen. Did she say where Frank is?"

Chewing and swallowing quickly, Dave swiped his forearm across his mouth as he processed facts for retelling. "Uncle Frank's gone. Aunt Helen asked me to help her get the sign off the shop. So I did. But I busted it 'cause it was stuck to the wall. Can I have the rest of your sun tea, Mom?" Dave asked, plucking up a brownie crumb from the plate.

Automatically, Joy handed the glass to her son. Bewildered looks all around the table indicated that even though Dave's account was obviously missing a few key details, there was just enough substance to cause concern.

"You were just walking along and Helen called you over and asked you to take the CLIP AND CURL sign off the front of the building?" Rusty queried.

"Yeah. She had a ladder out but she gets dizzy up high, so I said I don't get dizzy. And she said I should just climb up there and take it down. But the sign busted in two and one piece fell off. And Aunt Helen started laughing really hard. And she told me to just leave it exactly the way it was. It looks weird, but Aunt Helen says she likes it."

An uneasy silence settled like fog over the picnic table. Rusty finally said, "I'd better get going."

"Work is callin' my name, too," Hal said. "With the size crowd I've seen around the SATURDAY STORE so far today, I know we'll see a lot of traffic this afternoon."

"Thanks, guys," Al said. "I owe you. Collect anytime."

Fred hung back and pulled Al to one side. "I'll give you a call in a few minutes, once I see what's what going on."

"Thanks, Fred. Dave could be confused." Even though Fred was editor of the *Prairie Rose Chronicle*, Al knew he wasn't searching for front-page news. Fred fully appreciated that the friendship between Al and Joy Jenkins and Frank and Helen Wilson stretched long and deep. Attendants for each other's weddings, they often vacationed together, and it was a rare Friday night that they didn't spend at one house or the other. Since both couples' parents had relocated to warmer climates, the Wilsons and Jenkins had filled the roles of family for many holidays and celebrations.

"Come see our piano, Dave, before you go back to work." Joy loaded glasses on the tray as she spoke.

The three Jenkins were admiring the addition to their living room when the phone rang. "That'll be Fred." Relief coated Al's voice as he headed for the kitchen. He was back in an instant. "Come on, Dave. Your mom and I will walk you back to work." He shot Joy a look she knew well: *Don't ask; not with Dave here.*

"Good idea," she said lightly. "We want Dave to keep his reputation as a good employee."

"Luke likes me," Dave said proudly. "He says pretty soon I'll be as good on the new cash register as I was on the old one. Then I can check groceries again, not just stock shelves and clean. I like to check groceries. I'm sick of dusting."

Chatting all the way to LARSON'S GROCERY, Dave didn't notice if his parents' pace was faster than usual and their farewell was brief. As soon as Dave had entered the store, Joy tugged Al's sleeve. "What is it?" she said, matching his stride.

"Trouble. I don't know what kind, but Fred thinks we should check it out." Half a block later, the front of THE CLIP AND CURL came into view.

At least the front of what used to be THE CLIP AND CURL couldn't be missed.

A jagged-edge sign above the door now simply read D CURL with no evidence of THE CLIP AN in sight.

Joy clutched Al's arm and gasped a wordless sound. They took off running, the echo of their feet slapping the sidewalk rang like distant gunshots.

Al reached the combined barber and beauty shops first and flung open the door. He stopped so abruptly on the threshold that Joy collided with him. "Hello, Helen," he said evenly, noticing the two customers just in time. He met Sadie's piercing gaze knowingly. Her choice of the chair closest to the beauty shop side ensured she wouldn't miss a single word from Helen's lips. Al expelled an audible puff of air. *It can't be good to have the town's worst gossip already on the scene.*

Helen worked at the sink shampooing Rachel Lindquist's hair; that woman's requisite wheelchair was parked against the wall. Al pursed his lips. *Rachel would have come up the ramp by the back door so she may not know about the sign. But it's a sure thing Sadie does.*

"Hi, guys," Helen said a little too brightly. She had refreshed her make-up and only a discerning friend would know she had been crying.

Joy was that friend. She noticed.

"Hello, Helen; 'lo, Sadie; hi, Rachel," Joy's eyes never left Helen's flushed face.

"No customers for Frank today?" Al asked offhandedly. Not only was Frank not working, his side of the business showed no signs of any activity that day—no stray papers or magazines, no barbering tools scattered around, and the ultimate give-away: a perfectly clean floor. The only human touch was somebody's forgotten seed cap dangling from the hook on the wall where it had hung for months. The joke was, if the owner ever showed up, Frank planned to charge him storage fees. But that memory didn't spawn a flicker of a smile today.

The waiting area spanned the two sections and was empty except for Widow O'Dell who studied a seed catalog with all the interest of a zealous farmer—which she was not. The town's seamstress hadn't even managed to grow a respectable geranium since her husband—a true green thumb—had died twenty years ago. Joy turned a suspicious eye toward Sadie. "Didn't you just have a permanent last week?" she asked in her don't-mess-with-me teacher voice.

Chin jutting, the woman replied defiantly, "Yes, but Helen didn't trim around my neck as much as I like. And I won't be paying for this, either," she added, scowling across the room. Helen massaged conditioner through Rachel's hair and offered no response.

Rachel's words floated upwards from her position at the sink, "Helen and I have been chatting about those fancy tomato cages Hal has at THE GENERAL STORE. We both have always used stakes and ties, but we're ready to try something new."

In spite of the moment's underlying concerns, Al smiled to himself. *Bless her.* Unerringly, Rachel had chosen one topic to which Sadie had nothing to contribute and one that constituted valid beauty shop conversation but allowed for no juicy tidbits. "We'll leave you to your discussion, ladies, and head over to the café for a cup of coffee," Al said. "Why don't you call there when Frank gets back?"

"Frank is..." Helen straightened her back and turned toward them with an unreadable expression, "...at home. But I can take care of you, Al, in about half an hour, or so."

"Okay. We'll be back, Helen." Joy steered Al toward the door.

Outside, they let their eyes drift up to the mutilated sign: D CURL. "There's trouble, all right." Joy's voice quivered. "Oh, Al—I'm scared and I don't know why."

"Let's find Frank and get some answers," Al said grimly.

No words were spoken until they knocked on the Wilson's side door before opening it—a privilege based on many years of friendship—and Al called out, "Frank? You home?"

A distant thud and then "In the bedroom" floated down the steps. It didn't sound like an invitation, but this was no time to stand on ceremony.

Al sucked in his breath and grabbed Joy's hand. They climbed the steps with pounding hearts. Even though the four of them had been friends for nearly thirty years, Jenkins' trips to the Wilson's bedroom weren't the norm.

Thumps and bumps assured them they would find Frank in the second room on the left. By pushing an already-ajar door completely open, they gained a view of what had thudded, thumped and bumped. Drawers hung haphazardly open. Hangers lay strewn around the room. T-shirts, slacks, socks and shaving items littered the chair and bed and spilled onto the cedar chest. "You taking a trip, Frank?" Al asked with forced casualness.

One incongruous thought flitted through Joy's mind: *Frank never planned to go to work today, not dressed like that.*

Wearing faded jeans that rode his hips and a polo shirt that had seen the inside of the washing machine many times and was now tucked haphazardly into a beltless waistband, Frank studiously avoided Al's eye. "Yeah."

"This came up awfully fast. We just saw you and Helen last night and you didn't mention a trip. Is she going, too?" Joy asked, fear throbbing in her temples.

"No." Frank's lips tightened.

"Where you headed?" Al asked, bending to catch a pair of swimming trunks just before they slithered off the bed.

"California."

"Any place special?" Al's questions persisted, despite Frank's obvious disinclination to talk.

"The Bay Area, okay?" Frank's voice had a razor's edge.

"San Francisco? That's quite a trip. Are you planning to fly?"

"Jeez, enough with the questions!" Frank was clearly miffed to have Al on the offensive.

"Oh, I don't think so. Not at all. I've got plenty more I think deserve an answer," Al's voice rose in pitch and volume. Joy squeezed his hand in their standard *Careful!* signal. He took a calming breath. "For starters, why isn't Helen going with you? It's been your shared dream for years to see California."

Joy added, "When Luke and Cate came back from their honeymoon in Mendocino last November, you and Helen really started talking about it again. In fact, right around Christmas you mentioned you were doing research on the Internet for a trip to the West Coast."

"Hey, back off, you two! I've got a lot of packing to do and I don't need you preaching at me. Do you mind?"

Al stepped back as if struck. "*Preaching?* What on earth could be misconstrued as preaching? Good grief, man! You and I have been friends since college and our wives grew up together. But now all of a sudden I can't get ten words of explanation from you? You and Helen are obviously having some kind of a tiff. At least let us try to help you guys work through whatever's going on."

Frank shrugged. "Nothing will get better if I stay." He turned his back to dig through a drawer of underwear, tossing several pairs of briefs across the room to the bed.

This is no fairytale. Joy felt an icy hand squeeze her heart. *How could Al and I have missed seeing our best friends were in trouble?* "You have the right to choose the path you take, Frank..." She choked and blinked back tears and shot a look at Al.

"...but this one appears to be pretty rocky." Al thrust his hands through his short-cropped hair.

Frank snorted. "As usual, you two can drag out an old song to fit every possible situation," he said sarcastically, sweeping a handful of change off the dresser. "This doesn't concern you two. This is between Helen and me." One coin escaped his efforts to stuff the money into his pocket and rolled under the dresser.

"Of course it concerns us—we're all friends!" Joy protested.

Al's temper flared, "I thought it was bad enough when you blew off helping me move the piano. But then we have to learn from Dave that Helen has taken the sign off the shop, and now we find you packing for California and leaving your wife behind."

Frank straightened up. "She's taken the sign down? That bitch!" He kicked a shoebox across the floor and loose papers flew out of it.

Joy crossed the room in three strides and slapped him across the cheek. "That's uncalled for, Frank! I don't know what happened between you and Helen, but calling her nasty names doesn't fly with me. She's been your wife for twenty-eight years and is the mother of your two wonderful daughters and the best friend you'll ever have besides the two of us. I *will not* allow you to talk about her like that, especially when she's not here to defend herself."

Frank rubbed his cheek gingerly. "Call off your woman, Al," he said, half-heartedly faking a cowering stance. "She's got a wicked right-hook!"

"I'm not sure I want to," Al said darkly. "If Joy hadn't lit into you, I might have and then you'd be sporting more than a red cheek. Want to talk about what's going on?"

"Nah, I'm sure Helen will fill you in. She's got a list of grievances a mile long and is dying to air them."

"And you're going to California." Al watched Frank roll several pairs of jeans and walking shorts and stuff them into the suitcase. He appeared to be packing up everything he owned. "How long you planning to be gone, anyway?"

"Ask Helen," Frank said succinctly. Looking around the room, he grabbed up a paperback book and a pair of reading glasses from one bedside table, knelt to gather up the scattered papers and jammed them haphazardly back into the shoe box. "I'll call you when I get there and let you know how to reach me in case the girls need me, or something."

"Downright generous of you, Frank," Al drawled acerbically. "Good to know you're thinking of your girls in some fashion. I'd actually rather sit down and talk right now than wait for a phone call that may never come—which is a good possibility if your promises are as solid as the way you honor all the years of our friendship."

Frank's color heightened. "I have nothing to say you'd like to hear. Trust me on that one." He disappeared into the bathroom and came back with a toothbrush and a rolled-up tube of toothpaste that he added to a shaving kit. Snapping the locking tabs on one suitcase and zipping up another, he kicked a dresser drawer shut. He plunged one foot into a nearby shoe and knelt beside the bed, lifting the spread in search of its mate.

Numbly, Joy swept up the pile of hangers off the bed and walked into the closet. *The last thing Helen needs is to come home to face Frank's mess.* The stark reality of what was happening hit hard when Joy stood inside the closet. Blinking back tears, she carefully replaced hangers on the half-empty bar. Helen's workday blouses and slacks, Sunday dresses and casual clothes hung on one side. On the other side, only Frank's winter suit and wool slacks and yard-work clothes remained. Half the shoe rack was vacant. Half the shelves were bare. The closet looked like a freak storm had blown through, leaving an odd mixture of *untouched* mingled with *demolished* in its path.

Joy choked on tears she could no longer control and backed blindly from the closet, closing the door on the agonizing scene. Hands thrust into his pants pockets, Al stared at the man he felt he no longer knew. Pointedly ignoring them, Frank collected the bags he had packed and attempted to load himself up for one trip.

Any other time, Al and Joy would have gladly helped him, teasing about his penchant for saving time versus saving his back. Not today. Today, they followed Frank down the steps, cringing each time a suitcase banged against the wall he and Helen had so carefully wallpapered. Frank led their sad parade down the hall, through the kitchen and out to the detached garage where he piled the luggage into the passenger seat of his pickup.

Al and Joy stood off to one side, dazed and confused. Frank went back into the house, returning with his summer straw hat riding cockily on his head. An obviously heavy cooler bumped against his leg—more evidence Frank had been very busy that morning. He also carried his summer jacket, a baseball cap, a bag of potato chips and the small case both Al and Joy recognized as his portable barbershop. But Frank wasn't responding to calls from shaggy-headed homebound men today.

Al scraped the bottom of his dwindling supply of civility; one sad song from the past surfaced. "So, you're gonna be traveling on?" It was a rhetorical question. The responding phrase *if I stayed here, things just couldn't be the same* bugled so clearly in his mind that he flinched as if Frank had shouted the words back at him.

Frank's face hardened. "Get this into your head: I'm leaving." He climbed into the truck, shut the door and inserted his key in the ignition. The engine roared. Rolling down the window, he stuck his head out the window. "Take it easy." He put the truck in reverse. Gravel spit out from beneath the tires as he backed out the driveway.

"'Take it easy'?" Joy repeated incredulously. "Frank's leaving Helen and we don't know why, and we're supposed to take it easy?" A combination of fury, sadness and alarm sickened her.

"Come on; we told Helen half an hour, and it's been that and more." They automatically reached for each other's hand and walked back to Main Street, stunned into a heavy hush.

They found Helen alone and busily sweeping up snippets of hair. Frank always teased her about collecting hair for the birds to line their nests, but she refused to toss out something that could give her feathered friends a cozier abode in the trees behind the Wilson's house. If Frank had been here, he would have had some snappy remark about the birds.

But Frank was on his way to California. And Helen was sweeping for the birds as if they were her biggest concern.

Al's shoulders sagged briefly, but he promptly took charge. He closed the blinds on the barbershop side and crossed the room to do the same on the beauty shop side after turning the OPEN sign in the window to read CLOSED. "Come on, ladies. THE CLIP AND CURL is officially closed for the weekend. I'm buying you Cate's lunch special, and then I'm grilling hamburgers for our supper. We better eat a decent lunch so you won't notice I'm not as good on the grill as Frank is." Neither woman commented on the obvious gap in his agenda between lunch and supper—it went without saying they'd be together. Hopefully, Helen would be talking.

With Joy on his left and Helen on his right, Al led the grim trio to CATE'S CAFÉ. The room stilled when they entered, but Al heedlessly navigated the two women to a corner table. "Cate, three lunch specials, please, when you get a minute," he called over his shoulder. Pulling out the chair that would put Helen's back to the room, he seated her and positioned Joy next to her, claiming the chair that faced the room for himself.

"Looks like the SATURDAY STORE is doing a good business today. Folks must be stocking up on summer reading." Al's voice was pitched to carry. Anyone hoping to learn dirty details of the morning's hot story would be sadly disappointed. Al nudged Joy's knee beneath the table.

While Helen fussed with the napkin holder, Joy looked across the street where the sign in the window of Prairie Rose's most unusual business announced in a continuous scrolling loop: *May 25—Books on Broadway Comes to Town!* "It's perfect timing," she agreed, her volume level matching Al's. "Nothing beats the combination of a good book, a summer day, and a hammock."

Coming from behind the counter, Cate Larson pursed her lips thoughtfully. There had been only one topic of conversation in the past two hours: *What was going on that had severed the* CLIP AN *from the* D CURL*?* Having been the brunt of town gossip herself in the past, Cate admired Al's take-charge actions. She knew Helen's appearance at the café could help dim the town's spotlight on Wilson's misery, if only momentarily.

Cate served the three at the corner table and lingered for a few moments of small talk before moving along to jump-start stalled conversations around the café. Gossipy speculation was on temporary hold, which made for a quiet room since only one subject had currently been revving its engine. But with Cate's subtle prompting, attention shifted to the best way Bert could trim tree branches away from the electrical wires in his back yard, and veered off to speculation about the town softball team's chances at the game tonight, and finally idled around recent plans to resurface Main Street.

At their table, Al kept up a steady patter about Tina and Robyn, the two Wilson girls who lived in Minot where they co-owned a bakery. When that subject ran dry, he eased into an account of Dave mastering the new cash register's intricacies, making much more of the limited details they knew than Joy would have dreamed possible. She had never loved him more than for helping Helen survive the tumult that had swept through the quiet streets of her life.

Finally, Al pushed back his chair and stood beside the table to announce loudly, "May I have your attention, neighbors and friends? With Frank out of town, it's me manning the grill in our back yard.

You all might want to run home and shut windows because the smoke's gonna fly tonight!"

Al's words paved the way for them to exit on a wave of good-natured, if awkward, teasing. Within minutes, they sat in the Jenkins' living room.

It felt odd to see only three pairs of feet meet on the massive ottoman. The place where Frank's size-twelve sneakers always rested was a gaping hole. The end of the couch he called his "assigned seat" was glaringly empty.

Memories of many previous Jenkins-Wilson discussions lingered in this comfortable room. This is where they planned trips together. Around this circle, they argued the pros and cons of buying or leasing cars, and vinyl versus steel siding. This was the scene of struggles over major purchases and minor decisions. It was here the two couples laughed and cried over the joys and sorrows of parenthood.

But on Saturday afternoon of Memorial Day weekend, the alarm had sounded for *Man Overboard.*

"Helen, we have no right to insist you to talk to us, but we sure hope you will," Joy said softly. "We went over to your house after we left you at the shop so we know Frank has taken off to California."

"He said you'd tell us what's going on. Will you, so we can at least try to help? What's happened?" Al asked.

Helen pulled an afghan around herself like a shroud. Burrowing into the sofa cushions, she closed her eyes. Joy and Al shared an uneasy look as a brief pause grew into a lengthy silence.

Finally, Helen opened her eyes wide and words spilled out, "Frank's got another woman. He's gone to be with her. I told him he had to choose, and he picked her."

Joy and Al had been ready to hear about money problems, or arguments over vacation plans, or sharp words about in-laws, or disagreements about remodeling the shop.

Not this. Never this.

"What?" Al choked out. "*Frank?* An *affair*? What…? This is more than I can fathom."

"Same here," Joy said, blood pounding at every pulse point. "I can't believe it—I mean, I don't disbelieve *you,* but there's got to be some…"

Helen flushed. "I understand your confusion. I've spent three weeks fluctuating between denial and murderous intent."

Al's eyes darkened. "Three weeks! Where have we been? Two questions are jumping around in my head: *Why?* because I can't understand how Frank would want anyone but you, and *Who?* because I'd like to go over and kick the snot out of her for hurting you. I plan to whup the answer to *why* out of Frank someday, but can you tell us *who*?"

"In some ways I don't know much about her, and in other ways I feel like I know far more than I want to. He met her on the Internet, and I guess he's been calling and e-mailing her every day for months. I've been so stupid. I guess I thought I knew Frank," she said with poignant sadness.

"Well, yeah!" Al snorted. If the grip he had on the arms of his chair was any indication of what he'd do to Frank, it was a good thing he was not nearby. "So did we."

"They met in person once, that I know about," Helen continued in a lifeless voice, "when he supposedly went to a barbers' convention in Denver at the beginning of April. I found out later they had the whole thing planned and spent the weekend together."

"Oh, Helen! I'm so sorry." Joy hoped she wouldn't throw up; the way her head was spinning, that was a distinct possibility.

"When he told me about Denver, I lost it. I had wanted to go along, but he said one of us should keep the shop open so we wouldn't lose too much money. And here that jerk has been spending money on…her. Lots of money I see, now that I look back at the credit card statements."

"You said he met her on the *Internet*?" Joy asked as that fact pushed its way through the muck. "How does a person meet someone over the

Internet—and get to know them well enough to, uh, whatever? I know it's in the news about perverts and porn sites and such, but this is *Frank* we're talking about!"

"I don't know. I only learned about it three weeks ago when I went downstairs to put in a load of wash." Helen's voice was a monotone. "Frank was in the exercise room and didn't hear me in the laundry room. He wasn't working out at all; I could tell he was talking on his cell phone and at first I thought he was talking to the girls, until I realized no father would talk like *that* to his own daughters."

Al muttered, "That low-down, rotten cad."

Helen bit her lip as a blush flooded her cheeks and continued along her neck. "I pushed open the door and saw him leaning up against the wall with his eyes closed and his hands were, uh, busy and...I'll spare you the sordid details."

"Oh, Helen! How awful for you!" Joy blurted out.

Two angry red blotches sprouted on Helen's cheeks and life returned to her voice. "I marched in there and grabbed the phone before he could stop me and I screamed into it, 'I don't know who you are, but the man you're talking to is my husband and the father of our two daughters!' and I threw it against the wall."

"Good for you!" Al said. "What did he do?"

"He started ranting and tried to make it *my* problem. He said I should feel pretty dumb for acting like an idiot when I didn't even know who I had hung up on. He picked up the phone, real worried I had broken it, and said he'd been talking to another barber. Then that creep said he'd forgive me this time, but wasn't making promises about the next time I go off my rocker like a wild woman."

Al's eyes took on a steely glaze. "You catch him sex-talking on the phone and he turns on *you*? You should have aimed that phone right at his crotch."

Helen smiled sadly. "Yeah; he stormed off and when he got in the shower, I hit redial on his phone. A woman with a real throaty voice answered, so I pretended to be the phone company and said we'd had a report of a problem with her line. She said there was no problem—she had just been talking to her boyfriend in North Dakota and the line had been perfectly clear. She giggled when she said 'boyfriend.'"

Joy stared at Helen with a new respect. "Wow. It's amazing you had the presence of mind to use redial, Helen."

"I know—I've surprised myself a lot lately. Of course, after I hung up, I realized if she had caller ID, she could have called my bluff." She shrugged. "Sometimes, it's like if I can keep from thinking about it, it won't be true. Other times I get so mad at Frank, he's lucky to be alive."

"I sure wish I had known this before Frank drove off," Al said grimly.

"You can't believe how hard it has been to look across the shop everyday and see him laughing and talking with customers like nothing was wrong. Do you know what code-name he used for her number on his phone? 'Longings.' I found that out by checking his phone after he'd sneaked out of bed to call her again in the middle of the night. That was the last straw. I woke him up and gave him an ultimatum: her or me."

"I feel sick hearing how horrid life has been for our two closest friends—and we've been totally clueless, even though we practically live in each other's back pockets," Joy said, blinking furiously to stem the tears threatening to undo her.

"It's been pretty bad. We've had some knock-down, drag-out fights lately. But, even though it wasn't a conscious decision, neither Frank nor I wanted you two to know. We always envied your marriage."

Joy said sadly, "We thought your marriage was great, too."

"It hasn't been. Not for a long time. But I'd thought we were holding our own until this all happened. Things were better back when the girls were around. And whenever we could be with the two of you, it was like your good stuff rubbed off on us. You may not have noticed, but we rarely cancelled for Friday nights. All the troubles we had during the week seemed to disappear then. But afterwards, we'd go home and it was just the two of us again."

Al and Joy each saw their own shock mirrored in the other's face.

"This morning I went over to the shop alone because Frank was dilly-dallying. He timed his arrival for five minutes before the shop opened. He had no intention of working today—he was just biding his time before he dropped the bombshell about going to California to live with her. *California!*" Choking on the word that had symbolized so much for so long, Helen lost control and dissolved into wracking sobs.

Joy sprang from her chair and gathered her friend into a tender hug as Helen's tears found release. Al passed the box of tissues from the end table to Joy. She pulled out several and pushed them into Helen's hand.

"*I* can hardly understand what's happened—what do I tell the girls? And what will I do for money? I can't make it on the income I can bring in alone." The torrent of Helen's words was muffled against Joy's shoulder.

"Don't sell yourself short, Helen. A place named D CURL could do a booming business in North Dakota—it sounds French and fashionable." Al smiled gently and garnering a tremulous smile in return.

Joy caressed Helen's shoulder. "People will soon know you're the innocent party in Frank's big fiasco. And that's what it is—this is Frank's mess, not yours. He's going to come to his senses and come crawling back, begging your forgiveness."

"I don't think I can ever forgive him," Helen said morosely. "He not only lied to me, but he has *longings*," her voice cracked, "...for another woman—and made love to her. This is so shameful for us."

"Him, Helen. Shameful for *him*, not you," Joy corrected her firmly. "I wish we'd been more alert. The four of us have seen each other almost every day for years and talked about everything under the sun, and we've been there for each other through thick and thin. And yet, we had no idea you guys were in such pain."

"Don't beat yourselves up about it. Remember *I* didn't know anything until three weeks ago. Apparently the man I've been married to all these years has amazing powers of subterfuge. But I'm not entirely innocent—I hid stuff from you guys, too. Frank and I fought right up to the minute we hit your back porch last night. I wasn't sure we'd fooled you when we begged off earlier than usual. I *did* have a headache and Frank *was* tired—I'd yelled at him for such a long time Thursday night that I gave myself a headache."

"I guess we have just gotten so used to each other that we don't pay as close attention to clues as we should," Al said grimly.

"There's probably nothing you could have done. I know you would have tried, but something broke loose inside Frank when he turned fifty in January. He started saying he'd never really lived. He talked a lot about how you, Al, have at least seen some of the country. He couldn't figure out why someone like you who grew up as an Army brat would come from out-of-state to go to school at NDSU. Frank only ever lived in North Dakota and once he turned the big 5-0, it seemed like a noose around his neck. And I guess I must have seemed like the proverbial ball and chain."

"So he started investigating California?"

Helen nodded slowly. "One day when he seemed particularly down, I said maybe we should just go to California—you know, chase the dream, even if only for a few weeks, rather than waiting for some magic moment. It seemed like a good idea at the time, but you'll never know how often I've wondered how this all would have turned out if *I* had done the research. He spent gobs of time on the computer, but I thought he was planning our fantasy, not the destruction of our marriage."

The back door slammed and Dave appeared in the arched doorway separating dining and living rooms. "Hi, Aunt Helen. Where's Uncle Frank?" he asked automatically, eyeing the empty spot looming like a specter.

"Hi, Davey," Helen said, harkening back to the name that signaled a happier time in everyone's life. "Uncle Frank has gone to live in California."

"He should have taken you with him," Dave said matter-of-factly.

"He needed to make this trip alone, so it's just me joining your family for supper tonight. Guess what, Dave? Your dad's grilling hamburgers!" Dave failed to notice the jovial veneer on her words was thin.

"Oh, no, not Dad! We need Uncle Frank."

"We'll be fine without Uncle Frank, Dave. This will give your dad's hidden talents a chance to sparkle." Helen's feeble smile circled from Dave to Joy to Al.

"Let's bake pies, Helen," Joy suggested. Working together in the kitchen as they had thousands of times, the two friends seemed unable to come up with any topic of conversation other than the immediate situation. Finally, they quit trying and just talked, woman-to-woman.

Three pies in the oven, they pulled up chairs and poured iced tea. Often Helen's thoughts were jumbled into sentences that made little sense; sometimes the sequence of events was mixed up; sometimes tears muffled her words. But Joy let her talk. Finally the calming influence of a quiet kitchen and a good friend worked their magic and she visibly relaxed. "Frank accused me of missing signals that he was unsatisfied. Unsatisfied! How do you like *that*? I'll admit, it's been a long, long time since much about our marriage gave either one of us a thrill..."

"Have you told the girls...anything?" Joy asked, gently shifting topics.

"That's yet to come. They know nothing. I haven't breathed a word to anyone because I kept hoping I would wake up and discover this was all just a nightmare. But now the girls are going to demand answers and I have none to give."

"They may surprise you." Joy looked out the window at Al and Dave working together over the grill. Al's idea for a barbecue tonight was inspired. Life had to go on—and as it did, things would sort themselves out. But tonight, Helen needed the company of friends who shared her pain and didn't shovel blame onto her plate like a condiment for tossed salad, burgers and peach pie.

When the crickets began to sing, Dave said, "Aunt Helen, may I sleep at your house tonight? I could sleep on the couch and watch your TV turned down low, and I'd answer the door if anyone comes."

Helen look startled by the suggestion and was on the verge of rejecting it, but then stopped and smiled across the table at the young man she had known and loved since his birth. "You know, Davey, I think I'd like that. You can watch TV as late as you'd like because you don't have to go to work tomorrow. I'd like knowing you're downstairs."

"Okay!" Dave gave her a high-five and helped himself to another slice of pie.

Watching their son and their friend walk down the street together in the dusk, Al and Joy leaned against each other. "Dave is full of surprises, isn't he?" Al mused. "He managed to bring the first authentic smile to Helen's face that I saw all day."

Joy nodded and blinked back the tears that sprouted in the corners of her eyes. "Remember when he was born and we were going through such hard times, knowing he would never be like other kids? Dave had fallen asleep in her arms and she kissed his nose and said, 'This little guy is going to have a heart of gold and you'll feel like parents of a million-dollar kid.' It's been true before, but tonight, I've got that feeling again."

"I'm glad Helen is a recipient of her fulfilled prophecy. Let's go upstairs, Joybells," Al breathed into her ear. His embrace felt strong and secure.

"I'd like that," she whispered, "even though it seems selfish or disloyal to find solace in each other when our friends are hurting so badly. Do you know what I mean?"

Al nodded, his chin bumping on her head. "That's exactly why I want to be your lover tonight."

Putting a compact disk of Olivia Newton-John hits on continuous play, Al adjusted the volume and selected the bedroom speakers. He then led Joy upstairs, each tugging the other's clothing loose until they stepped into the shower, beginning a night of comfort, reaffirmation and discovery.

The knowledge their friends' marriage tottered on the brink of destruction added a bittersweet aura to their pleasure. As she drifted back from the edge of satiation in her husband's arms long after midnight, Joy whispered against his cheek, "I love you. I honestly love you." That declaration, borrowed from the music that filled their ears, blended their hearts.

"Ahh," Al murmured. "All I could do is echo you." His words formed the safety net beneath Joy's sleep that allowed her to sink into oblivion and find sweet rest. But Al stared at the ceiling in the darkness and wondered how a man like Frank could be blown so far off course...and why.

Joy stirred, knowing instinctively the love of her life was struggling with burdens almost too heavy to bear. She rose up on one elbow and traced his eyebrows with a gentle fingertip and whispered, "Remember that Jimmy Buffett song? *Come Monday...*"

"*...it'll be all right*? I'm not sure that's possible, Joybells. But please, God, make it so."

Chapter 3

Memorial Day morning, homeowners found handwritten notes wedged between screen doors and doorframes or slid beneath doors if a crack allowed such. A childish scrawl on the card in the Jenkins' doorway informed them: *I wiLL dElivr stUf for you 25¢ PEtEy GUddmAn.* His telephone number started on the front of the recipe card and ended on the back—below a recipe.

Al slid the card across the breakfast table to Joy. "I saw more of these on our neighbors' doors, so it appears Petey is recruiting business in a big way." In the pre—Frank's disaster days, the card would have spawned a good chuckle, but neither Al nor Joy felt much like laughing.

Joy set her juice glass aside and picked up the card. "So it seems. He told me he earned a quarter last summer when he helped a visitor find Pastor Tori, so I imagine this idea has been brewing ever since. I wonder if June has missed her recipe cards yet?"

"We'll see to it she gets Gingered Carrots returned, at least," Al said. "Maybe I'll give the kid a jingle. He can return the miter box I borrowed from John Caston. That's worth a quarter to me, because I don't feel up to standing around shooting the breeze with folks today, and ol' John does love to chat."

He propped Petey's card against the sugar bowl, reached for the phone and punched in the four numbers found on the front side and turned the card over for the remaining three numbers. "Hey, Rusty, how ya doing? Thanks for your help Saturday. No major aches and pains, huh? Good. Say, is Petey around?" He drummed his fingers on the kitchen table and whistled softly as he waited: *You're my lady of the morning.*

Joy wagged a finger in his direction. "Watch it, first-graders are pretty sharp—I wouldn't put it past this one to notice his former teacher looks especially refreshed, shall we say, this morning."

Al shot her an air-kiss and lifted a cautionary hand. "Good morning, Petey! I found your card in our door this morning and I'd like to hire you to deliver a package to Mister Caston. Could you pick it up today? Good. We'll see you in a few minutes." He disconnected and pushed back his chair and nonchalantly whistled again: *You're my lady of the morning.*

She laughed, but the sound seemed meager, even to her own ears. "Okay, okay—if you're that desperate for compliments, yes, you gave me all the loving I'm needing! You didn't give me a chance to be subtle about telling you how much I loved...this morning...and last night," she said, watching Al move away. "Hold on there, Big Guy." She pushed back her chair.

He halted in the kitchen doorway. Letting the screen door close softly behind him, he held out his arms. She nestled in close, rubbing the top of her head beneath his chin. "Good thing Petey's on his way, huh, or we wouldn't get much done today," she murmured.

"Frank's an idiot. I can't imagine loving anybody but you, Jingle-bells."

Joy arched her back within the circle of Al's arms to study his face. "As usual, we're on the same wavelength. I keep thinking about how Helen must feel, knowing Frank's *visibly* been with her, but *emotionally* and, apparently, *physically*, he's been straying. He could hardly have done anything to hurt her more." Her expression turned grim. "I wish I'd slapped him twice."

"Whoa, there! Even though I'm furious with the guy, I have to remind myself that Frank will eventually turn that truck around. We'll be seeing him again someday which means if we let ourselves start hating his guts, it's going to be pretty hard to help them get back together."

Chin jutting, Joy said, "I still think he deserves at least one more swat."

Al squeezed her hard. "I'll be in the garage waiting for Petey." He patted his pants pocket. "Got a quarter right here to pay the young entrepreneur. What's on your agenda today?"

"I'll be rubbing and scrubbing this old house until it shines like a dime," Joy caroled, giving her hips the rhythmic swivel that matched the tempo. She knew her mood affected Al's and they both infected Dave with whatever emotions they felt. Even so, she was fully aware her cheer-up-the-troops efforts fell short.

Al ran his hands slowly along her waist and down her backside. "Let's clean together, and then take a run over to see Helen. She's had enough time alone."

"I love you," Joy said softly.

"Right back at you, Double-U-O-M-A-N," Al said, completing that round of their natural-as-breathing routine.

The squeal of bicycle brakes and the sounds of a boy-soprano voice chirping "…I use my little compass to help me find my way…" signaled Petey's arrival.

"Hi, Petey!"

"Hi, Missus Jenkins. You sure look pretty!"

Giving her husband an *I told you so!* glance, Joy smiled at Petey. "Are you getting lots of calls for your new business?" She linked arms with Al as they stood together in the garage doorway.

"Yup. I got a big jar to put my money in and when it gets full, my dad says I'll get a bank account so our house isn't robbed." His eyes widened and Joy hid a smile. The idea of a robbery and the resulting hoopla held as much fascination for Petey as a jar full of earnings. She winked at Al.

"What kinds of things have you delivered so far?" Al asked.

"I've been pretty busy," Petey said dramatically. "Even before I handed out cards, Missus Lindquist paid me to take a bag of canning jars to Missus Thompson—and I didn't break any of them. And I got a bunch of nails from the GENERAL STORE for Father Donovan. Well, *first* I got the money to pay for them from Father Donovan and *then* I got the nails and delivered them," He sighed loudly. "Father Donovan gave me a quarter *and* a dime. And I just took Miss Meadows' cat back home; it was hiding in Missus Stenson's garage. I hope I don't have to do *that* job ever again. That stupid cat jumped out of my basket and I had to climb a tree to get it."

Al and Joy laughed outright, envisioning the episode even as Petey investigated his arm. "Let me put some iodine on your scratch. My husband has some in his First Aid box in the garage. We'll get you all fixed up and you can make the delivery to Mister Caston."

"Thank you, Missus Jenkins," Petey said after Joy had swabbed and bandaged his arm. "I'm glad I won this compass when I got an A+ on your quiz." He fiddled with the compass that hung by its chain from a belt loop on his jeans. "If you ever want me to deliver anything for you, I will only charge you a dime because you are the best teacher I ever had for first grade."

"I wouldn't think of paying less than a quarter," Joy said solemnly. "That would be taking unfair advantage of a student and that's against my personal policies."

"I didn't know that." Petey's mouth formed an *O* as he contemplated this moral issue; he was clearly troubled by his inability to reward his teacher. Suddenly, his face brightened. "How 'bout if I do two errands for you for each quarter?"

Al quickly transformed a hoot into a cough and spun around to busy himself at his workbench. "We'll see," Joy said vaguely. "Meanwhile, I know Mister Jenkins is glad to have you make a delivery for him."

Minutes later, Al came into the kitchen chuckling. "What a kid. He shook my hand! I gave him a bungee cord to help keep things—like the miter box—in the basket if he gets a little wild on the curves."

"Good thinking. Did you mention not to use it on cats?" Joy asked with a broad grin.

"Oops! Anyway, after he pocketed his quarter, he stuck out his hand. 'Thank you, Mister Jenkins. Please call me when you need stuff delivered.' It was all I could do to keep from ruffling his hair."

"I predict Petey will have a jar full of quarters when school starts. Remember last summer how he spent hours racing around town, signaling every turn and calling out 'Turning left!' He told me he was pretending to be a taxi driver and practicing finding all the best routes between houses."

"Now he's got a compass and knows out to use it! We'll have to call on him every week, or so, to encourage him."

Two hours later, the vacuuming and dusting were done, two loads of wash hung on the clothesline, and the bathroom and kitchen floors sparkled.

"Enough for one day—I don't want to take unfair advantage of the guy I love," Joy said. They had worked to the background of Barry White's seductive music, aware they risked an emotional overload with his voice and lyrics filling their minds, but also knowing music and shared chores had gone hand-in-hand for their entire marriage. "Thanks for showing me you love me in so many ways, Al."

"Nothing says 'I love you' like the sound of a vacuum cleaner, huh?" His voice cracked in the middle of his attempted humor.

"Nothing, at least not to me." Joy sidestepped a pail of soapy water to kiss the man who personified what Barry White merely sang about. "Hey, are you okay?"

Al started to nod, but then shook his head. "I'm a mental wreck. I didn't fall asleep until nearly dawn. I thought working together this morning would take my mind off everything going on with Frank and Helen, but every single song we heard only made it worse. If it was a happy song, I thought of the good times we've had with them, and every sad song predicted what life is going to be like until Frank comes to his senses."

"We can't banish music just because it make us think and feel and hope and despair. It is meant to give a release for emotions." Joy ran her index finger along Al's jaw line and continuing down his chest where she tapped on his heart. "A release in here."

"I know. It's just...oh, let's go see Helen. We're not helping anyone sitting here letting a bunch of old '70s songs make us feel blue."

Unaware she had visitors so close at hand, Helen had cranked up the volume on the stereo in her own living room. The last notes of a song rumbled across the lawn as Al and Joy approached. Then, the air stilled as if the mere touch of their feet on the Wilson's porch triggered the next song. At the precise moment Joy touched the door, Helen belted out along with Marvin Gaye, *How could he treat my heart so mean and cruel?*

"Good grief. Shall I cut the power?" Al asked with a sad smile. Helen's standing defense of her marginal singing abilities was *That's why I play French horn and stay clear of the choir!*

"No way. She's asking the same questions we are. Like I said, music is a release."

They sat down on the steps and let the music pound against their ears and hearts. Al circled Joy's shoulder with his arm; they leaned their heads together. The song and Helen's voice faded. But before they could stand up, Al and Joy heard the familiar introduction to *Mockingbird.* Helen's voice nearly drowned out Carly Simon:...*find me some peace of mind...if that peace of mind won't stay...find me a better way.*

"Oh Al." Joy swallowed a lump the size of her fist.

"It's rough stuff, Jinglebells, this business of being friends with a messed-up couple."

"Let's go give it the old college try." Joy pushed up off the step. "Helen," she called through the kitchen door. "Can we come in?"

Helen's head appeared in the doorway from the hall. "Good timing, Jenks," she said, using the abridged name a two-year-old Robyn had dubbed Al and Joy over twenty years ago. "I need help moving furniture." She disappeared from view. Muffled muttering followed the sound of a heavy object hitting the floor.

Al and Joy gawked at their surroundings. The kitchen was stripped bare as if in preparation for a thorough painting. The cupboard doors were wide open, revealing bare shelves. Many drawers were pulled out and empty. Only the major appliances remained in place. "Maybe she's cleaning for therapy," Joy whispered. "Come on."

They stepped into the hallway where they had to squeeze between a nightstand and a twin-bed mattress. Joy bumped into a coat rack and jumped when an umbrella swung against her back. A zippered clear plastic bag held the Santa outfit Frank and Al had shared through the years when all three kids still believed enough to set out cookies and milk.

If Helen had been a fan of moving furniture over the years, this wouldn't have been quite so dramatic. But the truth was, the Wilson's furniture hadn't shifted positions once in three decades except for carpet cleaning—and then it was always put back in precisely the same place. Al had once joked the Wilson home was the perfect place for visually impaired to gain confidence in navigating solo because nothing ever moved. Helen's mantra was *If I liked it here before, I'll like it here now.*

Had either Al or Joy been called upon to express a coherent thought, each would have failed miserably. The living room's gleaming hardwood floor was lost beneath an odd collection of furniture from all over the house. Whatever didn't fit in there, spilled out into the connecting dining room and hallway. Dressers, a bookcase, Helen's quilting frame, a bucket of mops and brooms, bed frames and mattresses, an overflowing box of photo albums, a filing cabinet, Frank's exercise equipment, tables, lamps, chairs, desks, a clothes-drying rack, plant stands, a stepstool—it was all jumbled together with a haphazard array of boxes.

"Helen! How on earth did you move all this stuff by yourself?" Joy croaked.

"Adrenalin is a marvelous thing. So is anger. Anger is highly underrated as a powerful force. Plus, Dave was here; he's strong. And he brought me bunches of boxes from the grocery store." Helen's voice was shrill and uneven. Considering she had worked as a beautician for the past thirty years, her hair mirrored the house's appearance—one disheveled mess.

Joy bit her lower lip until it stung. Untidy hair and a living room that mimicked the ravages of a tornado on the ten-o'clock news: *This is one troubled woman.*

Al had an additional concern: *Dave helped? He hasn't said a thing to us. That's not good—Dave needs to talk things through to understand them.* Forcing himself to speak calmly, he asked, "What's going on with all this stuff?"

"See, it's like this. I called the girls to tell them about their dad, and said they should come get whatever they want. I didn't get through to them until this morning because they'd gone on a shopping trip to Fargo." Helen's words tumbled like logs rolling into a river, jamming from time to time and lurching loose. "They've been saying how they need furniture, so this is their lucky day." Her pitch now lurked close to hysteria. "They're going to rent a truck and come get stuff later today."

"But…" Al blinked, unable to absorb what he saw. "…they can't possibly fit all this into their place."

"Of course not! Some of it I'll take with me. That's where I need your help—getting me moved into the apartment behind the shop."

"The apartment?" Joy echoed numbly.

"Yeah. I don't want to sleep here another night. Getting my stuff out of here will make this place look better before the girls get here."

Look better? How does one give havoc a pretty face? Joy perched on the couch arm since the rest was loaded with upended dining room chairs. "Helen, may I say something? I know this is a hard time, but I hate to see you making such big decisions so quickly. I mean, Frank's only been gone a matter of hours, really. In the big picture, that's a pretty small percentage of your lives together. Maybe you should just hold off on disbanding the house for a couple of days."

Al asked reasonably, "What if Frank comes back to work things out? Getting rid of furniture before you give that a chance to happen is a little drastic, isn't it?"

"Why don't you come stay with us?" Joy offered.

Helen turned a stony gaze on them. "Furniture can't save my marriage, but getting rid of constant reminders of Frank's betrayal may save my sanity. Now, are you going to help me, or do I hire it done?"

"Of course we'll help, as long as you're sure this is what you want..." Al paused in hopes Helen would change her mind. Realizing this wasn't about to happen, he continued reluctantly, "I'll get the pickup." He met Joy's eyes with a worried look and touched her shoulder as he squeezed past her.

"I can't remember much about the apartment, Helen." Joy resisted the impulse to rub her temples where a sudden headache pounded. "How big is it?" Even though Frank and Helen had started out in the apartment, this house had been their home for most of their married lives. She knew the apartment opened on to the alley, and connected to the shop through an inner door. It had stood empty except for one- or two-night rentals—to those willing to camp out on army cots—over the Fourth of July when the number of out-of-town visitors burgeoned.

Helen rattled off the amenities: "There's a living room and dine-in kitchen and a bedroom and bath—oh, and a decent-sized storage closet. The laundry's in the shop, so that's all I need. Dave and I went over there on Sunday and he helped me measure the rooms and clean up the cobwebs. The stove and refrigerator both work fine. When I came home, I figured out what furniture I want to take with me."

Whatever Joy had imagined was happening over at the Wilson's house on Sunday didn't include this flurry of activity behind closed doors. Sunday morning, Dave delivered a note to them from Helen: *Jenks: I need some time to myself—I'd like to spend Sunday alone. Helen.*

Every natural impulse propelled Joy to want to ignore her friend's request, but Al's advice had made sense. "She knows where we are—we'll check in on Monday morning. I can't imagine she'd get much out of church, anyhow. She appreciates Dave's company, so let's just let them be."

Crying, staring into space, pacing—those would have been expected activities. But, bulldozing the remnants of one's life into a heap in the living room? Without warning, words from her first graders' musical masterpiece floated to the surface of Joy's mind:...*to help me find my way...*

Helen was in desperate need of a compass. Maybe north *had* moved.

"When did you pack all these boxes?" Joy asked, waving at chin-high stacks filling every inch of floor space not occupied by furniture.

"It all sort of mushroomed." Helen looked startled as if seeing the accumulation for the first time. "I started moving the heaviest furniture to the living room Saturday night with Dave's help. Yesterday, I packed boxes and moved small stuff. I've kept at it today. It took surprisingly little time to pack up my life," she said with a shuddering sigh she quickly swallowed.

Joy spoke past a lump in her throat. "What about Frank's things?"

Helen's eyes turned to steel. "I could care less about Frank's stuff. Dave took a bunch of it to the garage. It can stay there and rot, for all I care. I'll have a rummage sale for whatever the girls don't want—but not here. I'd rather do a sale in Minot where people won't come just to get juicy tidbits about my miserable marriage."

Joy noticed some boxes were marked "Girls" or "Sell" while others said "APT" in big black lettering. At this point, Helen didn't seem amenable to sitting down for a sensible chat about decision-making, so Joy bit back her advice and merely offered, "What can I do until Al gets back with the truck?"

"Come upstairs with me. I couldn't get the hallway mirror down by myself, and the last thing I need is seven years of bad luck!" Her laugh sounded tinny. "I think it will make the apartment look bigger, don't you? Let's see, do I have the screwdriver? Yup, right here in my pocket! And it's the right kind of screwdriver, too. Why do they have to make different kinds of screw heads? That's what I want to know. It sure makes life difficult, because you've usually got the wrong screwdriver." She seemed compelled to fill every second with nervous chatter.

Joy held the mirror in place while Helen removed the screws and brass braces anchoring it to the wall. They reached the bottom step with the mirror just as Al pulled into the driveway.

He parked as close to the back door as possible and had tossed several tarps and ropes in the truck bed. Joy applauded mentally: *Good job—not that we can forestall the inevitable rumors, but the less anyone sees of what we're doing, the better.*

She knew that along the route between house and apartment, a silent alarm would sound, alerting citizens to trouble in their midst. Flowerbeds would suddenly need weeding—at least those nearest the sidewalk. Ancient bones would creak their way out to porch swings, ostensibly for a bit of fresh air. Like birds diving for road kill, inquisitive children would swoop next to the truck, picking the bones of the current mystery: *What's happening at the Wilson house?*

Drama wasn't usually served up along these streets, so one couldn't blame folks for paying attention when the curtain lifted right on their own doorsteps. But this was one time Joy longed for the anonymity of a metropolis.

By mid-afternoon, Helen, Joy and Al had made six trips with the pickup. The single bed and matching dresser from Tina's old bedroom, Helen's sewing table and the bookcase and rocker from Robyn's room packed the small bedroom at the apartment. The quilting frame claimed one closet corner. "I'm still going to teach you to quilt, Joy," Helen said with forced gaiety. "I can't have you getting lazy on me, now that you're retired!"

The round table and four accompanying chairs from the Wilson's three-season porch just fit into the cramped kitchen where Joy had lined the windowsill with pots of Helen's prized African violets. "I need all four chairs," Helen insisted. "When the girls come, they sometimes bring a friend."

In the living room, two matching overstuffed chairs, a rocker and footstool, the glass-front china cabinet and the entertainment center vied for floor space. Helen's cedar chest now doubled as a coffee table. A healthy fern, a sprawling ivy, and Helen's prized Christmas cactus each occupied plant stands positioned by windows like sunbathers eager to catch the sun's rays.

Al's idea to hang the big mirror opposite the living room windows not only magnified the light, but filled blank wall space. Joy eyed the other dismally bare walls and suggested hanging one of Helen's quilts.

"I've got just the one," Helen said, opening the cedar chest. "I wanted to enter it in the State Fair, but I can always take it down to show."

On the next trip back to the house, Al stopped by his own workshop and found a dowel. Helen threaded it through the loops she had sewed on in preparation for showcasing her work for judges. Al pounded in several nails and soon the quilt was hung. "Perfect," Joy pronounced.

Over the years, Frank had displayed an otherwise untapped artistic flair when he selected the pictures that had hung throughout the Wilson's home. Helen now wanted nothing to do with them. The only pictures she agreed to display in the bedroom were a framed history of the girls' lives from birth through college graduations that had hung in the upstairs hallway at the house. Noticeably missing was the previous focus: Frank and Helen's wedding picture.

While Al cleaned the ceiling light fixtures and checked window latches, Joy and Helen unpacked several boxes of the basics: dishes, linens, and food supplies. "Let's call it a day," Helen said, at last. "The rest can wait."

"We'll stop for today, but only if you come over for supper. The girls should be here soon, and I've got spaghetti sauce simmering in the crock pot." Joy's offer was her only hope to soften the blow for Robyn and Tina. All too soon the girls would see the brutal reality of what had thus far only been words coming across the telephone.

Helen nodded. "Thanks. The café's not open today, and I haven't exactly been little Suzy Homemaker lately so my cupboard is bare. Thanks for all your help, Jenks."

Joy climbed into the pickup and scooted up close to Al on the bench seat for the short trip back to the house, soaking up his warmth and nearness. "There's the rental truck; the girls are here." Helen's voice low and shaky. "Goodness, why did they get such a small truck? They must have just gotten here—they're still in the truck."

Al tooted the horn and Tina and Robyn waved. Even before the pickup stopped fully, Helen leaped out and ran toward her daughters. Robyn reached her first and flung her arms around Helen; they swayed in place. Tina stood by, watching the scene with an eerie sense of detachment.

"Hey, Tina." Al called out softly.

"Hi, Uncle Al; 'lo, Aunt Joy." Old habits lingered—Al and Joy and Frank and Helen had filled the roles of aunt and uncle for each other's children since their births. The affectionate names lingered even when Dave, Tina and Robyn reached adulthood. "Is Dad really gone?" Tina's eyes clouded over.

Al nodded. "He left Saturday morning." He felt her shoulder slump beneath his hand.

Robyn and Helen separated and, brushing their hands across their eyes, turned toward the others. "You're all coming to our house for a spaghetti supper," Joy announced, "so let's head over there. We didn't have much lunch and I, for one, am ready to eat. We'll come back and load the truck later."

"Sounds good," Tina said. "It took so long to locate a truck, we just grabbed sandwiches and sodas at a convenience store and ate on the road. Memorial Day weekend is *the worst* time to rent a truck, we discovered. We'll just jump in the back of your pick-up like when we were kids, Uncle Al. Come on, Robyn." The girls climbed in and Tina slapped the side of the truck in their standard *Ready!* signal.

It didn't take long to get angel hair spaghetti cooking, and prepare garlic bread for the oven, and toss a salad. Shredding carrots and slicing mushrooms, the Wilson girls listened with the same incredulous disbelief Al and Joy felt. Helen gave a more detailed accounting of their father's recent actions, her tongue loosened in the presence of family and friends.

Tina and Robyn exchanged worried glances as their mother frequently stopped slicing tomatoes and flailed the air with the knife to punctuate key points. Her voice spiked harshly at times, or plunged into whispered and tearful disjointed murmurings.

Helen ended the sad discourse with, "I wish your father hadn't left town without at least talking to you girls. I hope you'll both have an opportunity to hear his side of the story." Her words showed more graciousness than Joy could believe she possessed.

Talk was put on hold while they took their places at the table. Al held up his hand before the first bowl was passed. "I'd like to say a blessing—and even though what's on my mind may seem sacrilegious, I think God will understand."

The four women looked at him with varying degrees of puzzlement. He reached out his hands to Joy on one side, and Robyn on the other, each of whom reached out to Tina and Helen to complete the circle. "Dear God," Al began, "this isn't the traditional table grace, but I know You understand how hard these days are for Helen, Robyn and Tina." He squeezed Joy's hand as he began to sing Marilyn Sellars' heartfelt prayer, "One Day at a Time." By the third measure, Joy joined in, her eyes clenched tight against the pool of tears that sprouted. Her voice and Al's blended softly, and she felt the gentle pressure of Tina's hand:*…yesterday's gone, Sweet Jesus…give me the strength to do everything I have to do…*

In the stillness following the last notes, they began the rituals of passing food and taking first bites. It was a quiet meal, at first; Al's alteration to a familiar ritual had provided shelter in a time of storm.

But they soon ventured back into conversational tide pools, with Tina reviving the topic floating beneath the surface. "Personally, I think Dad's a jerk. He's throwing away the best things in his life. At least, that's how I *thought* he considered his family."

Robyn's lip quivered. "Are you doing okay, Mom? Do you want to come stay with us for a while?"

"No, no, honey. I'll be okay. I've got a business to run…" her eyes darted nervously around the table, and she finished in a rush: "…and Al and Joy helped me move today."

Tina lowered her glass to the table with such speed, water sloshed out and dripped off her hand. Robyn's forkful of spaghetti landed on her salad plate. "You moved?" The girls' unison voices jumped an octave between words.

Helen nodded nervously. "To the apartment behind the shop. It's more than enough room for me. I want you to come see it after we get your truck loaded."

This news unnerved the girls; it was the screw's final twist, capping their father's abrupt defection from the family. Tina and Robyn wept quietly, daubing tears on Joy's soft cloth napkins.

"Mom, you can't move there—you need sunshine!" Tina protested. "The apartment windows face either the alley or other buildings."

Robyn choked out, "You can't give up your birdhouses and the garden! Why can't Dad move into the apartment and you stay in the house?"

"Girls, your dad's not here. He's made his move—and it's to California. If I stay in the house, it will only remind me of things I want to forget, so I'm taking the apartment." Mired by her daughters' despair, Helen struggled to rein in her own emotions. Nervously, she drummed her spoon against the palm of one hand.

Joy tossed a pleading glance at Al, but he merely shrugged. This situation was beyond even his abilities to bring sense from confusion. Finally, he offered the best advice he could muster: "Eat up, ladies. I know it's hard to think about food, but we need to eat." He picked up his own fork again and forced bite after bite down his constricted throat while the women half-heartedly pushed food around their plates.

"Uncle Al, how could Dad get so off-base he would run off with another woman?" Robyn asked, at last.

Al pushed his plate away. "If I knew the answer, I'd tell you. This whole thing has mystified and angered Joy and me as much as anything in our lives. I want you all to know, we are here for you, just like always. We'll get through this together."

"Right now, we need some extra muscle to help us load a truck." Tina stopped to blow her nose. "Can Dave help, too? Where is he, anyway?" The fact she just now missed him at the table indicated the state of her heart and mind. Tina had long been Dave's staunchest ally in playground fights and his steadiest friend during childhood's cruel moments.

"Since the grocery store is closed for the holiday, he's helping Luke paint the walls. I'll call him and see how close they are to finishing. He'll be glad to help, and will be thrilled to see you girls," Joy said.

Fortified by food and friendship, the girls held up amazingly well when they faced a living room stacked high with packed-up memories. "Mom, are you sure this isn't rushing things?" Robyn asked. "What will Dad say when he comes…"

"That's the least of my worries," Helen interrupted. "As far as I'm concerned, he burned all his bridges behind him. If I have to stay one more night in a house I shared with the man who betrayed my trust,

I'll go crazy. If Frank ever comes back, I want him to realize what he has destroyed."

A paint-spattered Dave soon joined them and, by nightfall, both the rental truck and the garage were loaded with furniture and boxes. The house echoed hollowly as they searched nooks and crannies for left-behind objects.

"What's going to happen to the house, Mom?" Tina asked. "And all the stuff in the garage?"

"Eventually, I'll have a sale. And I'm going to talk to Milt Browning about putting the house on the market. He'll know what I have to do since it's in both your father's and my names. In the meantime, it will sit empty. There's not much of a rental market here, you know."

Unspoken words and trembling emotions rattled at roller-coaster speeds with the six of them tumbling along a nauseating ride. Solid ground seemed very far away and there was nothing to hold on to. They fanned out around the house.

In the master bedroom, Al pulled a screwdriver out of his hip pocket and removed a light-switch plate Robyn had painted in first grade. It could easily be replaced with a plain one; this one should be a happy memory where Helen would see it in the apartment.

Joy checked the laundry room and found a forgotten bag of clothes-pins. She closed the door, not wanting that room with its heart-wrenching revulsions to be Helen's last visual memory of the house.

Tina and Robyn lingered in their childhood bedrooms and met in the hallway where they mutely clung to each other. Robyn broke away and pulled her sister along to the attic stairs. Up in the partially finished crawl space, she reached behind a board into a special hidey-hole and pulled out a small box. "Remember?" she whispered, not trusting her voice.

Tina nodded and held out her hand. She lifted the cover and their heads brushed together as they explored forgotten treasures: a birthday-cake candle that couldn't be blown out; the ring that had declared

Jimmy Peters' love first for Tina in third grade and then for Robyn when Tina rejected him; and finally, the only thing the girls had ever stolen: an unopened bag of lemon drops from LARSON'S GROCERY—too tempting to ignore at the time, but too guilt-laden to enjoy in the end.

"Lots of memories, huh," Robyn said.

"Yeah, and lots more that don't fit nicely in a box." Tina pushed herself off the attic floor and brushed off her pants. She reached out a hand to her sister.

Downstairs, Dave lugged the last few items that didn't fit in the truck out to the garage and locked the door behind him, hesitating only briefly before he rehung the key on a hidden hook. *Uncle Frank said 'Always remember to put the key back, Dave,' so I better, even though he's gone.*

Out in the kitchen, Helen climbed up on the counter to check on top of the cabinets and found a dust-covered plastic Easter egg. Tina and Robyn appeared just as she made the discovery of an ominous note still inside it, a warning a much-younger Tina had penned: *This is my candy if anyone eats it I hope you get bad poops.* "I guess the secret's out: I rarely clean on top of my cupboards. This has been here for twenty years!" Their laughter sounded empty; it was time to leave this house of sadness.

Darkness descended as they walked two-by-two to the shop's alley entrance. The night's quiet shadows mirrored their moods. "Do you really want to run the shop by yourself, Mom?" Robyn asked as Helen opened the door. "Why don't you just close it for a month or so, and come help us with the bakery? After all, you taught us most of what we know."

"Thanks for the offer, sweeties, but if I close the shop even for a while, people will go elsewhere for their cuts and perms and I'll never get them back. Plus, it will give me something to do besides plot how to get even with your father." She stepped inside ahead of her guests.

"Believe me, with the state I'm in, it would be a real downer to have your mother moping around the bakery."

The thing was, no one had really seen Helen moping around at all. She was all spit and vinegar, and get-outta-my-way.

An exhaustingly animated Helen conducted a quick tour. They left through the door to the shop, waiting while Helen took a few minutes to trim the straggly hair around Tina's ears, and soon they were out on Main Street.

Beneath the streetlight, Robyn turned and noticed the mutilated sign first. She gripped her sister's arm. The girls stared at the sign: D CURL.

"I told your mother it adds a French touch to Main Street," Al said lightly, the sight of the girls' dismayed faces piercing his heart.

Dave promptly filled them in on his role in the unfortunate destruction of the sign, but his words fell on numb ears. They had seen and heard too much in the past few hours to fully absorb any more than this final shock.

Al walked between the girls as all headed back to the loaded rental truck. "Tina and Robyn, this has been a great blow for you, for all of us. Even though your mom is understandably angry, I'm confident your dad will be back. Things may be kinda tough for a while, but it will sort itself out."

"I've got to say, Mom doesn't seem all that traumatized, but I guess that's her way of coping. Do you really think Dad will come back? I mean, there's no home left for him to come to, but can he and Mom ever..." Tina couldn't finish her question.

Robyn reverted to childhood and slid her fingers into Al's hand. But this was no freckle-faced kid skipping along beside him. This was a young woman in anguish, seeking comfort from a trusted family friend. "Ever since Mom called us, we've been ripped apart."

"That's how Joy and I feel. We missed all the signals, and we've known your parents longer than you have. Hey, we even got together with them Friday night and had no clue at all that Saturday morning our world would explode."

"The last time we talked to Dad," Robyn said, "he was saying stuff like, 'Next time we come to Minot, I'll bring my drill and fix that door for you.' Nothing about, 'Have I told you about my plan to destroy your lives?'"

"For our part," Tina said, "we wasted most of that phone call moaning about how we lost the bid for the Senior Center's breakfast rolls. It never occurred to me to ask my folks how their marriage was doing."

"Joy and I know some of how you feel. But one thing you need to realize—your dad won't find happiness in his new life, not the way he went about it. He and your mom may have had problems no one knew about, but he didn't solve them with this cockamamie decision he made." Al's stride lengthened as frustration with his long-time friend flared once again. The threesome covered the remaining distance to the Wilson's yard, each locked in a brooding silence.

After tearful hugs all around, Tina revved the truck's engine and the girls pulled away from the curb. A bottomless sigh escaped Helen's tight lips as she watched her daughters roll away.

Dave waved until the truck was out of view. "Can I walk you back to the apartment, Aunt Helen?"

She took his arm. "You're on, Davey. G'night, Jenks. Thanks. See you tomorrow—it's a brand new day."

CHAPTER 4

Tuesday morning truly felt like summer. School had been out for several weeks, but it took Memorial Day before people left spring behind and started thinking about summer. Grade school kids made the traditional pilgrimages back to the schoolyard to enjoy the beginnings of a three-month recess filled with jump rope contests and hopscotch rhymes, swings and teeter-totters, tree houses and impromptu ballgames. In the shadows of the very building they had longed to escape just days earlier, they embarked on the rituals of childhood.

Helen flung open the front door to the D CURL and made a phone call to Bismarck even before opening the blinds. Within an hour, her phone was ringing and she carried on spirited and mysterious conversations that left her regular customers curious and sent them scurrying on their way with morsels of news as fresh as their haircuts.

Stitching speculation to far-flung fantasies, rumors blanketed Prairie Rose:

"Frank's definitely gone and must not be coming back for a while, at least. I heard Helen talking on the phone to someone about coming for a one-week internship, she calls it."

"The wife's been saying I need a haircut...maybe I'll see if Helen can fit me in and see what's what..."

"Good thing she can barber. She's going to need lots of business to stay open."

Over backyard fences:

"Where do you suppose Frank disappeared to?"

"If we knew that, we'd know why he's gone. And we don't."

"Can't be good."

"Got that right. And Helen's as close-mouthed as a clam."

Around the tables at CATE'S CAFÉ:

"The Wilson girls were in town over the weekend and loaded up a truck of furniture."

"No! Hadn't heard that. We didn't get back until late from Crosby. Is the house *empty*?"

"Yeah. Sadie said Helen moved into the apartment behind the shop. Al and Joy helped."

"Maybe I'll go buy me some stamps and see if I can learn anything from Al."

"You'll be wasting your time. I heard Al's mad as hops at Frank, but that don't mean he's talkin'."

Around the gas pumps at ED'S GARAGE:

"Mitchell said Helen asked him for Justin Campbell-Lampman's phone number. What's that about?"

"You don't suppose she's asking him for a loan, do you?"

"I doubt it, though he's sure got the dough and she can't be taking in much. The shop's paid for, but still, there's living expenses."

"If Frank's gone for good, she's gotta be planning ahead for retirement, you know."

And so it went—hearsay blew around town like feathers at a chicken plucking.

Mildred Windsor was scheduled for a permanent after lunch on Tuesday and stopped by the café a full hour before her appointment. Her rationale that she didn't want to be late didn't fool anybody. The bottom line was she needed to gather the full body of hearsay before stepping foot in the beauty shop.

Her conversation with Betty about what to call the shop now that the name was chopped in half on the sign was interrupted by Calvin's nasal voice coming from a cluster of men at the next table. "How much does one of those permanents cost, Mildred?"

"Thirty-five dollars, last time I had one," she responded. "Why?"

"How long does it take?"

"A couple of hours."

"But Helen can do other things while you're under the dryer, right?" Calvin persisted.

Frustrated by this intrusion on her limited time to collect data, Mildred said brusquely, "It takes a while for the permanent to set, so she fits in haircuts, and such."

Meaningful nods circled Calvin's table. With Mildred's grudging help, at that precise moment Prairie Rose launched a campaign destined to accomplish what small towns do best: take care of their own.

For the remainder of the week, the shop's business was brisk. Helen was so exhausted at the end of each day, it was all she could do to close up the shop, slap together something resembling supper, and fall into bed. One night she dozed off in the bathtub and awoke with goose bumps. Her paperback novel had sunk to the bottom of the tub. "That's fitting—it was just some sappy story about love, anyhow," Helen scoffed as she wrapped a towel around her chilled body. "Such nonsense about finding true love deserves to drown."

The second week in June, two young women from the North Dakota Cosmetology School arrived. Madeleine and Cassie began the summer-long parade of Lisas and Heathers and Julies and even a Dylan and a Max, each pair arriving on a Monday evening and returning to NDCS for Friday classes. Helen requested two interns each week so they could keep each other entertained during off-work hours. The interns stayed in the sleeping rooms above the SATURDAY STORE, these arrangements initiated by Helen's mysterious phone call to Justin Campbell-Lampman.

The stylists-in-training gained valuable experience with Helen's help and example. They washed heads, but learned much about the fine art of small talk. They came to recognize the difference between customer service and just doing business. They saw how careful supply orders affected the bottom line. They witnessed the details of scheduling that kept things flowing. They cut hair for those clients who gamely bought into Helen's homespun philosophy: "The only difference between a good haircut and a bad haircut is two weeks—and a good hat."

In addition to helping Helen keep the shop open, these assistants provided her with someone to talk to who didn't know all the dirty details of her life's recent upheavals. They found her amazingly interested in their thoughts and dreams and ideas and goals. Each Wednesday night, Helen cooked dinner-for-three and they talked long after the dishes were cleared. Back at school, more than one young hair-stylist would decide Helen Wilson was about the best mentor they would ever have.

Helen seemed to be doing fine. At the Jenkins' house, it was another story. Joy watched Al warily. He slept poorly, ate half-heartedly, and spent a lot of time staring off into space. One evening, she talked him into a walk. As they strolled the quiet streets, she could tell he was trying to conduct a normal conversation, but his heart just wasn't in it.

Passing by the Wilson's deserted house was inevitable—it would have taken a conscious decision and a circuitous route to avoid it. As it came into view, Al stopped abruptly. "Oh, that makes me angry! Look at that lawn, Joy. Who did Frank think would mow his grass while he's out cavorting in California?"

"I doubt if he was thinking much about home maintenance when he left," Joy said dryly. "And remember, he didn't know Helen would move out."

Al snorted, "Yeah, like Helen's ever been able to get that mower started. He knows she floods it every time. It looks terrible." He looked back at the Marshall's home. "I'm surprised Bob or one of the other neighbors hasn't mowed it, just so they wouldn't have to look at it every day."

"Bob Marshall might have, but he and Trudy are on a ten-day vacation. You could mow it, Al," Joy suggested mildly. "Or, we could send Dave over."

"And what kind of statement does that make? It would look like we're covering for Frank."

"Maybe...or it could be an act of friendship for Helen."

"I doubt if Helen gives a rip if the lawn grows waist-high."

"But the neighbors might. They're probably as confused about what's going on as we are, and not sure what to do about a lawn going wild."

Everything Joy said made sense, but Al wasn't able to let his tirade die. "If I lived next door, I'd be over here mowing," he sputtered.

Joy didn't reply. She heard the sorrowful resignation in Al's voice, but recognized something of the old Al in his words. Sure enough, after work the next day Al headed over to Frank's garage with a gas can, and unearthed Frank's lawnmower from the garage. Putting it away an hour later, he muttered, "That's more than you deserve, Frank."

Joy had cold lemonade waiting for him and hugged him tightly when he returned home. "I *love* a man who gets all hot and sweaty doing the right thing."

"Yeah, well you'll never know how close I came to *not* doing anything so don't figure me for any saint. And don't go telling Helen I mowed, okay?"

"I won't need to. Remember, Sadie's right across the street and I bet her phone was busy before your first swipe around the yard!"

The last weekend in June, Justin Campbell-Lampman appeared for a by-now predictable visit. He had first set foot in Prairie Rose a year earlier, drawn from New York City to the northwest corner of North Dakota when his idol—BJ Kendall, world-renowned golfer—had reopened the golf course in an event that put Prairie Rose in the sports-world spotlight.

On his return trips, Justin monitored the considerable success of the ingenious business venture he had launched during that first visit. As on-site managers of the highly successful SATURDAY STORE, retirees Mitchell Young and Lewis Clifton enjoyed a special relationship with the closest thing to a celebrity the town could claim among their citizens.

When Justin financed renovating the old Manchester Hotel into the once-a-week rotating business that brought big-name stores to a refurbished building in a small town, Prairie Rose reaped more than increased Saturday traffic. The village gained a can-do attitude that subtly infused each citizen. Justin may have provided the impetus and the initial resources, but it was the people of Prairie Rose who kept the flame lit.

Though only in his mid-twenties, Justin's business acumen, combined with significant financial resources, allowed him to take a gamble on a small town willing to think big. Founder and CEO of the New York–based CAMPBELL-LAMPMAN CONSULTING in his East-Coast life, Justin's trips to North Dakota provided an escape from his fast-paced high-stressful life as he immersed himself in the calm and acceptance he found in Prairie Rose.

This trip was no different. He had relaxed in the skies above New York even as he heard the pilot say, "…sit back and enjoy the flight…"

At the Williston airport, he quickly picked up his rental car and headed down the familiar roads. From the minute Gail Harker opened the door to welcome him back to THE JOHANSON HOUSE BED & BREAKFAST INN on Friday night, Justin felt as if he had just shrugged on a comfortable old sweater.

He complimented Gail on her new curly hairdo and talked with her for a few minutes before heading upstairs to his room. He took time, as always, to open the window and listen to the silence. An hour later, he walked over to Luke and Cate's for dinner and time with their four-month-old adopted son and his partial namesake, Justin Edward Larson, now called Juddie.

An evening's conversation with friends ensured a restful night's sleep for Justin. Fully refreshed when the sun streamed in his bedroom window, he dressed quickly and headed downstairs. "Good morning, Gail! Something smells great."

"Turnovers. Help yourself to coffee and juice and I'll have a hot one in front of you in a minute." Since Justin's first stay at the B&B, it had become their habit to share these uninterrupted early-morning moments. As unlikely as it would have seemed a year ago, their friendship had grown steadily. Gail Harker, young widow and mother of two, received housing and a modest salary in return for her services as on-site B&B manager. Justin Campbell-Lampman, with his New York accent and tailor-made wardrobe, had an innate knowledge of things totally foreign to Gail: computers, investments and how to succeed in the Big Apple.

None of this made any difference as they faced each other across the table. He downed two turnovers—one rhubarb, one raspberry. "There's nothing like this in New York!" he praised. With Gail supplying local updates, Justin learned Eric and Amy Carter would arrive within the week, moving into Luke Larson's house that had been vacant since Luke and Cate married in November.

"I know Amy's the new first grade teacher, but what will Eric do?"

"He put an ad in the paper that said he can build patios, decks, sheds and I heard he got several jobs from that. I'm glad he doesn't have to remodel an old house to live in. It's nice he can start working for pay right away."

"At one time, I'd thought about buying a house here," Justin remarked casually.

Startled, Gail looked up from stirring cream into her coffee. "Really? I didn't know that."

"Yeah, I even talked with Milt Browning about it. But I have everything I need here at the B&B, and no worries about pipes freezing when I'm not around. Besides, with my own house, I'd have to learn how to bake turnovers!"

"You could still come here—I'd sneak you one!"

"I'd rather get my breakfast fair and square, not creeping up the alley for handouts."

The mental image of Justin standing by the back fence, waiting for her to lob a hot breakfast treat to him amused Gail and she led their laughter.

"Besides, I'd miss our early-morning chats," he said.

She took a slow sip of coffee and met his eyes. "So would I," she agreed softly.

Footsteps overhead forewarned of others awakening. After meeting his fellow lodgers and talking with Jillie and little Alex, Justin ambled off to meet Mitchell and Lewis. Weather permitting, they liked to claim a picnic table at the park, but with the Boy Scouts busily painting and repairing damaged tables in preparation for the Fourth of July, the men met at CATE'S CAFÉ instead.

After a quick visit to the SATURDAY Store, Justin crossed the street. He stopped short just inside the café's door. His eyebrows raised and his jaw dropped when Mitchell and Lewis signaled him from across the room. Both men's gray heads sported a jumble of wiry curls. The men looked like models for billboards warning children not to play with electrical sockets. As if coiled tresses weren't enough of a shock, Lewis had grown a mustache, and a straggly goatee sprouted from Mitchell's chin. It took all the good breeding Justin possessed to calmly greet the men.

Cate called out a welcome and followed him to the table with coffee. Justin's gaze swept across the room as he lifted his cup for the first satisfying swallow. *Yikes!* Coffee spewed out of his mouth and he grabbed for a napkin and mopped up quickly. Mitchell and Lewis met his feeble smile curiously, but he didn't attempt to explain his embarrassing breach of etiquette.

Damage repaired, he gripped the mug and looked around again. From the counter to the tables spreading across the café, one thing was startlingly different. *It's like a reunion of Art Garfunkel look-alikes—the only heads in this room that aren't curly are Cate's, mine, and two bald guys!* He caught Cate's eye and raised his eyebrows in a silent query; she winked knowingly.

Uncannily reading his mind, Mitchell leaned forward, already studying Justin's head. "You know, you've got a lot of hair, Justin. Ain't that right, Lewis?"

"Yeah, thick, too," Lewis agreed, squinting at Justin's precision-cut hair.

"Ever think about getting a permanent, Justin? Helen could fix you right up for thirty-five bucks, plus tip. And you come often enough for touch-ups. No need to pay rip-off city prices."

Lewis nodded sagely. "If your mustache is any indication, I bet you could grow a mighty nice beard. She trims them, too; real reasonable."

Panic blended with humor to form an outrageous mental cocktail as Justin imagined returning to New York looking like someone zapped by lightning. His clients were Big Business, leaning towards designer suits and silk ties or scarves, professionally laundered shirts or blouses with jewel-studded cufflinks or brushed gold bracelets. They looked sleek and successful, and expected the consultant who gave them more bang for their bucks to look the same. In Justin's other world, the wrong haircut could kill an encounter. No telling what a wild and woolly version of a rag doll would do to his business. He didn't intend to find out.

Without warning, a chill settled around him; just as suddenly, he felt feverish. He met his tablemates' persistent stares and wondered if he looked as nauseous as he felt. "Helen? I thought Frank is the barber," he said in a lame attempt to resume the conversation that sagged heavily on his end.

"You might as well know," Lewis said. "You're practically one of us, now." The men began a garbled account of the goings-on at the D CURL. Justin learned why Prairie Rose women—including Gail, he suspected—matched Shirley Temple lock-for-lock, and why men with enough hair to comb now required seed caps one size larger than usual to accommodate their curly heads. Their story also helped Justin further understand Helen's interest in the sleeping quarters above the SATURDAY STORE.

"When Helen first permed us, we looked real nice. We haven't got the hang of daily maintenance, so some of us tend towards frizzy. Apparently, there's a lot more to it than just shampooing and towel drying," Lewis said ruefully, running his hand over his scalp.

"But you probably wouldn't frizz up much at all, Justin," Mitchell said soothingly.

Justin's adopted hometown had piqued his interest since the first day he drove into town, but this was beyond anything he had previously experienced. Finding himself with a nervous tumult in the pit of his stomach and no words of wisdom regarding hair, he stepped on to the solid ground of business talk. "Everything seemed fine at the store when I stopped by earlier."

"Sure is," Mitchell said and opened his notebook.

An hour later, Lewis stuck his pen in his pocket, and signaled for a coffee refill. "Say, we've got a dandy idea for celebrating Doctor Alex's birthday to run past you." Listening intently, Justin realized he could barely remember Mitchell and Lewis any other way than curly. Their interesting proposal shot every concern right out of his straight-haired head.

Later that day, Justin walked quickly from the B&B to the D CURL. He held the door open for a high school boy just leaving and stared at the startling appearance of that lanky fellow. The boy greeted him, "Hey, Mister Campbell-Lampman!"

"Hi, Chad." He blinked and stared, slack-jawed, after the retreating teenager he had hired for the remodeling project the previous summer.

The door squeaked and Helen looked over her shoulder. "Hello, Justin. Are you okay?"

"Yeah, I'm fine, or I will be after you work your magic. I was playing with Gail's kids this afternoon and a piece of Jillie's gum got stuck in my hair. I'm hoping you can cut it out without too much damage."

"I have pretty good luck with gum-cuts!" She brushed a towel across a chair. "Have a seat. You're my last customer for the day, at least in the shop. I'm going to go over to Rachel's when I finish up here to set her hair. She's taking off on a trip in the morning, so I said I'd come to the house for her to conserve her energy. All that to say, if you don't mind, I'm going to close up before we start."

"Sorry to show up so late. Would you rather I come back tomorrow?" he asked as she flipped the sign from OPEN to CLOSED and adjusted the blinds.

"Heavens, if you roll around on that gum all night, it will be a real mess in the morning. No, this is fine. Rachel isn't expecting me any specific time." She waved him into the chair, tied a cape around his neck, repositioned a few essentials within her reach and spun him around to face the mirror.

Justin spoke while she contemplated the sticky situation. "That boy who just left here—Chad—he can't have needed much help from you. He was shaved as clean as a billiard ball!"

"That's precisely what he needed—a close shave," Helen laughed.

"He's quite the contrast to all the curls I've seen around town."

Helen rested her hand on Justin's shoulder, the comb she held bushing against his ear as she met his eyes in the mirror. A transformation swept over her face like windshield wipers clearing fog from a steamed window.

"What you've seen—bald and curly—is friendship. THE CLIP AND CURL, or the D CURL, as I'm sure you noticed," Helen added wryly, "is a solo business these days, and everyone knows it. Before I could lose sleep over making it financially, boys like Chad suddenly want shaved heads, men insist they've always dreamed of curls, women decide this is the summer to get a tint, and girls of all ages walk in with pictures from magazines and say, 'Make me look like this!'" She stepped aside and pulled a tissue out of a box and blew her nose loudly.

"This town is filled with good people, isn't it?" Justin said softly, remembering Lewis and Mitchell's persistent interest in his hair.

She nodded and sniffed into a second tissue. “And you’re one of them, even though you may think of yourself as a New Yorker. I can’t thank you enough for allowing me to rent those sleeping rooms for my interns and at a dirt-cheap price, too. If they had to stay at the B&B, I couldn’t afford them. It’s an imposition to ask folks to house total strangers in their own homes, week-in, week-out.

“That space stands empty weekdays, so everyone’s a winner. I’m sorry about your personal situation, Helen. Mitchell and Lewis told me Frank is gone.”

“I wasn’t up to going into all the details when I called you; sorry. People in town have helped me so much, but I just can’t tell them how much…yet.”

“I know what you mean. I lost someone last September and I still find it difficult to talk about it.”

“I’d heard. I’m sorry for your loss,” she said sincerely.

“Loss comes in different shades, but it’s all pain-colored.”

Helen tipped her head thoughtfully. “You’re sure right about that. Do you have anyone to help you make it through?”

“I see a grief counselor back in New York. But when it gets bad, I come to Prairie Rose. That’s the best therapy for me. I love this town.”

“I do, too, but it’s such a small place. My troubles are so embarrassingly personal. Even though I’m mad enough to spit tacks, this is my girls’ hometown. I want people to remember Robyn’s beautiful music, and Tina’s remarkable athletic abilities—not their parents’ unfortunate lives. So I keep my mouth shut.”

“It’s lonely, isn’t it, when you feel there’s no one to talk to?”

“I used to be the ‘Helen-who-can-do-anything-you-want-with-your-hair.’ But now I’m the ‘Helen-who-did-God-only-knows-what-to-her-husband.’ Let me tell you, it’s no picnic living here these days.”

“I’m sure if I’d grown up here, it would be hard for me, too.”

“Do you think I’d be better off to move away?”

“Only you know the answer. When the dust settles, you’ll know what to do.”

"What bothers me most is my silence is alienating my friends. Even knowing that, I can't make myself spill my guts. It leaves people wondering what on earth has happened. I don't want pity, but I sure miss having people sit in this chair and just *talk*—like you're doing now. They weigh every word like they were being charged by the syllable. I never dreamed how much I'd miss normal conversations about new shoes and grandbabies and vacuum cleaners that quit working and the pros and cons of flu shots."

"I discovered people really don't know what to say, so rather than say the wrong thing, they say *nothing* not realizing how much we need *something*. Here's what worked for me: I told one person as much as I felt comfortable sharing, and gave them permission to talk to everyone else."

Helen nodded pensively and spritzed his hair, ruffled it with her hand and combed it back into place. They shared a comfortable silence while she clipped a few more hairs and offered Justin a hand mirror. Spinning the chair around, she asked, "How's this?"

"Wow!" Justin exclaimed as he examined the back of his head from several angles. "You didn't even leave a dent. I had visions of a hole back there the size of the Holland Tunnel. What a relief!"

"Luckily, I honed my barbering skills over the years, or no man alive would let me near his head."

"What do I owe you?"

"Not a thing—consider it part of my gratitude to you."

Justin extracted a bill from his wallet. "Take five—consider it a tip. Don't argue with me!" He wagged his finger. "You've done something I thought was impossible."

Helen pocketed the bill and automatically reached for the broom. Leaning her chin on the handle, she said, "I like your idea of giving someone permission to talk for me. May I practice on you?"

"Absolutely."

Helen straightened her shoulders and met Justin's eyes. "Frank left me for another woman. He's in California and we'll probably get a divorce. I hate him now as much as I once loved him." She swallowed hard and clutched the broom so tightly her knuckles whitened. "But I'm determined to survive."

"That's important, and I know you'll make it. Frank made a big mistake," he said, quietly.

"Thanks." She loosened her grip on the broom and set it aside. "If you don't mind my asking, how do you make it through the roughest times?"

"I don't mind at all," Justin replied. "Most of the time, I do okay, but some days, it's not so good. Too many not-so-good days in a row, and I know I've got to plan a trip to Prairie Rose. Even though I've never been a religious person, whenever I'm here, I go to church. Pastor Tori always says something that pulls me together again."

"I let the church habit slide after Frank left, mostly because I just sit there and cry which only makes people notice me. If I steel myself against crying, I get nothing out of the service because it takes so much effort to be strong that I have nothing left to devote to listening."

"This is the voice of experience—try coming late, sitting in the back and leaving early," he suggested with a crooked grin.

"Maybe I'll see you there tomorrow," Helen said slowly, opening the door for Justin. "Save room for me in the back row."

"Consider it done. Thanks, Helen."

"No, that's my line, Justin. Thanks for the best conversation I've had in over a month."

Walking over to Rachel's home, Helen breathed in the fresh air and said aloud, "I need to get out more." By the time she reached Rachel's, she had decided to bring a bird feeder and a couple birdhouses from the old house to go outside her new back door. Her step lightened as she vowed, "Then, I'll fix up a little space where I can sit outside and enjoy my birds, again." She *yoo-hooed* and entered Rachel's open door, nodding her head resolutely. "That's what I'll do."

A damp-headed Rachel greeted her in the kitchen. "Thanks for catering to an old woman's whimsy, Helen. I just couldn't garner enough *oomph* to get to the shop today."

"No problem, Rachel. I just told myself I need more fresh air, and coming over here gets me started on that goal. So, you're taking a trip," Helen said, falling into her usual conversational pattern as she pulled a comb from her pocket.

"I sure am. If you see any straggly ends, please trim them. I'm sure I'll look like quite the wild woman the next time I come to the shop."

"Oh, this isn't a short trip?"

Inexplicably, Rachel's cheeks reddened. "I really don't know at this point. Alex and Tori will keep an eye on things, so I'm under no constraints to return any specific time. I wanted you to come over and help yourself to flowers—they're growing profusely and it's a shame to waste them. In fact, take some home with you tonight. I've got a vase you can fill."

"You know me and flowers—I'd be happy to water and weed for you, too, if Alex and Tori need help."

"I'll let them know; they're coming by later for last-minute instructions. Now, tell me about your interns. What a marvelous idea you had, Helen, to bring such energetic young people to town!" Rachel adeptly changed the subject while Helen worked steadily. Within minutes, the task was accomplished and supplies put away. Rachel rolled her wheelchair to a hallway cabinet and directed Helen to select a vase.

Back home, Helen put the flowers in the center of her table and sat down to enjoy an egg salad sandwich loaded it with onions—something Frank detested. After selecting a compact disk of hits from the '70s and adjusting the volume on the CD player, she propped her feet up on the ottoman for a relaxing evening. She settled into the rocker with the latest issues of several women's magazines she would take to the shop on Monday. As she had told Justin, she was determined to survive Frank's annihilation of their marriage. Beginning tonight, she planned to reclaim all the songs she loved, stripping them of their previous association with good times and bad.

"You can yank the rug out from under my feet, Frank, but I'm hanging on to these songs—you can find new songs for your new life," she announced to the empty room. "The Jenks and I have squatters' rights to the '70s music. You're the one who moved on."

Flipping magazine pages, she listened to the music with half her mind and replayed her conversation with Justin in the other half. Justin's voice mingled with the musicians':

...Loss comes in different shades, but it's all pain-colored...

Carly Simon sang...*I haven't got time for the pain...*

...Frank made a big mistake...

Gordon Lightfoot sang...*Getting lost in her loving is your first mistake*...and Helen shook her magazine in the air. "You'd better believe that, buster!"

...I go to church...

Earth, Wind & Fire sang...*How's ya faith? 'Cause ya faith is you...in our hearts lie all the answers...*

...pick one person...and give them permission to talk...

The Spinners sang...*Wear a pretty dress...too many dreams have died...*

Helen let the magazine slide off her lap to the floor and leaned her head against the rocker's high back. Who to pick to spread the word? One idea pushed itself up through the surface and scared the living daylights out of her. *I must be losing my mind! Such a thought is plum crazy.*

But as she contemplated her options, that radical idea made more sense than anything else. To expect either Joy or Cate to spread the word would make them look like faithless friends. Both kept as close to her as she would let them, but what she couldn't explain to them was how heart wrenching it was to be around happily married people right now. Besides, neither woman had ever been known to talk about another person's private affairs, so she could hardly expect them to suddenly adopt the role of authorized blabbermouth. Maybe Rachel could have helped, but she was leaving town—and being quite evasive about the length of her absence.

No, this required a professional talker, and one who would be around.

Helen looked at the clock. It was only 7:30. Chuckling, she picked up the phone, forcing the humor out of her voice when the call was answered on the third ring. "Hello, this is Helen. Are you busy this evening? I'd like to come over to talk to you about a new, uh, dress." *Wear a pretty dress…too many dreams have died…*"A pretty dress," she added.

Fifteen minutes later, Helen knocked on Widow O'Dell's door.

Sadie peered through the screen door, eyes like black walnuts in her age-lined face. The two women were soon surrounded by stacks of fabric Sadie pulled from her trunks like rabbits from a magician's hat.

"Thank you for letting me come over on such short notice. I just decided tonight that I need something to take my mind off all my troubles, Sadie. I didn't even think about needing material, that's how upset I've been lately. Thankfully, you have a nice assortment on hand. I really like this soft yellow one."

"It looks good with your coloring, and it's an easy fabric to care for," Sadie said agreeably, still stunned at her good fortune. *Surely, she'll let some juicy details slip. I just have to get her talking…*

"I need something cheerful these days, and yellow fits the bill. Can I confide in you, Sadie?"

Startled speechless as her silent wish was granted, Sadie nodded jerkily and leaned forward. Suddenly, her eyes narrowed. *Wait a minute; no one confides in me. Is this some kind of a trick?*

Sensing Sadie's suspicions, Helen widened her own eyes to inspire trust. She modulated her voice and spoke the ten words she had rehearsed on the short walk to Sadie's house. Ten words destined to put Sadie in the catbird seat: "Frank has left me. It came as such a shock." She stared at the braided rug beneath her sandaled feet.

Sadie pressed her fingers against her lips for a moment, tiny squeaks escaping despite her efforts to suppress them. "I knew he'd left, and suspected it wasn't…Oh, my, I can't begin…I mean, how terrible for you."

"There's another woman."

"Oh!" Sadie's blue-veined fingers now did a tap dance on her lips. "I didn't realize Frank had a wandering eye." Sadie's forehead furrowed as she conducted a quick mental census of local women. *Who could it be?*

"Neither did I. We were married for nearly thirty years and in all that time, I never *once* suspected him of infidelity. Now, we'll probably get divorced."

"Gracious! What happened?" Sadie attempted to veil her excitement with a respectable shroud of concern, but her eyes gave her away: *Details!* they shouted.

Helen purposely gave her own spin to Sadie's question. "He turned fifty this year, and that made him feel old. I guess he just wanted someone who wouldn't remind him of his age."

Sadie scoffed, "If that isn't just like a man. Always looking over the fence for greener grass. What woman would want an old goat like him anyway?" Realizing too late what her thoughtless remarks implied about Helen, Sadie had the sense to clench her teeth before the insult could compound itself. Her goal now was to steer clear of anything that could eradicate this unprecedented event in her long and lonely life.

Helen bit back a wild giggle, wishing Frank could hear Sadie's assessment of him. "He found a sweet young thing and headed off to live with her in California."

"California!" Sadie snorted derisively. "That figures." Raised eyebrows, sniffs and head-jerks punctuated her words with upper-case disdain: "That whole state is a Hell-Hole of Reprobates. Filthy heathens, everyone of them, who don't have the First Regard for God, morality, purity, Honor—any of that. Frank is going to Die of Sexual Diseases, and he's going to expect You to give him a Christian Burial. Don't do it, you poor thing. He made his bed, *Now Let Him Lie In It.*" The last remark's potential innuendo registered and Sadie blushed furiously. Flustered, she spoke quickly, "Let's measure you for that new dress." She wiped at her wispy hair with a fluttering hand.

Helen stood straight and still while Sadie wrapped the tape around her, made notations on a tablet, and draped the yellow yardage around her like a sari, standing back to view the effect. "I have everything I need. Now we'll have tea," Sadie said and disappeared into the kitchen.

Forcing herself to sit quietly beside Sadie at the dining room table for a cup of herbal tea and an oatmeal cookie, Helen reached the last step in her mission. "I have a favor to ask of you, Sadie."

Sadie's cup landed noisily on her saucer. "Anything, anything at all," she said fervently, reaching across the table to pat Helen's hand.

"I, uh," milking it shamelessly, Helen lowered her eyes, "I can scarcely bear to talk about this...this whole mess. But I feel like I'm alienating people by not telling them what's on my heart. I mean, I feel so all alone now." A dramatic pause, and then carefully orchestrated a rush of words: "I know people wonder where Frank went and if he's coming back, but I can't find it in myself to tell the same story over and over again. It's just so hard...Would you...no, I can't ask you to do my dirty work..."

Sadie sucked in her breath. "Of course you can! I'd do whatever I could do to help you—just ask, my dear."

Helen allowed her lower lip to quiver—Sadie need not know that hoots of laughter were more likely to escape than heart-wrenching sobs. "If you could just...help me tell folks the barest details...just enough so their imaginations don't go crazy..."

"You've told no one else? What about Joy Jenkins and Cate Larson?" Sadie asked suspiciously. "You three are thick as thieves, it seems." Tact was not her middle name.

"We're all friends, but they're so happily married that being around them makes my situation all the more painful." Helen pulled a tissue out of her pocket and daubed her eyes.

Sadie squared her shoulders and leaned back in her chair. Her eyes blazed, her voiced stilled. Helen could almost see the mental wheels turning beneath the *Three-Step-Silvery-Moon* hair she touched up every month for Sadie.

The seamstress twisted a gingham apron string in her hands. *It seems too good to be true: the facts behind the fiction, details only Helen and that scoundrel Frank know—and I'm being given permission to speak! People will be seeking me out…no more cold shoulders. Mercy, I need a new dress, too!*

"Of course you can't talk about it, your poor thing. Why, I'd be…" The widow choked in search of a word. *Happy? Delighted? Thrilled beyond belief?* She coughed delicately into a handkerchief. "…I'm willing to help in any way I can. I will give only the scantest details—just enough so people realize the anguish you feel. It's the least I can do for a long-time friend."

Friend wasn't the word Helen would have chosen, but she didn't quibble with the person who would perform a necessary service for her. "Thank you, Sadie," she allowed her voice to quiver, "from the bottom of my broken heart. Please know how grateful I am." She pressed Justin's five-dollar bill into Sadie's hand. "This is the down-payment on my new dress."

Sadie trembled. *To be given such a mission! No more slip-sliding on the rails of gossip—this is a ticket to ride!* To mask her jubilance, she cleared her throat and turned all business. "A down-payment is hardly required. I'll have this dress ready for you in the next few days. You need something to cheer you up and you deserve it more than anyone I've ever known. If you *ever* need someone to talk to, you can count on me, Helen."

Like a horse at the starting gate, Sadie had heard the whistle and was ready to race. Impatiently, she waited for Helen to move along the hallway to the front door, across the porch, down the steps, out of sight on the sidewalk.

Closing the front door, Sadie leaned against it until her heart slowed to a steady beat. After filling the teakettle for morning tea, she paced the kitchen floor beside the telephone. There it hung on the wall—waiting, ready. If only there were someone she could call right now. *No, be patient. This is far too important. You need to plan your way through this one.* With that resolved, Sadie cleared the table and returned to the living room and sat down in the very spot Helen had occupied to contemplate this most unusual evening.

Out on the street, Helen glanced at her watch: 9:00 o'clock. Never had an hour produced such fine results: Sadie, with Helen's blessing, would have tales to tell, and Helen had reclaimed her *zing*. Up until now, she had been fueled by anger; now she was rejoining Life with a capital *L*. Frank may have wounded her, but she wasn't dead.

"So there," she said as she turned off the lights and crawled into bed. "You may have stomped on my heart, Frank Wilson, but you didn't smash my ticker flat. And Sadie's none too crazy about you, either! I'll bet she is going to be awake all night, plotting and planning her strategies." Lying in bed, she replayed her conversation with Sadie and laughed so hard she had to sit up to breathe.

Then, she remembered she had left the stereo on. Padding barefooted into the living room, she reached to push the button, and hesitated. Turning on a lamp, she searched through her music collection. She found the song she was thinking about, turned off the light and danced solo in the moonlight to *Seasons in the Sun*. The poignant refrains released her from the place where Frank could hurt her any longer:... *We had joy, we had fun...goodbye to you, my trusted friend...*

CHAPTER 5

Sadie hit Main Street on Monday morning with a sense of giddiness she could barely conceal. Several times she had to force herself to slow down to her normal pace. She searched the streets for her first encounter. *No one. They must all be at the café. Sadie, you're going to the café!*

Sadie had always suspected it to be true, but today she could almost see it happening: she appeared, and conversations ground to a halt. No one wanted to be guilty of giving her any information to spread, no matter how innocent it might be. *Hmmph!* Today she alone had News-with-a-capital-N and the authority to spread it. *Heavenly days, I believe my heart just skipped a beat!*

"May I join you, ladies?" she asked a table of three. She had gotten up during the night to practice that very question before the mirror, working on her smile, perfecting her body language. *Not too sweet, not too eager.* She ignored Ethel, Dorothy, and Betty's lack of enthusiasm and failed to give them time to invite her before she pulled out the remaining chair and plunked herself down.

"Hello, Sadie," Betty said belatedly.

"My, don't you all look nice this morning. It's as if you just stepped out of Helen's beauty shop!" Sadie twittered, airing her best conversation-starter first.

Ethel, Dorothy and Betty stared at her blankly. That's when Sadie realized Ethel had been crying and actually looked rather blotchy and drained. She felt like sobbing herself. *Isn't that just my luck—not only have I wasted my first chance to spread the word, but I'm not likely to hear first-hand what's wrong with Ethel, either.*

Squirming beneath the trio's chilly reception, Sadie felt like a tire with a slow leak and knew she better move along before she went entirely flat. "I can see I've interrupted your conversation. I'll just go sit with…" She looked around the room. *Tilly-fally! Only one empty chair.* "…with Harvey and Bertha."

The three women she deserted stared after her and turned back to each other. Something had seemed different about Sadie when she'd approached them—that fact alone unfurled a red flag in their minds. Dorothy summed up their feelings succinctly: "Sadie must not be feeling well—she seemed almost pleasant." The others nodded, and Ethel resumed her account of the late-night TV movie that made her sob every time she mentioned the heroine's tragic death.

Across the room, Harvey and Bertha Thompson stoically bemoaned their fate. To be picked out of a crowd by Widow O'Dell was no honor. Sadie was undeterred by their lack of warmth. Since she had gotten no bites on her last venture, she figured her bait was still fresh: "My, Bertha, don't you look nice this morning. It's as if you just stepped out of Helen's beauty shop!"

Bertha's stiffened. "You know full well, Sadie O'Dell, that I wear a wig."

Before Sadie could justify her thoughtless remark, the front door opened to admit Amber and Tyler Larson, carrying young Juddie. Cate had been winding her way toward Sadie with the cup of tea she knew Sadie preferred over coffee, but quickly changed courses. All around the café attention turned to the baby.

Oooohs and *ahhhhhs* and *cootchy-coos* and silly questions addressed the infant as if he could talk:

"Aren't you growing like a weed?"

"Are you treating your Grandpa and Grandma nice?"

"Where'd you get those big brown eyes?"

"Look how he flings those chubby little arms around!"

Forget that baby! Sadie wanted to roar. *He'll be here for the rest of his life, and I've got hot-off-the-griddle news! News you all are itching to hear—I know you are!*

Harvey and Bertha gave each other a silent signal and stealthily disappeared. Sadie looked back to see only empty chairs and a dollar bill fluttering on the table.

She gripped her purse in frustration. Though she didn't often admit it, she knew it was unlikely anyone would purposely join her. *What a waste this whole trip has been. I lost my audience twice, and that silly baby robbed me of my tea.*

As if Cate felt the daggers shooting from Sadie's eyes, she promptly kissed Juddie on the head, returned him to her mother-in-law's arms and resumed her duties. "Sorry, Sadie!" she called out. "Your tea has cooled. I'll fix you another—and throw in a doughnut to make it up to you."

Yesterday's Sadie would have huffed about the indignity of it all; today's Sadie had reason to swallow every disgruntled word. When Cate approached her table, Sadie looked up with an expectant smile, startling Cate. "My, don't you look nice this morning. It's as if you just stepped out of Helen's beauty shop!"

"Actually, I did! Don't tell anyone," Cate said conspiratorially. "Helen sometimes sneaks me in before I open the café. Mum's the word, okay?" Cate winked and returned to her duties.

Sadie stared blankly after her. Twice in twenty-four hours she had been trusted with confidential information. Granted, Cate's tidbit hardly ranked up there with the full scoop on Helen's shattering tale, but still it showed trust. She felt the weight of this burden and vowed to carry it without mishap. If anyone *ever* learned Cate got her hair cut before dawn, they wouldn't hear it from Sadie O'Dell. *No, sirree-bob!*

She looked around the room, eavesdropping shamelessly, but learning nothing that equaled the secret she longed to share. No one mentioned the D CURL; no one breathed Frank or Helen's name; no one was talking hair.

Sadie's best shot at opening a conversation had failed miserably three times. Surreptitiously, she pulled a paper out of her pocket and looked at the very short list she had compiled the previous night. She mentally crossed out the first line: *My, don't you look nice* was a dismal failure. Resolutely, she pushed back her chair, paid her bill, and marched out.

From where he was arranging the window display, Luke saw her coming across the street and groaned inwardly. Since Sadie was usually a first- and third-Wednesday morning shopper, he wasn't expecting her today; there wasn't time to slide what Dave called *Widow O'Dell's oatmeal sign* in place.

Ages ago, having tired of Sadie's bemoaning what she considered the extravagant price of a cereal "that's about as simple a food as God ever made," Luke had scrawled a sign to keep her quiet. *Oatmeal $1.00 or two for $1.75* it read, and he hung it in place on appropriate Wednesday mornings until after Sadie left the store. She regularly bought two boxes of oatmeal and said nothing more about escalating prices.

Luke envisioned boxes of oatmeal piled high on Sadie's kitchen counter, behind the couch, under the bed. Everyone knew she made nothing but oatmeal cookies or oatmeal cake—no frivolous chocolate from *her* kitchen. Anyone who tasted her baked goods knew that her recipe for meatloaf included oatmeal, as did each loaf of banana bread and every batch of muffins. She prided herself on having eaten oatmeal for breakfast every day for over sixty years. The door opened to admit the invincible widow whose body was well fortified by oatmeal.

But Luke need not have worried about the missing signs. Sadie latched on to a cart and rolled it aimlessly along the aisles. He watched the feather on her sensible straw hat bob right past the cereals, move along to canned goods, halt briefly by the cottage cheese, and back-track to review the week's special on carrots.

When she headed for check-out, Luke noted her cart held little of substance: a frivolous box of mints, a carton of whipping cream, two perfect bananas she would surely insist were so soft he should only charge pennies for her to take them off his hands, and a can of generic sink cleanser.

Luke rang up her items without comment. Sadie allowed the firm bananas to go by without argument, and pulled the required amount out of her coin purse without her usual review of every line on the cash register slip. She picked up her bag and turned to leave.

"Are you feeling okay, Sadie?" Luke asked.

"Hmm? Yes…I feel quite well. Why do you ask?"

"You seem, uh, a little quiet today. I know you live alone, so I wanted to be sure you're not ill."

Sadie looked at Luke in surprise. *An opening!* "Speaking of living alone…" She sidled up to the counter and leaned in close. "We must keep our eye on Helen. She's alone now, you know. Frank left her and went to California. He's got another woman. Helen's devastated. They'll probably divorce."

Luke's mouth opened and his lips moved but they couldn't catch up to his speeding thoughts, so nothing came out.

Sadie picked up steam, emboldened by her success in making it up the first steep grade. "I believe I'll take her a batch of oatmeal cookies. I'm making her a new dress, you know. She needed something to cheer her up, she said." Luke's face communicated his disbelief and Sadie bristled. "That's right—she sat in my living room Saturday night and told me *everything*."

Luke sighed and said firmly, "Sadie, I…"

"If you don't believe me, you can ask Helen," Sadie said curtly. Abruptly, she picked up her bag of inconsequential purchases and strutted out the door like a majorette leading an invisible marching band.

Luke hooked the stool behind the counter with his foot and dragged it beneath him in one fluid motion. Sinking down, he stared at the door. "*What* was *that* about?" he asked aloud. Even replaying the details offered no illumination as to why Sadie would have the scoop on the Wilson's personal disasters.

Thinking back to the week following Memorial Day weekend, Luke remembered Dave Jenkins had mentioned bits and pieces of the sad saga, but when Luke had suggested that perhaps Helen would prefer to tell her own story in her own time, Dave had agreeably halted his comments.

Maybe I should have let Dave talk—he could hardly have done the damage Sadie's bound to inflict. Luke picked up his pricing gun and grimly attacked a carton of pickle jars, slapping sticky tags on each lid. Only when he had priced the whole case did he realize that in his irritation with the town gossip, he had misplaced the decimal point. They were mighty fine pickles, but hardly worth $179.

He called to Dave who was stacking sweet corn in the vegetable case and asked him to watch the counter and redo the faulty pricing. Within minutes, he was sitting at the counter at the café and watching steam rise from a cup of coffee. "You planning to drink that, or are you translating the smoke signals?" Cate teased, easing on to the stood beside him.

Luke smiled absent-mindedly. "You seen Sadie today?"

Cate's brow furrowed. "Matter of fact, I have. She was in earlier, hopped tables for a bit and disappeared. She told me I looked real nice."

Luke looked at his wife and nodded thoughtfully. "You do, but didn't you think that was a bit odd, a compliment coming from Sadie?"

"Didn't have time to give it much thought; your folks had brought Juddie in for a few minutes, so I was distracted. Why are we having this conversation about Sadie, anyway?"

"She just came to the store and dropped a bombshell. She not only seems to know an awful lot about Frank and Helen's private business, but she claims Helen told her all the details in person. And get this: supposedly, Helen sat in Sadie's living room Saturday night and had that conversation. Usually, I just give Sadie wide berth and don't pay attention to anything she says, but…"

"I saw Helen this morning when she cut my hair and she didn't say a word about any such nonsense. I'll talk to her again once lunch is over," Cate said grimly. "We'll get to the bottom of this, hopefully before too much damage is done by that silver-haired motor-mouth."

Luke spun around on the stool and stood up. "Sounds good. I'll see you later. Not sure when I'll get here for lunch—there's a new produce delivery guy and I want to go over a few things with him. If you're gone, I'll figure you're over talking to Helen."

Cate stood and turned, coming up nose-to-nose with Luke. At that proximity, there was no reason at all not to kiss him squarely on the lips. So she did. Twice. He smiled and turned to a table of retired men enjoying their morning coffee break, "Gotta love this small-town friendliness, huh? For the price of a cup of coffee, a guy can get a kiss that gives a better buzz than caffeine!"

One man teased, "Can't say I've noticed you paying for the coffee! Must be nice to be married to the owner."

"Oh, yeah. Verrrrry nice," Luke said and winked at Cate as he left. The past seven months had been like heaven for Luke and Cate. Most newlyweds wouldn't think that adopting a newborn just months into their marriage would be a good thing, but they weren't a typical couple.

Cate's thoughts were troubled. *Granted, I've only been married a few months, but I can't imagine how demoralizing it must be for a wife to have her husband reject her. To live with someone for as many years as Frank and Helen were married, and then this betrayal of all that is sacred...*There were no answers. And, Cate admitted sadly, Helen asked no questions—so even if Cate had answers, without questions, answers were useless.

Cate had attempted dinner invitations for Helen, invited Helen to ride along to Crosby to pick up café supplies, offered help when she found Helen contemplating wallpaper borders at THE GENERAL STORE. Nothing had been accepted. It was as if Helen wanted little to do with Cate, even though she was unfailingly polite and outwardly friendly. She maintained a host of excuses; either the girls were coming, or she was cooking for the interns, or she had plenty of help. There was no room in her life for old friends, it seemed.

Cate may have stopped asking, but she hadn't stopped worrying. The door swung open and Alex and Tori Johanson entered. "How on earth did the doctor and the minister manage time off together?" Cate teased.

"When Tori showed up in my office looking so tantalizing, I told Lulu I was taking an early lunch with my best friend!" Alex tweaked Tori's cheek.

Tori—*nee* Reverend Victoria Dahlmann, pastor of both the PRAIRIE ROSE COMMUNITY CHURCH and rural INDIAN HILLS UNITED CHURCH—had moved to town two summers ago. Initially, she had privately considered this North Dakota line on her resume to be her starting point; she had every intention of doing a good job for a few years and moving on.

But that was before she discovered her first and dangerous love, Alexander Johanson—long known as Zan, to her—could revitalize high-school passions with the same skill with which he showed up along Main Street to reopen his grandfather's medical clinic.

Cate pulled out an empty chair and straddled it. "That's what's been the problem." She thumped her forehead with the palm of her hand. Alex and Tori looked at each other blankly.

"Uh, we're gonna need a clue before we can participate in this conversation," Alex drawled.

"Your remark about being best friends just cleared the fog—somewhat—for me. Though I've got to admit, I can't believe she's so desperate that she's reaching out to Sadie..."

Tori shot Alex a puzzled look and peered into her friend's face. "Was that our clue, Cate?"

Cate slowly focused on them. "Sorry. Luke was just in and said it appears Helen has told all the details of the past month's Wilson drama to none other than Sadie." She watched Tori's eyes darken. "Obviously, that's troubling."

"So your theory," Alex said, "is that Helen refused to open up to trusted friends, but has confided in the infamous Sadie O'Dell?"

"Yup. Weird, huh?"

"Are we sure Sadie has her facts straight?" Tori asked, fully aware of the potential for error, having been the subject of one of the widow's most damning miscalculations of what was truth and what was sheer fabrication.

"I intend to find out that very thing."

"I'd be happy to come along for moral support—how about if we swing by her place this evening?"

Cate nodded. "I was thinking about after lunch, but there's no guarantee she'd be alone. This evening is a better idea. I'll hold back three pieces of pie."

The day dragged by so slowly that Cate was sure the clock on the wall had died. Finally, she closed up and carried supper home in a cooler. At the appointed time, she met Tori outside the Rectory gate.

As they walked along, Tori voiced their common concern. "How do we bring up the topic?"

Cate arched an eyebrow. "I was hoping you had some seminary secret up your sleeve for how to deliver bad news."

"That would have been helpful. Must have skipped class the day they gave that out!"

"First we knock, and maybe inspiration will strike." Cate knuckled-knocked on Helen's apartment door.

It took a few minutes—just long enough for Tori and Cate to exchange wondering glances—before Helen opened the door. "Well!" She looked back over her shoulder furtively. "This seems to be my night for company!"

"Oh, are you in the middle of something? Sorry; we should have called," Tori said.

"Um, that's okay." Helen made no move either to invite them in or step aside to allow them entrance. "Could we make it another night?"

Cate and Tori looked quickly at each other. *Not a good idea, but we can't talk if Helen has other company.*

Helen picked up on their hesitancy and asked, "Was there some special reason you wanted to see me tonight?"

Tori nodded, but Cate spoke first and carefully modulated her voice so it wouldn't carry to Helen's invisible guest. "We thought you needed a heads-up about a situation involving you. You can call either of us for the full story later. Here's the deal: Luke got concerned when Sadie trotted into the grocery store today. Did you know she's talking around town about your personal business?"

Helen hooted. "Did I know? Of course I knew! In fact, Sadie's in my living room right now telling me all about it."

Cate jerked back as if slapped.

Tori swallowed the *What?* that nearly made it past her vocal cords and said with unbelievable calm, "We'll let you go, then, Helen. As long as you're aware, I guess we have nothing to worry about."

"Oh, I'm aware—I just can't believe it took her so long. Thanks for coming by—catch you both later," Helen said brightly and closed the door. Tori and Cate stood like stone statues in the alley.

Finally Cate sighed. "I've got three perfectly good pieces of pie here. Luke figures I'm gone for the evening, so if you invite me over, Alex can have Helen's piece. I want to ask him something."

"Let's go." Tori led the way to the Rectory's back gate. Two solid tri-colored furry bodies plummeted off the back porch and raced across the yard to welcome them enthusiastically.

"Hey, Cino!" Cate greeted the four-year-old male Bernese Mountain Dog and bent to scratch him behind the ears. Cali, a year younger and a mere half-weight female compared to Cino's 130 pounds, kept pace across the yard. When they reached the back door to the Rectory, she leaned against Cate's leg and raised soulful brown eyes. Cate hooted. "Oh, you sweet thing! Didn't I show you enough affection? All right, ear-scratches for little girls, too!"

"Good grief, dogs—I've barely been gone fifteen minutes! Come on in, Cate. Hey, Zan!" Tori called out, using the name created years ago when their love was young. "Home are the sailors, home from the sea. With nothing to show for their trip, either," she ended glumly.

"I didn't expect you for hours, or I'd have joined the dogs in the back yard! I'm sure they gave you enough of a welcome you didn't miss me!" Alex's eyes lingered on Tori in the living room doorway, but he included Cate in his broad smile.

"We had a quick and unsuccessful—or make that unnecessary—trip. Helen had company, and guess who?" Cate challenged the lanky doctor who was surrounded by a tottering stack of medical journals. His laptap computer's cord and cable snaked behind the couch to unseen sockets.

"Was it Frank?"

Cate snorted. "I never took you to be a happily-ever-after kinda guy, Alex."

Tori laughed. "Oh, but he is! He believes in love, enduring love, love unshaken by incredible odds—remember, he waited ten years for me!"

Alex batted his eyelashes furiously. "And I'd do it again in a heart-beat—but we're avoiding Cate's question. Out with it."

"It's a good thing you're already sitting down, Alex: it's Sadie."

Alex puckered his lips around a low whistle. "First Helen's rumored to be at Sadie's and now Sadie's at Helen's? What gives?"

"Beats me. Helen seems delighted Sadie's talking about her—right, Cate?"

"Yup. She was almost giddy."

Tori returned to the kitchen and Cate sank into an overstuffed chair. "Is it possible Helen has gone over the edge? And that's a serious question, by the way."

"She *is* under a great deal of stress these days," Alex said.

"Or, could it be we're just too danged happy in our own marriages for her to deal with right now?" Cate asked, looking up as Tori returned and distributed pie all around.

Alex twirled his fork thoughtfully between bites. "Let's not waste the considerable skills of our own Reverend Tori Johanson. What's your take on this, Love?"

Tori set her plate aside and pulled one leg up beneath her. "We're thinking there's one happy ending to this story that goes like this." She held up five fingers and ticked off the points on her fingers. "Frank sees the error of his ways, truly repents, comes back home, Helen magnanimously forgives and forgets, and all live happily ever after. What if Helen sees it completely opposite?"

"You're saying," Alex chimed in, "what if Helen sees no future for them and would rather die than take Frank back again? That's a whole different situation. Made all the worse if Helen's perception is that all her former friends support what she suspects are conflicting opinions."

"It's just a theory," admitted Tori.

"I still think they could work it out," Cate said. "Frank did a dreadfully stupid thing, but it hardly constitutes a pattern. Not that I'm saying I wouldn't be responding just like Helen if it happened to me."

"Maybe they could get back together, but sometimes things can't return to the way they were," Tori said.

When Cate left half an hour later, they not only had no answers, but had added several more questions. Back home, she rehashed the puzzling evening with Luke. He listened intently, rolled his eyes and offered his assessment: "This situation has gotten about as goofy as it can get."

* * * *

In California's Sierra Nevada Mountains, a man drove east through the night, gripping the steering wheel of his pickup and gulping truck-stop coffee from a thermal mug. He listened to the garbled voices of callers to late-night radio hosts, mingled with disjointed snippets of songs that alternately faded or blasted his ears. Despite the crisp mountain air, he rolled his window down in a desperate attempt to stay awake.

Coming around a bend above the snow line, he hit a slick spot and the truck spun out of control. His wallet—tossed on the dashboard after his last stop for gas—slid out the window and skittered a hundred yards away from the overturned truck as it rolled off the road. It was hours before anyone found him and by then he was incoherent from the cold and shock and the pain of his injuries.

"Call these plates in," said the highway patrolman as he double-checked the numbers on the battered license plate. The flashing lights atop his vehicle sliced the eerie blue-black night. He ripped a sheet out of his report book and handed it to his partner. "Someone in North Dakota's going to be getting a dreaded phone call tonight, unless I miss my guess. This fellow's in pretty bad shape." The whine of an ambulance pierced the thin mountain air. "The plates are all we've got to go on, if it's even his truck. And that's anybody's guess since I don't see any other ID."

*   *   *   *

Tuesday morning, an unknown driver in an unfamiliar red convertible parallel-parked on Main Street, ruining the three best angle-parking spots in front of the Post Office. "What's going on?" Joy asked a gaggle of townsfolk who had gathered outside LARSON'S GROCERY in contemplation of the offending vehicle.

"Did you see that girl going into the Post Office?" someone finally responded.

Joy shook her head. "If this is her car blocking all these parking places, she's not from around here. Anyone else knows to pull in, nose first." Following her instincts, Joy headed to the Post Office. The door's bell jangled and startled Al's only customer who was obviously the parallel-parker.

At first glance, the champagne-blonde woman was not particularly beautiful, nor did she possess any one memorable feature. Though her astounding head of hair did qualify as interesting, there was just too much of it for Joy's taste, and the style shouted *Look at me* a bit too loudly for this part of the country.

Skyscraper hair on one end and kiss-of-death high-heeled sandals on the other made it difficult to accurately judge height. But as Joy stepped closer, she realized her own five-foot seven inches easily dwarfed the stranger.

As a package deal, this young woman sizzled like a just-lit fire-cracker. In fact, she required warning labels on every visible inch of skin—and there was plenty of that. Minimal material was invested in the tank top that her torso stretched to Spandex-testing limits. Her frayed-edge denim cut-offs ended four inches above North Dakota decency. Smooth tanned legs made the long trek down to the strappy sandals that offered negligible foot support.

Joy's antennae went on full alert. "Hello," she said guardedly as she crossed the room to the service window. She turned to look at her husband who stood stiffly behind the counter.

"This is Blyss," Al said in an odd voice. "Blyss is looking for Frank," he added pointedly.

"Oh," Joy said, sending that one word on a five-note skid. *This is just like Californ-i-a.* She looked quickly at Al, expecting a wink that signaled he was reading her mind. But he was too caught in the snare of a *bushy bushy blonde hairdo* to play the music game.

"I just couldn't stay in California after my Frankie left. I miss him so much! So I'm here to surprise him," the young woman said in a breathy voice, obviously continuing a conversation already in-progress. Her bottle-green eyes widened above a tapered finger with weapon-length nails as she tapped her full lips in the standard *Shhhh!*

signal. "I'm here to give moral support while he settles up with his nasty ex-wife. Then, we can go back home and get married."

The Post Office door swung open. Harvey Thompson's eyes made the circle and came back to rest on Blyss. The ubiquitous unlit pipe in his mouth did a little vertical dance. Nervously, he twisted his seed cap from one side to the other, settling it precisely in its original spot on his permed salt-and-pepper hair. He straightened his shoulders and jingled the coins in his pocket. "How-do, Miss." His face burned. "'Hello, Joy," he added belatedly and nodded nervously at Al.

Fireworks had just singed Harvey Thompson.

"Can I help you, Harv?" Al asked more curtly than he realized. Harvey looked startled and glanced first at Al, then back at Joy. She attempted to offset Al's abruptness with a smile, but her efforts fell short of encouragement.

"Uh, sure. I need a book of stamps. Need to get the new ones. First class." He stepped up to the window and pulled out his wallet. The women stood like sentries on either side while Harvey transacted postal business. Each inconsequential word between the men bounced off the high ceiling and rattled around the room like pennies in a tin can.

After Harvey paid for his stamps, he then remembered he needed postcard stamps, too. Finally, he tipped his hat at Blyss and left. Al closed the cash drawer with unnecessary force and resumed the interrupted conversation with equal intensity. "There's something you need to know, Miss...what's your last name, again?"

"Hathaway. Blyss Hathaway," she responded and raised the long dark eyelashes that framed two deep and enticing emerald pools. "What's that?"

"Huh?"

"What is it I need to know?"

Hey! Quit flirting with my husband! Hello? Joy clenched her fists. Her fingernails bit into her palms and she welcomed the pain—it kept her from slugging this velvet-tongued stranger.

"It's important, so listen carefully." Al leaned in close to the barred window; his voice cut through Joy's incensed thoughts. "Frank doesn't have an *ex*-wife. He has a *current* wife, and contrary to what he may have told you, she's anything but nasty," he added darkly.

Blyss shrugged, wisely saying nothing, though her cosmetically enhanced lips formed a sneer.

"Something else you need to know is that Frank's not here," Joy said firmly. "And even if he were, I can't imagine he would be so stupid as to invite you to stay here with him."

Laughter pushed words past Blyss' parted lips like a babbling brook dancing across glistening stones. "Oh, he's here, alright! He just doesn't know *I'm* here. We had just the *teensiest* argument," it would have been difficult to slide a Change-of-Address form in the space demonstrated between her thumb and index finger, "so I've come to say I'm sorry. I flew into that little-itty-bitty airport in Williston and rented a car and here I am! All I need to do is find Frankie."

"*Frank's* not here." Joy repeated, biting her words off clean and crisp. *Enough with the Frankie business!* Al heard her end-of-discussion punctuation loud-and-clear, but Blyss either missed or chose to ignore such signals.

"I've been driving around town looking for Frankie's truck for almost half an hour," Blyss fussed. Her lips curved into a little-girl pout. "It shouldn't be so hard to find a person in a town this size. Amazingly enough, I saw a B&B a few blocks away so I'll get a room there if it's not a complete dive. If you see Frankie before I do, will you have him give me a call? Oh, where's the best place to get a vegetarian meal?"

The first response that flew to Joy's mind was *Find something in Williston on your way back to the itty-bitty airport!* but she grudgingly offered, "There's only CATE'S CAFÉ, but it's hardly vegetarian and isn't open for supper during the week. You could pick up some things at the grocery store."

"Oh, I don't need much." Blyss perched her French-manicured hands on a trim waistline. "Just a salad and nuts will be fine." She gave a finger wave and clicked her way to the door on the four-inch stiletto heels.

Al moaned and clapped the palms of his hands against his temples. "Oh, man, what a mess."

"That little...hussy...is trouble."

"You ain't seen nuttin' yet. We've got to get to Helen before someone else does. You know, between the two of us, we could have knocked ol' Blyss out cold and dragged her out of town," Al said. "There's not a judge on the bench who would put us away for that deed. In fact, we could get rewarded for doing a public service."

"It didn't take long for her to get my dander up. You're right, though, Al. Job-One is to talk to Helen. *That's* not a conversation I'm looking forward to."

Al expelled a gust of meaningless sounds, ending with absentminded tongue-clicks. "I'm afraid it's going to have to be you, and by yourself, too. Wendy's coming in to cover me for lunch, but I'm afraid this can't wait that long. Blyss could be heading straight for the café."

"I'll go. Can I have a hug first?" she asked wistfully.

Al was beside her in an instant. Joy leaned against his chest and molded herself to the familiar lines of his body. "Thanks for not ever being a ramblin' boy like Frank."

"That kind of California life is more than just too hard to build—it's beyond my comprehension. I've got everything I ever wanted right here in my arms." Their lips met and Joy stood on tiptoes to soak up every ounce of loving from Al's kiss. When Al slowly pulled back, she entwined her fingers behind his head and said simply, "More."

He didn't need a second invitation.

Finally, street noises reminded them where they were. "Whoops. We may have just broken a federal law." Al kissed her nose.

"If anyone's disgraced government property, it's Blyss. She could have exploded right out of those clothes and we'd be toast."

"Hmmm?" Al smoothed Joy's ruffled hair.

Joy looked quickly at her husband and knew that while Blyss Hathaway may have attracted Al's attention briefly, *she* held his soul. It was a staggering realization. "I love you so much, Al, that if I were to kiss you again here and now, we *would* be breaking laws right by Stella's post office box. The next customer would have no choice but to call the Postmaster General and have us booted out on our naked behinds!"

"Yikes, better get a move on, Jinglebells. I need this job—remember, we're living on my income now!" He swatted her behind playfully.

Joy floated down the sidewalk fueled by high-octane love, but anchored to the ground by the guide-wires of the tough job awaiting her.

Helen looked up when the beauty/barber shop door opened; she waved her scissors in greeting. She was halfway through cutting Howard's hair and motioned Joy to take a chair while Howard continued to air his woes about a wasp's nest under the eaves of his house.

Joy picked up a magazine and idly thumbed through it. When the story ended and several other customers had offered and debated advice, Helen called out, "You look pretty good to me, Joy—did you think you need a trim?"

"Nah, I just stopped by to entice you to take a coffee break at the café."

"Sounds good. I'm almost done with Howard, then Betsy and Sally can take over for a bit." Joy saw one intern shifting wet towels from the washer to the dryer in the hallway at the back while the other worked behind the counter. After a few minor instructions and a major dose of encouragement, Helen washed her hands and led the way to the door. "The number for the café's by the phone—call me if you need anything."

Both girls nodded and smiled with nervous excitement.

"What a fun surprise!" Helen said brightly as they stood outside the shop. "I can't stay away long, though. These two just got here yesterday. I hope Cate still has cinnamon rolls this morning."

Joy hadn't thought much beyond getting Helen out of the shop. She realized, too late, they were heading to the one place in town where private conversations could happen, but rarely did. A person could sit on a chair and loudly proclaim government secrets and hardly get any attention, but sit in a corner and talk softly—even if only about the best way to remove catsup stains—and the whole world tilted closer to hear.

Knowing the magnitude of her mission, Joy regretted suggesting the café; the park would have been a better place to conduct this conversation. But before her frazzled mind could suggest that alternate plan, Helen pushed open the café's door and stepped inside. Joy followed, looking more like a doomed prisoner than an eager customer.

As luck would have it, the only places open were at the counter. Helen headed for two empty stools. Sliding in beside her, Joy knew there would be no talk of any serious intent—not at the U-shaped conversation pit where every comment was considered open to discussion.

Lucy centered two glasses of ice water in front of them, then positioned coffee cups in place and hit the mark twice with a stream of rich, hot brew. She nodded approvingly when Helen said hopefully, "Any cinnamon rolls left?"

"There's one with your name on it. Be right back."

The saucer-sized roll arrived. "Doesn't this look decadent? It's been dry wheat-toast and black coffee for my breakfasts all month so I plan to enjoy every crumb, and I may just lick the plate! Plus, I'm using cream—and lots of it—in my coffee today." Helen slathered butter on the hot roll, slid her knife along the outer ring to cut off a first bite, closed her eyes dreamily and cradled it on her tongue. Good manners tossed aside, she said around her mouthful, "I'm in heaven!" Swallowing slowly, she looked at Joy's coffee and water. "Hey, want any? I can share one bite!"

Joy shook her head and smiled weakly. "Just coffee for me, but thanks anyway." She couldn't help comparing Helen today with Helen from Memorial Day weekend. In mood alone, the two Helens were a night-and-day contrast. She observed her friend more closely. "Are you losing weight, Helen?"

Helen giggled as she licked her fingers. "I was, until I sat down here!"

"On purpose?" Over the years, the two women had bemoaned the five and eight pounds, respectively, that seemed permanent fixtures on their hips.

Helen's laugh trilled. "When your husband leaves you, the pounds just fly off! Hey, don't look so worried. I'm not wasting away on account of Frank's dumping me. I'm just accepting the facts—and eating healthy stuff. If that constitutes a weight-loss program, so be it."

Joy noticed Helen's wedding rings were gone and her class ring was back. It fit just fine. There was no more puffiness about Helen—she was trim and heading towards sleek. "You look great, Helen."

"I'm happy with how I look—and that's what counts."

The café door opened and heads automatically turned. *No!* Joy hoped the word echoed only in her mind. Usually, a person's entrance into the café got minimal, or at least short-lived, attention. He or she got and gave a wave or two, found a place to sit, and chatter continued without missing a beat.

Not this time. Not when the person in the doorway was Blyss Hathaway.

Blyss scanned the room; only Joy knew what she wanted. *And that's what I was supposed to be telling Helen—not talking about weight loss.* She moaned aloud, causing Helen to study her curiously.

There's not a second to lose—do something. Now! Joy resorted to desperate actions: she jostled her arm just enough to dump a glass of water in Helen's lap, and then faked a recovery move that also pushed the buttered cinnamon roll and coated knife into the soggy mess. "I'm so sorry!" she fibbed. Reaching, as if for the napkins, she knocked Helen's coffee cup sideways on its saucer. A lazy stream of creamy brown liquid dribbled over the plate's edge, picking up speed as it sloshed along the counter.

At first speechless, Helen yelped just as the first splat of coffee landed. All eyes turned toward her. Lucy scurried over with towels and sympathy and the three women sopped up the mess. Even while helping clean up, Joy knew the disruption she had devised was only temporary. "Let's go so you can change into dry clothes. May we use the back door, Lucy?"

"Sure," Lucy agreed amiably, efficiently setting things right at the counter.

Out in the alley, a soaked and sticky Helen turned to Joy. "What was *that* about? You never were a very good liar."

Joy blushed and confessed, "I was desperate to get you out of there, and that was all I could come up with. Sorry. Come on, I'll walk you back to the shop so you can change."

"I'm fine—just confused and more than a little messy. First, you want me to go to the café; then you want to get me out of the café. Which is it? In or out?"

"Both. My plan was to get you in, thinking we'd have a nice quiet talk about something I wanted you to hear from a friend. But then we ended up sitting at the counter where anyone who can't hear everything we say can still read our lips. Then, uh, someone, um, came in and I had to get you away because I hadn't talked to you yet."

Helen dropped down on the alley steps behind her apartment. "You're obviously all bent out of shape. Sit down and start talking."

"There's no simple way to tell some things, anyway, so maybe it's for the best we didn't talk at the café, because it's not exactly good news, and bad news is hard to tell in public..."

"Joy! Out with it, already!"

"Okay, here are the facts, blunt and straight-out. You know that, uh...person who Frank, uh...went, uh, left you, uh..."

"You obviously have trouble talking about two-timing Frank. If you're talking about his girlfriend, yes, I'm aware she lives and breathes in California. So, why are we talking—or, in your case—not talking about her?"

"She is the reason you're one soggy mess. She walked into the café and..."

"What?" Helen leaped to her feet and spun around to face Joy. "How would you know it was her? *I* don't even know what she looks like."

"Long story, short?"

"No-no-no-no-no, let's have the whole story—just quickly. No lolly-gagging with unnecessary details."

Joy felt woozy and closed her eyes briefly in hopes her world would stop spinning. "I knew nothing about her—other than what you've told Al and me—until about an hour ago. Blyss Hathaway—did you know that's her name? Anyway, she parallel-parked on Main Street and that's what got my attention initially. When a car isn't angle-parked, it's a dead give-away a stranger's in town."

Helen rolled her eyes. "Joy!" she said in a voice sharp with frustration.

"Okay, okay! Several people—Wally and Lester are who I remember, oh, and Linda..." Helen's paralyzing stare pushed her onward, "...saw her going into the Post Office and they seemed so dumbstruck I decided to check it out myself."

"But how did you know she was Frank's mistress? Ooooo, ick, that's that first time I've ever said *that* out loud." Helen's shoulders sagged and she pursed her lips tightly. "I can't believe the potholes in my life, sometimes."

"Honey, I'm afraid you're in for a whole stretch of bad roads until that woman leaves town—and I wouldn't count on that happening right away. Like I said, I went to the Post Office and there she stood. Al sort of introduced me and said she was asking for Frank. She said he left California about a week ago to come back and take care of a few things." *I'll tell the truth and nothing but the truth, but, please, God, I just can't tell Helen the whole truth right now.*

"But he came without her?"

Joy moaned inwardly at the pinprick of hope evident in Helen's five words. It was the first glimmer of anything but anger or revenge Joy had heard since that fateful weekend in May—and the timing couldn't have been worse.

"Yes," Joy said slowly, "she says he drove back. She flew to Williston and rented a car there to come find him. She wasn't having any luck just driving around town, so she stopped at the Post Office to ask for directions. Since no one has seen Frank, she didn't learn anything. She plans to stay at the B&B until she finds Frank."

"So it was Blyss Hathaway coming into the café when you dumped a perfectly good cinnamon roll on my lap?" Helen arched an eyebrow at Joy.

"Yeah. My plan was to sit down and have a talk with you so people wouldn't come into the shop knowing all about...her, when you didn't know a thing. My intentions were good, but the timing stunk."

"You are hardly to blame for any of this," Helen said graciously, falling silent as she contemplated painted toenails sticking out from beneath her stained and sticky slacks. "What's your impression of her? I hardly got more than two blinks in before you drowned me. And since I didn't realize I was seeing the...person...who butchered my marriage, I wasn't paying much attention to anything except my lap."

"Well..." Joy stalled, "she's quite the, uh...looker."

"*Looker*? That's the best you can do? Do you think she's pretty? Ravishing? Sexy?"

"She's not what I'd call pretty—but I can see how Blyss Hathaway could capture and hold a guy's attention. Even Harvey Thompson almost forgot how to breathe when he came in to buy stamps."

"That's great," Helen said glumly, "Frank spends all these years with someone like me and jumps ship for someone who makes old men drool." She paced a tight circle in the alley, skidding to an abrupt stop to ask, "He's coming back to divorce me, isn't he?"

Joy dodged that bullet. "She seems under the impression he's going back to California after his trip here."

"Unless I shoot him in the kneecaps—and he better hope I don't aim high," Helen said ominously. "Part of me wants to look him in the eye and give him what-for, and part of me wants nothing to do with him or this Blyss-person. Blyss," she scoffed. "That's gotta be a made-up name. Don't hookers usually have street names? I bet she's a hooker."

"I'm not defending her, but do you think a hooker would follow a client halfway across the country? They're usually in it for the money, and it's not like Frank is worth chasing across the continent. Money-wise, I mean."

Helen snorted and flopped back down on the steps. "The way he was doling out the cash on her, she probably thinks he's loaded. Keep me posted. If you do see Frank, tell him...no, scratch that; tell me. And come by the shop sometime soon—you do need a trim around your ears."

Joy stayed on the alley steps for several minutes after Helen went into her apartment. Birds chirped in the trees; kids called out to each other; and in CATE'S CAFÉ, there were a dozen people getting their money's worth of fresh gossip. She took a deep breath, startling herself when it emerged as a lingering sigh.

Frank, you're a full-fledged tornado and Blyss Hathaway is your siren. She laughed humorlessly. "That's what I should have told Helen. Blyss is a siren." She headed off in pursuit of her original mission which now seemed inconsequential: strawberries from LARSON'S GROCERY.

Within the hour, water and pectin reached a boil on the burner of Joy's stove. Stirring a bowlful of sweetened mashed fruit into the bubbling pan, she watched it stain the water until the mixture was a cheerful red. Distractedly, she poured the lumpy liquid into the waiting wide-mouth jars, covered them and put them on a rack to cool.

Considering this was the first batch of her traditional summer jelly, the familiar process brought her little joy. Every year since the first summer of her married life she had responded to Al's urging: "You're going to make strawberry jam this year, aren't you?" with several dozen jars sparkling on the kitchen counter.

Tradition had shifted to include Dave when he arrived in the family. Once Dave started speaking, Al taught him to chime in on the *forever* part of "...strawberry fields forever..." and Joy once overheard Al whispering to Dave, "Sing 'forever' real loud and maybe Mommy will make strawberry jam today, Davey!"

Young Davey obliged, "*Fo-ebah*!"

For the men in Joy's life, once strawberry season arrived, it was *strawberry fields fo-ebah* hummed in the car, whistled in the garage, sung loudly in the shower. It was the song of the season, forming the daily reminders and broad hints until Al and Dave knew strawberry jam was a certainty.

Since Dave took his cues from Al, when Al's music died on Memorial Day weekend, no one had sung "...strawberry fields *fo-ebah...*" this year. Just when Joy had begun to hope life could get back on course, at least for her family, Blyss Hathaway had driven into town. Marking the day with strawberry jam seemed almost sacrilegious.

Chapter 6

Focused on one narrow goal, Blyss Hathaway barely noticed the commotion preceding Joy and Helen's rapid exit from CATE'S CAFÉ. While Lucy swabbed the floor with a damp mop, everyone else stopped conversations to stare at Blyss. She took advantage of their attentiveness. "I'm looking for Frankie Wilson. Can anyone tell me where I might find my man?" At that, even Lucy looked up and the swooshing mop sounds stopped.

Even those men not blatantly ogling Blyss were clearly mesmerized by her alluring presence.

Sadie says Frank and Helen are splitsville because he's got another woman. And here comes Hot-Stuff looking for Frank.

Her man, she says. Ho, boy, this is something, ain't it, now?

The women were incensed by her audacity.

How dare she come prancing into town looking like that? If she was my daughter...Lord, have mercy—she's young enough to be my daughter.

Look how all these old coots are sittin' at attention. She ought to be ashamed, flouncing her unh-unhs from here to kingdom come.

"Would someone just tell me where Frankie's house is?" Blyss was becoming more disenchanted by the minute with this small town's lack of charm. For the sixteen people in the room, she could have walked off a soap opera set—especially with a question that matched the daily dramas played out on the TV screen. She was The Other Woman in pursuit of The Wayward Husband. But this crowd wasn't used to having lines in the small-screen scripts. They needed a commercial break to discuss amongst themselves what happened next—and Blyss wasn't going anywhere.

Cate came in from the kitchen with a plate of coconut cupcakes in time to hear Blyss' question. One quick glance around the room during the ensuing silence, and she knew she needed to take charge. "We could tell you where Frank and Helen's house is," she allowed the slightest emphasis to rest on Helen's name, "but that wouldn't do you much good because Frank's not there."

Blyss met Cate's gaze and held it steadily. "What makes you so sure?"

"If Frank were back, his neighbors would have mentioned seeing his truck, and he would have shopped for groceries and come in for coffee. None of that has happened—that's how we know. If you're looking for Frank, you're looking in the wrong place."

Blyss to Cate, Cate to Blyss, back to Blyss: it was like watching a tennis match. Would there be a face-off over the net?

Blyss pursed her lips. Her chest rose and fell in a silent sigh—sending most male blood-pressure readings to dangerous heights as the men watched that abbreviated blousy-thing struggle to do its job. "I'd like to check for myself. I'm planning to stay at THE JOHANSON HOUSE BED & BREAKFAST INN, so if any of you hear anything, give me a call there." She pivoted 180 degrees on the balls of her feet and sashayed out the door.

Whereas the exit of a stranger usually generated hours of speculative talk around the café tables, Cate knew this time was different. No one had come close to understanding the reasons behind the limited facts Sadie dished out about the demise of the Wilson's marriage. With this newest development, the plot had not only thickened—it had turned into a slimy mess. It was one thing to think about mud and quite another to get splattered.

Cate mixed refill rounds with several half-hearted attempts to spur conversation, but dangling an enticing tidbit from the morning news about teaching chickens to play tic-tac-toe didn't get more than a distracted "You don't say?" from Charlie. When Charlie, who would usually beat a topic to death before letting it go, had nothing to say, Cate knew the situation needed air.

"If anyone does see Frank, let me know, okay? I'll talk to him and get his take on things. Even though that girl may be the reason he left town, I doubt he'll be too happy to find her waiting for him," Cate said.

Distinct relief spread across the room. Voices soon drowned out the soda machine's hum. The only further mention of Blyss came from Harvey, who had the distinction of knowing a few more details than anyone else present. "She's got an awful lot of sail for such a little ship, if you know what I mean," he said.

Oh yeah, we know what you mean.

Over at the B&B, Gail Harker rushed to the door when she heard a protracted *toooooot* in the driveway. It was not only early in the day for guests to arrive, but it was also early in the week—hardly a usual time for drop-ins. She could see a bright red convertible with creamy leather seats in the driveway and waited curiously on the steps. A young woman emerged, already speaking. "Sorry about that honking! This is a rental car so I didn't know where the horn is. I hit it by mistake."

"No problem," Gail said. "Can I help you?" If she hadn't known she was alone on the porch, she might have wondered where the man was who this half-naked person was trying to impress. *Or maybe she's always performing, in case someone's watching from the wings.* All too conscious of her rhubarb-stained hands, Gail flung her apron aside.

One ankle bracelet flashed in the sunshine as the woman ambled toward the porch. "I'm Blyss Hathaway." Her tone seemed to indicate Gail might have heard of her. "I'm looking for a room for one night, maybe two. Are you the proprietor?"

"Yes, I'm Gail Harker. Getting a room is no problem at all, at least until the weekend; then I'm booked solid, straight through the seventh of July. But I have a room available through Thursday this week.

Come in and we'll get you registered. What brings you to town?" she asked conversationally.

"I'm looking for my boyfriend, Frankie Wilson." Blyss' perfume flooded the narrow hallway leading to the living room.

Gail's instantaneous thought was *No!* She fumbled through the familiar rituals of handing a clipboard and pen to a B&B guest. While Blyss filled out pertinent details, Gail scrutinized the first person she had ever hoped would take offense at something and leave. *And I can help that happen.* "You realize we only serve breakfast. And the café's only open Friday and Saturday evenings in the summer," Gail warned.

"No problem. In fact, quite predictable for a Bed and *Breakfast*," Blyss said with an engaging smile. "I can pick up a few things at that quaint little grocery store."

Down, but not out. Round Two. "We don't provide televisions in our guest rooms."

"I'm a reader—I wouldn't even turn on the TV if there were one."

Time for the serious threats. "I have two small children. They're usually quite well behaved and stay in our family quarters. But sometimes they run and shout and the noise really carries." This had never been a problem yet, but Gail imagined that with a little hands-off parenting, it could happen.

Blyss sidestepped all the punches with ease. "I *love* children!" she trilled and signed her name with a flourish.

Then and there, Gail determined to put Blyss Hathaway in the smallest room with the poorest view.

Blyss tapped one blank line on the registration form. "I'll copy down the license plate number when I go out for my luggage—oh, wait! It's a rental car, so that information is right here on the key tag." Blyss slid the clipboard across the table to Gail and looked around the room with unfeigned interest. "This looks like a charming place. It must be an intriguing job, meeting people and hearing their stories."

Gail nodded, stood up and said curtly. "I'll show you to your room."

Blyss seemed unaffected by Gail's rebuff. Usually, the next comments from a first-time guest would be about the house's history or furnishings. Gail was so caught up in mentally editing her customary account to include only the briefest details that Blyss' question broadsided her.

"Gail, why won't anyone tell me where Frankie lives? I'm sure he's at his house. I should report that fellow at the post office—surely, government employees are obligated to be more helpful. And the café? Why, I've never been in a less friendly place. I came to surprise my sweet man, but everyone acts like I'm in town to rob the bank."

"That'd be hard to do; there's no bank," Gail muttered.

"So I've seen. There's not much of anything here, is there? Actually, finding a B&B is a shock."

"It's a surprising little town," Gail admitted guardedly.

"You're not going to tell me, either, are you?" Blyss said.

Gail's eyes narrowed. "You mean, where Frank lives? The answer to the question isn't the problem, Blyss. It's who's asking it. See, what you don't realize is this: Frank and Helen are part of Prairie Rose. It's like fabric, or a weaving; you pull one thread and it tugs at another, and pretty soon there's a hole and it never looks the same again."

"So everyone blames me for pulling the thread that wrecked the pretty little weaving?"

Gail knew her cheeks blazed, but she straightened her mental shoulders and spoke forthrightly. "It seems to me you're only thinking about the fake little world you and Frank created. You're not even worried about the ramifications of you showing up on the Wilson's front porch."

"Oh, you mean like if his wife answered the door?"

Gail ignored the question. "Frank left a jagged rip when he took off. You say you asked at the post office. Do you realize that's the worst possible place you could have stopped? Al Jenkins is more than the postmaster. He and Frank have been friends for over thirty years. And

Al's wife, Joy? She and Frank's wife have been friends since kindergarten, maybe longer."

Blyss opened her mouth and exercised her lips without a sound. She studied the bracelet on her arm—a gift from Frank. When she looked up, she caught Gail also eying the bracelet. Blyss looked at Gail's hand and noted a plain wedding band. Frank's gift cost enough to buy a dozen wedding bands—jewel-studded ones. Both women knew it. "So that's why no one would give me the simple answer to a simple question? Just because everyone thinks they're Frankie's friends and I'm a horrid person?"

"You were expecting friends and neighbors to ignore the mess Frank left behind. I'm not sure about how things work where you come from, but in Prairie Rose, we have our loyalties and principles."

Blyss stiffened. "I'm not leaving until I find Frankie, Gail. If you don't want me at the B&B, just say so. But I plan to stay until he shows up, even if it means I have to sleep in my car. If he truly isn't here yet, he will be soon. Do you want me to leave?"

Gail rolled her head back on her neck and stared at the ceiling. "On a personal level, yes; on the business level, no." She leveled her gaze at Blyss. "You're a legitimate guest. The only people I am to deny a room are suspected lawbreakers. What you've done unfortunately isn't against the laws of the land."

On the way up the stairs, Gail reveled in one wicked thought: *Anyone else, I'd warn; Blyss Hathaway can find out the hard way that she parked her car directly under a bird's nest!*

After several trips to the car to retrieve luggage, Blyss closed the door to her room and all fell quiet overheard. Within the hour, she came downstairs. Sunglasses wedged into her hair and an unbelievably tiny purse dangling on a gold chain from her bare shoulder, Blyss leaned against the doorframe and watched the peaceful living room scene: Gail reading to her children.

"And the princess said to the prince..." Gail's voice faded and three sets of eyes moved from the colorful pages to their guest in the doorway. "Going out?" she asked without emotion.

"Yes, I'm going for a walk and then shopping."

Gail's eyebrows arched. "Neither one will take long," she said, with mild humor.

Blyss seemed in no hurry to leave. "Hi, kids!" she said a little too enthusiastically. "My name is Blyss. What are your names?"

Gail nudged her daughter. "Jillie." The little girl was mesmerized by someone who looked nothing like any woman in her life.

"That's a nice name," Blyss said in the fake voice adults dredge up to use on children. "And what's your brother's name?"

Another nudge from Gail. "Little Alex."

"Lil 'lex" echoed the toddler.

"Oh, if you aren't the cutest little thing! I'd just like to eat you up! Gobble, gobble, gobble!"

Four little eyes widened on the couch. Jillie reached for her brother's hand and held it tightly.

"So, do you look like *Big* Alex, little guy?" Blyss asked, parking her hand on her hip. "If so, your daddy must be quite the handsome devil!"

"My son is named after Doctor Alex Johanson—as in THE JOHANSON HOUSE BED & BREAKFAST INN. He delivered little Alex," Gail said stiffly.

"Oh, isn't that cozy?" Blyss cooed.

Gail clamped her lips to staunch the angry words that threatened to spew out. When the bile subsided, she said, "To find Frank's house, turn left outside here and go to the corner; then go one block past Main Street, and it's a big white house with a green roof on the southwest corner."

"Thanks," Blyss drawled as she shifted her weight from one hip to the other. "What made you change your mind? About telling me."

"I'm hoping you'll see we're telling the truth—Frank's not here. Once you believe that, maybe you'll leave. Sorry to be so direct, but you asked, so I told you. I'll even give you a full refund if you don't spend the night."

"I can't leave until I find Frankie. I know he was coming here. He's worth waiting for. Haven't you ever loved someone that much?"

The lump in Gail's throat formed quickly and set like cement. Little Alex shifted on her lap, and she buried her nose in his little-boy smells. Jillie looked into her mother's face and twisted her body to peer even closer. "Are you crying about Daddy, Mommy?" she asked in a stage whisper.

"No, Jillie, your brother's hair just tickled my nose," Gail lied blatantly.

Jillie glared at the woman across the room. She hadn't understood half of what had been said but, with a child's instincts, she knew her mother didn't like this lady. "You made my mommy cry. She hardly ever cries 'cept when she thinks about my daddy," she said fiercely.

"Oh, now I understand, Gail—you got dumped, didn't you? You might still wear a wedding ring, but the guy who gave it to you is long gone, I'll bet. That explains a lot. No wonder you're so free with your opinions about Frankie and me. You want to dump all your own misery on me."

Gail slapped the storybook shut. Both children looked at her in surprise.

Jillie interrupted the chilly silence "My daddy's dead," she said sternly. "Quit talking so mean to my mommy."

"Be still, Jillie," Gail chided softly. "Please take your brother into the play room, and I'll bring your snack in a few minutes." Jillie pulled her brother off the couch and shot a daggered look at Blyss as they moved past her.

Both women heard Jillie's stage-whispered: "She's a bad lady!" and the little boy's echoed, "Bad lady!"

To her credit, Blyss said contritely, "You watched what you said; I spoke all too bluntly. Please accept my apology."

Gail nodded numbly.

Blyss stepped backwards into the hallway and then halted. "If I come back late and the place is locked up, how do I get in?"

"We don't lock our doors here." Gail's voice sounded tired. The last hour had been as draining as a marathon, and she still faced the monumental task of reassuring her children their world was safe and secure.

Blyss hadn't been on the streets of Prairie Rose for more than five minutes before phones started ringing around town:

Look out your window right now!

She just walked past my place and is heading your way.

Yes! It's that woman. Go look, and call me right back!

Sadie was in her back yard pounding nails in loose fence boards when she heard the Westhaver's cocker spaniel set up a ruckus. She knew Skippy's barks and decoded this one as *Stranger!*

She stood up just in time to look across two neighboring back yards and see the most astonishing thing beyond the Westhaver's fence: a pair of bare shoulders and a veritable bush of hair. The scene held steady, the character frozen in place, until two hands appeared out of nowhere, just like a puppet show with the fence hiding the rest of the action. Their sole action was to lift a jumble of curls high off a long, slender neck and then pull back, allowing the sun-kissed strands to fall back in place in a sensuous slow dance.

Sadie sucked in her breath audibly and gripped her hammer tightly. *Mercy!* She flew to her gate and marched down the sidewalk, past the Robertson's picket fence and the Westhaver's bridal wreath hedge. Skippy was living up to his name, leaping off the ground in wild bursts of ecstasy at finally having a legitimate reason to bark.

The women reached the corner at the same time and took each other's measure like chickens tossed into a barnyard fight. One was breathless from her race to the corner; the other perspired beneath the unforgiving North Dakota sun that held none of the orb's charm that attracts thousands to California beaches.

Sadie made no attempt to disguise her disgust for a stripped-down Jezebel roaming the streets of *her* town.

Blyss felt her heart pound as she stood face-to-face with a hammer-wielding, stony-faced senior citizen who looked ready to take on a street gang.

"Can I help you?" Sadie demanded, having never bought into the belief that streets are public property.

"Where were you when I needed you?" Blyss asked, with a nervous laugh. She contemplated the hammer and wondered how fast she could run, given the rough sidewalks, gravel streets and shoes that had seemed *so right* until this very moment. "Actually, if you'll just confirm I'm headed the right direction to find Frankie Wilson's house, I'll be on my way."

Sadie's eyes shot wide open and her mouth formed a perfect O. After a long pause, she snapped her jaw shut and squinted at Blyss. "You're That Woman, aren't you?" Her nostrils flared. "What's your name?" she demanded.

"Blyss Hathaway."

Sadie sniffed derisively. "I'll be hog-tied and flogged with a wet noodle. I never thought I'd see the day..." Her eyes narrowed as she looked at the parts of Blyss' body that seemed appropriate—which pretty much limited her to the neck and upwards.

"And you are...who?" Blyss asked.

"Sadie O'Dell. What brings you to town?" she asked curtly.

"I'm looking for Frankie."

"Oh, mercy me!" Sadie fanned her face with one hand and stepped back a pace. "It's one thing to come looking for his house, but to actually be looking for him...And you think you're going to find him at his house? Heavens, child—Frank's not there! He went to California to be with you, and no one's laid eyes on him since. You'd best go back home and be quick about it. There's folks here wanting to tar and feather you."

"I think I've met them already," Blyss said dryly. "This isn't the friendliest place on earth."

Sadie drew herself up sharply. "It is, if a person isn't toting a reputation as messy as yours." She waved the hammer in emphasis. It was Blyss' turn to step back. "And it wouldn't hurt you to put some clothes on, either. Clothes that fit and cover you up. Everything I see appears to be two sizes too small. Have you recently gained a great deal of weight?"

The nerve! Blyss' nostrils flared. "Thanks for your advice. Don't get bent out of shape if I don't take any of it." With that, Blyss sidestepped Sadie and flounced across the street without a backward glance.

Blyss crossed the street, walked up to the Wilson's porch and knocked a coded *tap-tap-tappity-tap* on the door. Nothing. She repeated her signal. Still nothing. "Frankie? It's Blyss, honey. Open up!"

Sadie grunted disgustedly on the opposite corner.

Blyss walked around to the side door—with Sadie moving along the sidewalk at the same pace, keeping Blyss in her line of vision. Repeating her knocks and pleas, Blyss peered into several windows, apparently taken aback by what she saw. Looking around the back yard for a moment, she headed toward the garage to try that door.

Sadie called across the street, "Told you—nobody's there. And he sure ain't living in no garage, so you're just wasting your time."

In a surge of anger, Blyss kicked a rock lodged in the driveway and winced as her bare toes took a beating. Limping back across the street, she started talking midway. "If you see Frankie, tell him I'm at the B&B. Looks to me like his wife cleaned him out and split town. We should be able to stay at his house. Then you'll be seeing a lot of me because we're going to be in town while he settles his affairs."

Sadie tipped her head back and examined Blyss through the bottom of her trifocals. "I can't *tell* you how I'm looking forward to that." She spun around and marched away in her sensible shoes, head held high beneath a sensible hairnet, and hammer bouncing against her sensible housedress.

Blyss allowed herself one childish gesture—she stuck out her tongue at Prairie Rose's self-appointed guardian of all things decent. Then she strode off in her treacherous shoes with their braided leather straps, head held high beneath her disarrayed curls. Her clenched fists bumped against skin-tight shorts. Each step she took set the little purse swinging like a pendulum on its chain.

She had lost any desire to sightsee, but skidded to a halt when the sign for LARSON'S GROCERY registered in her muddled thoughts. Inside the store, she jerked a cart loose from its companions and careened down the aisles, planting herself by the produce display. Holding a bunch of carrots by their tops, she jerked so hard on the roll of plastic bags hanging overhead that it spun out an incredible river of endless bags, spilling across fruits and vegetables and puddling around her ankles.

Observing the whole scene from his perch behind the counter, Dave hurried to her side. He looked from the pool of bags on the floor, back up one short tributary reaching to her hand, then across to the river leading back to the source. He ripped off one bag and handed it to Blyss. "Want a bag?" he asked, grinning.

She searched his face and words for sarcasm and, finding none, leaned over her cart and moaned. "This just isn't my day. Sorry about the mess."

From the meat counter, Luke had full view of the situation. Dave was already gathering up an armload of plastic bags so Luke didn't budge. His phone had also rung in the last half hour; he needed no introduction to this customer.

"You didn't do it on purpose." Dave pulled his eyes away from Blyss' rainbow-hued toes with rhinestones embedded in each nail and met her kneecaps so close-up that he could see the veins beneath her smooth coppery skin.

Dave rose slowly, his eyes moving upward along the trail past tanned thighs to fringed crotch to exposed bellybutton—with a sparkling belly-ring—to her ribcage to the breath-taking swell of womanhood. Dave may not have understood the word *cleavage*, but he had just met the dictionary definition.

Speechless in the face of such discovery, Dave clutched the trailing mess of plastic bags and hurried back to the counter where he thrust the whole bunch into the wastebasket beneath the cash register. He hiked himself up on the high stool and leaned against the back wall. Hormones trumpeted inside his head.

Ignoring Luke who busied himself weighing meat, Blyss hastily made a few selections and rolled her cart to the counter.

Relieved to fall back on a familiar routine, Dave punched in numbers and bagged apples, pears and bananas, carrots, lettuce, and tomatoes, and a can of mixed nuts. While Blyss searched for the right change, Dave asked, "What's your name?"

"Blyss Hathaway."

"I like that name."

She looked at him, startled. "That's the first nice thing anyone's said to me since I hit town. And you didn't yell at me when I made a mess—you're a nice guy; what's *your* name?"

"Dave Jenkins."

She stuck out her hand. "Glad to meet...oh-oh. Are you related to the postmaster?"

Hand halfway extended, Dave's eyes lit up. "Yup, he's my dad," he said proudly.

"Oh, I don't believe this!" She yanked back her hand and thrust her fingers into her hair, dislodging her sunglasses and sending them flying.

Dave rushed out from behind the counter to retrieve the glasses that had skittered across the floor to rest beneath the line of grocery carts.

"So," Blyss drawled, "I imagine you're another loyal Frankie Wilson fan—at least a fan of Frankie's *before* he broke all this town's commandments and ran off with me."

Dave mentally sorted through her words and shook off the ones that made no sense to him and grasped on to those that did. "I like Uncle Frank." he said and handed over her sunglasses.

Blyss stared at him for a moment, then turned away as something about Dave's guileless response triggered understanding in her.

Luke tensed behind the meat counter, ready to do battle if Blyss insulted Dave in any way. *Go! Start walking and don't look back!* Luke held his breath until the door closed behind Blyss and then hurried to the front.

Dave turned to him with a puzzled look. "Isn't she kind of early for the Fourth?"

"She's not here for the fireworks," Luke explained. *Unless setting them off just by her presence counts.* "She's looking for Frank, so we might be seeing more of her. Cate told me Blyss announced at the café that she's not leaving until she finds him."

"Uncle Frank's not here."

"We know that, but she's having a hard time accepting it."

"She's pretty, but sort of crabby, too, huh?"

"She's not getting what she wants—and that's not making her any happier," Luke agreed.

"Maybe she should just go home."

"Amen to that, buddy," Luke said fervently. "Now, we've got work to do. First, we need to replace the plastic bags. Then, would you like to take down the strawberry signs? I sold your mother the last crate today so we shouldn't advertise them anymore."

"Ooo-eee, I bet Mom's making jam! Wait 'til I tell Dad!" Dave headed off to get the ladder and a replacement roll of bags from the storeroom. He whistled *strawberry fields forever* so light-heartedly that Luke caught himself joining in on random notes.

The great thing about Dave's world, Luke knew, was that on any report of the day's activities, strawberries would get top billing. He wished with all his heart that strawberries had been more important to Frank than all of Blyss' considerable charms. Life was much easier for a guy who liked jam on his bread more than a tart in his bed.

* * * *

It may have been Blyss, the heart-stomping home-wrecker who returned to the B&B Monday night and holed up in her room with her bag of groceries, but it was Rosie the Riveter who hit Main Street at 9:00 o'clock the next morning.

Curls had disappeared beneath a bandana. Granted, that kerchief was knotted pertly over one ear allowing wisps of curly hair to peek out, but Blyss was serious business today. With the dark-gray work shirt's short sleeves rolled up and the shirttails tucked into the waistband of matching pants, she looked tough to the women and helpless to the men. The pants legs were folded just high enough to meet the tops of no-nonsense, mud-kicking work boots, allowing random glimpses of tanned legs no one could forget.

Looking like a poster-girl for WWII shipyards, she started at one end of the street and slowly made her way along the sidewalk. Carrying a pocket-sized spiral notebook, she paused in front of each building, jotting down cryptic notes before moving along to the next storefront.

What traffic there was, slowed to watch. Seeing a stranger engaged in such odd behavior was interesting enough, but realization soon dawned that this character—who could have leaped off the pages of history—was none other than the previous day's startling visitor.

Cate turned around after transferring a tray of warm cookies to a plate in the display case to find four customers clustered at the window. Coming up behind them, she saw enough to make asking questions unnecessary. She rolled her eyes and returned to her work, knowing that within seconds, the scuttlebutt would surface. *One, two, three...sure enough, here we go.*

"Ain't that the girl who was looking for Frank?"

"Nah, that one had hair from here to Friday."

"She's got hair—it's just all tucked under that scarf-dealie."

"What's she wearing, anyway? Is she some kinda lineman?"

"Ha! Even in that get-up, it's pretty clear she's no line*man*! She's whatcha call one-hundred-percent female! That's her, alright."

"But what's she doing? I thought she was here looking for Frank. It 'pears now she's casing the joints up and down Main Street. Could be she's planning a crime. Wouldn't that be something?"

"I think we ought to just walk out there and ask her what she's doing."

"Oh-oh, she's heading this way!"

There was a scramble for chairs; the door opened and Blyss strode in. Close up, the transformation between Blyss of yesterday and Blyss of today was all the more startling. Yesterday, she was quicksand for an unwary male heart; today she was new cement that formed a bridge from fantasy back to reality—or vice versa. Either way, a guy could get mired down.

No matter what she wore, Blyss set alarms clanging in every woman's head. Yesterday, they had dismissed her attempts to entice their menfolk as passing fancy. Today, they realized that even with clothes on, Blyss was a magnet capable of attracting even the rustiest iron filings.

No one needed to ask Blyss Hathaway a thing. She parked herself on a counter stool, pointed at the coffee pot and, when Cate arrived with one steaming cup, asked in an all-business voice that matched her outfit, "Are any stores in town hiring that you know of? I'm going to need a job if I'm going to stick around here."

Every woman on the premises thought, *Nobody's stopping you!*

Every man thought, *Let's see—surely someone needs help?* even though he knew that giving Blyss a reason to stick around would have the same results as inviting a tiger to share one's home.

Cate met Blyss' eyes squarely. What everyone heard her say was, "No, can't think of anything, off-hand." *Take the hint, kid* is what Blyss read in her steely eyes.

Blyss had met her match, but didn't back down. "How 'bout you? This place looks busy and, according to the newspaper, it's going to get even busier when the Fourth rolls around. I've done plenty of waitress work, so you wouldn't go wrong hiring me."

"I've got all the help I need already lined up," Cate said evenly.

Blyss spun around on the stool and faced the room like an actress fully aware her audience was hanging on her every word. "I'm staying at the B&B; if anyone hears of any work, please let me know." She reached for her coffee cup, tipped her head back to finish off the last swallow. Standing up, she dug in her hip pocket for a dollar and slapped it on the counter.

From a table in the center of the room, a murmured "Don't hold your breath," reached her ears. She stiffened and slowly turned her head, zeroing in on the red-faced culprit. Dag Colson instantly wished he'd followed his wife's constant reminder, *Watch your tongue, Dag!*

"Did you say, 'Don't hold my breath'?" she grilled him.

"Something to that affect," Dag replied with false bravado.

"Something to that *affect*? Don't you mean *effect*?"

"Whatever." Dag glanced at his tablemates in hopes of getting help, but found none.

"*Effect. Af' fect*—the noun, and note the different accent—means emotional response. *Effect*—the noun—signifies result, consequence, general purpose, intent. *Affect'*—a verb, with the pronunciation you used—means to produce an effect, to act on, to move or to change, to pretend, to tend toward. *Effect*, the verb, means to bring about, to accomplish. So, I believe you meant *effect*—the noun."

Dag stared at Blyss who seemed to tower over him in her red bandana and dusk-gray cotton work clothes. He felt as if she had kicked him in the solar plexus with those heavy-duty boots. He nodded slowly and felt a tic form in his right cheek. *Man, I hope she doesn't think I'm winking at her.*

Blyss didn't stay long enough to form any such opinion. Her long legs ate up the floor in four bites and she disappeared like a rock beneath the surface of a pond. But the ripples lingered.

"Good grief, Dag! What was *that* about? I thought Noah Webster was in here, for a minute there."

Dag shrugged self-consciously. "Looked more like *Missus* Noah Webster. Maybe that's why Frank turned up missing. He probably said some wrong word and she lit into him. I'll bet he's running like a scared rabbit if she gave him one of them speeches!"

Even Cate joined in the laughter. The town had seen its share of strangers in recent years—and even welcomed several of them into the fold, folks like Justin Campbell-Lampman with his SATURDAY STORE, and Eric and Amy Carter who would be arriving any day. Every Fourth of July the town rolled out the proverbial red carpet for thousands of tourists who flocked to town for the best fireworks around.

But there was no red carpet in Blyss Hathaway's future. Not in Prairie Rose. That was becoming clearer by the minute.

Blyss left the café and continued her survey of Main Street buildings. Standing beneath the mutilated D CURL sign, she chewed her bottom lip thoughtfully. Squaring her shoulders, she moved from the curb to the step and reached for the door handle. A distinct click sounded from inside. Blyss jiggled the knob. *Locked.* Muted sounds from within convinced her the shop wasn't closed. Leaning into the prickly bushes, she peered in first one window, and then the other—each time seeing merely her own shadow staring back at her in the bright sunlight.

Then, the door swung open and a nervous man quickly stepped outside and shut the door. Carefully avoiding eye contact with Blyss, he hurried toward the café. "Hey!" she called after him, to no avail.

She walked back to the door and pounded on it. "I know you're in there! There's only one barbershop in town and Frankie's a barber, so this has to be where he worked. Let me in!"

Silence reigned within and after a long moment, Blyss pounded one more time on the door, for good measure, and turned and left.

Meanwhile, over at the café, Carl held center stage. "Helen saw her coming and locked that door so quick, it was like seeing a magic trick! Whooeee, that got Blyss mad! She had thought she could just walk in. Wouldn't that have been something, though, if the two of them had lit into each other?"

Cate sighed and decided this dismal tale's time in the spotlight had to end. Expertly, she steered the conversation toward the upcoming parade, squelching each resurgence of the previous conversation with persistence until it fizzled and died.

There was plenty to discuss—preparation for the Fourth demanded every citizen's efforts. Flour and sugar flew off the grocery store shelves as Women's Guild members baked up a storm. Neighborhoods smelled of paint and varnish as folks completed crafts they hoped to sell. Others spiffed up the home place to exhibit town pride for strangers who would watch the parade from shady front yards. A select few dusted off their band instruments and practiced for the annual concert in the park. Shop owners restocked shelves in anticipation of their best day of sales—it truly was Christmas in July each year.

Last year's Fourth of July celebration had upped the ante on entertainment. Pastor Tori's friend, BJ Kendall—the golf pro—had come to town then to help re-open the PRAIRIE ROSE GOLF COURSE, leaving people wondering just how they would top, or even match, that achievement this year. Wisely, they decided not to try. It was back to the special brand of down-home entertainment that had brought hosts of visitors for many years before BJ Kendall even heard of Prairie Rose.

Committees met, To-Do Lists shrunk and then ballooned again. Delivery trucks roared around town like fighter jets, and Blyss Hathaway watched it all in bemused silence. Like a faithful old dog waiting for its master's return, she clung to the belief her Frankie was due to arrive any day.

Gladys, Lucy's sister from Iowa, arrived for her traditional working vacation at CATE'S CAFÉ. With extra skilled labor available, the ovens seldom had time to cool down, the dishwasher ran constantly, the electric meter spun, and Cate barely had time to pack Juddie's diaper bag with clean clothes each morning.

This year, Gladys arrived on Wednesday—one week before the Fourth. Even though she hadn't seen her sister since Christmas, it still wasn't surprising the first words out of her mouth when she pushed open the front door were, "Heavens! Who is that girl on Main Street?"

No one needed to ask, *Who?*

Blyss treated Main Street like her personal beat. Not one passing car escaped her scrutiny as she paced the sidewalks from morning to night. If any crime *were* to be committed in Prairie Rose, authorities would have an easy job apprehending the perpetrator: they could just ask Blyss for details—she would have seen it all.

Citizens watched her monotonous journey with more interest than such activity would normally hold, mostly because she gave them daily fodder for gossip. Her third day in town, Glen commented to his buddies at the café, "She's kinda like one of them chameleons, ain't she?" Everyone had to agree. Watching Blyss was like surfing channels.

Each day, she emerged from the B&B transformed. The only constant about Blyss was she always toted a book, though even it changed from day-to-day. In a town where there was no easy supply for books, only the staunchest supporters of the printed word considered themselves *readers.* For many, the weekly newspaper, a magazine scanned at the barber-beauty shop, and whatever reading was required in a Sunday's service pretty much covered their reading needs once they graduated from high school.

However, those with a yen to read always knew who had bought a new best seller and quickly got their name on the list once it was out for loan. It was these folks who eyed Blyss' changing assortment of books like a cat watching a bird's nest.

There wasn't much talk about Blyss at the D CURL, but that didn't mean Helen wasn't aware of her archenemy's many-colored-coat of personalities. After the pointed episode involving the locked door during business hours, Blyss made no further overtures toward the D CURL. By noon of the second Blyss-on-Patrol day, Helen had begun to take notes, though she would have been hard-pressed to explain why:

Wednesday—it's the Little-House-on-the-Prairie look; a schoolmarm with hair rolled into a bun—where'd she find hairpins, anyway? Shirtwaist blouse tucked into a flowing skirt. Complete with the wire-rim glasses—and a book the size of Wyoming.

Helen tucked her pencil away and turned to catch a curious look from the customer she had thought was still in the bathroom. Sally, in for a cut-and-color, knew exactly who was outside the window. "She's something, isn't she? If you don't mind my saying so, I can't imagine her with Frank."

"She's not with him now," Helen said dryly.

Thursday—She's acting like a wide-eyed innocent little girl with too-cute pigtails, bubble-gum pink princess-line dress and patent leather Mary Janes—good grief, even lacy anklets! No glasses now, so unless she's wearing contact lenses, she'll likely end up with little-girl banged-up knees.

Deciding the only way to see Helen was to show up at the shop, Joy called for an appointment and requested that Helen—not an intern—trim her hair. She fidgeted, wishing the shop were empty so they could talk, but promptly rebuked herself: *If the shop's empty, Helen's not making any money.* So she waded into a pool of inconsequential talk. "I noticed you put up a clothesline outside your back door, Helen."

"Yeah, but it's in the bird zone back there. I'm torn between wanting the birds to enjoy the feeders and feel at home in the birdhouse, and being able to hang out my sheets." Both women fell silent, each visualizing the full regiment of clotheslines permanently camped in an unused backyard.

Joy attempted another topic. "I'm really enjoying my piano. You'll have to come hear me play some evening. When Al brought it home,"*...on that fateful day when our lives fell apart...Why did I think this was an appropriate topic?* She stumbled on, "...there was lots of sheet music in the bench. His aunt had an interesting collection."

But she'd lost Helen to thoughts as dismal as her own. Anything she could think to say would only bring back memories, so she said little more. Luckily, the interns kept the chatter going with the other customers, which allowed Helen and Joy to float along on a raft of impersonal words. When Joy paid Helen, she blurted out, "I miss you, Helen," undercover of a burst of laughter across the room.

Helen carefully placed the bills in the correct register compartments and looked around the shop quickly before whispering, "I know." Two words, fraught with multiple meanings and no clues as to her intent. Lightly touching Joy's arm, she said, "Catch you later," and called to the interns, "Girls, I want to show you a technique I use to avoid scalp burn..."

Leaving the grocery store later that day, Helen passed a cluster of men on the sidewalk. She didn't have to ask who they were discussing when she overheard, "What's she driving, anyway? A semi-truck? I thought my wife had a lot of clothes!"

Friday—Wet-look (apparently, no time to dry off after her morning shower?) Tight T-shirt, hair all moussed back, short-shorts and flip-flops. Must think there's a beach nearby! She's only got a paperback today—doesn't want to lose a hardback book if a wave hits her, I guess.

At the café, Bernie held court from morning coffee break right through lunch. "...an' I says to her, I says, 'What are you doing, walking up and down Main Street all the time?' on account of I have a little experience, you know, with police work."

No one slowed his tale by debating whether traffic patrol at the State Fair back in the '50s truly constituted police work.

Bernie pinged his suspenders against his chest and continued, "…an' she says to me, she says real snooty-like, 'I doubt there's any law that precludes me from walking on Main Street.' *Precludes,* she says. Now if that ain't a two-bit word when a nickel word would do, I don't know what is."

Dag Colson, survivor of the previous infamous Grammatical Encounter with Blyss Hathaway, waved a warning hand. "Bernie, Bernie, Bernie! Did you learn nothing from my experience? You can't discuss words with her. She's got a head full of them and is just waitin' for someone like you or me to unload 'em on. *Beep-beep-beep-beep-beep!*" Dag sang out every dump truck's back-up tune and leaned backwards as if pursued by a ten-ton load.

When the laughter subsided, Bernie picked up his story again. "So I says to her, I says, 'We don't hold with folks doing what you're doing, *precluding* or not.' Believe me, that shut her right up. She's done plenty around here good Christian folks don't do, if you catch my drift."

All eyes turned to the street where Blyss strolled slowly past the café. Bernie blustered. "What I said may not have *stopped* her, but it sure gave her something to think about. It sure did."

An adolescent boy's hormones went into overdrive when he saw Blyss sitting on the steps outside the SATURDAY STORE. As she bent over the book resting on the step between her spread-eagle legs, her charms were in full evidence, apparently unencumbered by anything in the foundation-garment line. He tripped coming into the D Curl and sprawled across the floor, the door clipping him in the ankles. Blushing, he picked himself up and muttered, "Fix that step!" and chose a seat to wait his turn, ignoring the knowing winks and chuckles from the man in the barber chair.

Opening the shop's blinds on Friday, Helen yelped and jumped back, still holding the wand. Blyss walked a mere six feet away from the window, oblivious to her observer in the shadowy room. Helen grabbed her notebook. *Olé! Low-cut puffy-sleeved white blouse, off one shoulder. Yards and yards of bright-colored swirling skirt, ankle-strap high-heels, dangly jewelry and lots of it. Hair pinned off to one side with a huge white flower. Add a sombrero and she could be Miss Mexico. She's already mastered walking the dais. Wonder if her book is in Spanish?*

Picking dead blooms off the flowers in the alley after work, Helen heard young voices from a nearby back yard. Even though they never mentioned such in front of Helen, Blyss was the number-one topic of conversation among the teenagers:

"She's *always* reading something. That's why she's got so many glasses—she must have a pair to match whatever she wears. That is way cool!"

"Like, she doesn't always wear glasses. Me and Zoe have, like, seen her up-close twice. Like, once, she had green eyes and, like, the other time she had, like, these really, like, brown eyes. That's the beauty of contact lenses, dude—you can, like, change your whole, like, personality."

"It's so romantic—she's like pining away for her lover to come back—just like in those poems Mister Rowland made us read in Lit class!"

Helen slammed the door with extra gusto, muttering as she headed for the bathroom. "Pining away—I wish!"

Saturday—just in time for the SATURDAY STORE to open, of course—it's the biker-chick look. Spikey hair, leather vest zipped up over nothing-at-all—and showing plenty of all she's got. Tight leather pants with zippers up the legs and no room for pockets. Pointy-toed boots, reflective sunglasses. Whatever Blyss-the-Biker reads, I bet it should be hidden in a plain brown wrapper.

Gail brought rhubarb crisp to Helen on Saturday night. "This is my peace offering. I'm just sick about housing that woman. I'm not sure where she's staying now; I had bookings so she had to leave. I just wanted to warn you, she might have figured out a way to get into your old house."

"If she did, I don't care. There's nothing there anymore for me. If she's guilty of breaking and entering, it's a far lesser crime, in my book, than what Frank committed."

Sunday—the whore came to church! Wore a tailored suit and V-neck silk blouse with sedate pearl brooch and earrings. Hair looked decent, tied back with a long silk scarf that trailed down her back. Her little folding gold-framed glasses fit into her breast pocket—as if we needed anything to draw our attention to that part of her body. She read all the scripture readings and sang all the songs—she is a hypocritical minx, that one.

By Monday noon, Alex knew full well everyone was dying to know just what it was Blyss Hathaway had needed from him when she came to his office. The only word on the street came from Bertha Thompson who had just completed her weekly blood pressure reading. If she hadn't just sat down to finish copying a recipe for cornbread from a magazine when the door had opened and Blyss walked in, she would have missed the whole thing.

"I knew it was her when I heard those silly shoes of hers on the floor. Believe me, it's a broken ankle just waitin' to happen with them. Anyway, Blyss says to Lulu, 'I would like to see the doctor, please,' real persistent-like." Bertha leaned across the table. Her three tablemates slid their coffee cups aside. "Lulu says, 'May I ask the nature of your problem?' real professional. And Blyss says, 'I prefer to discuss that with the doctor,' which left Lulu with nothing to do now, but go knock on Doctor Alex's door and tell him he had a patient."

"You don't suppose that temptress has designs…" a delicate cough from a tablemate stilled the question. The door opened to admit none other than Alex; four women quickly resumed coffee drinking as he slid into place beside his wife.

"What's up, Doc?" Tori asked in a nonchalant undertone. "Word is, Blyss may be done with Frank and is making a play for you."

Alex caught Tori's wicked grin and coughed into his fist. "At the risk of looking guilty as sin, let's cut that rumor off at the pass." The kiss they shared across the table kicked the zest right out of current speculation.

Midway through their meal, Alex casually said, "Here's a medical tip you might enjoy: A person who does a great deal of walking...oh, let's say, like pacing a sidewalk for hours—or days—on end...that person is at great risk for blisters. Blisters on the heels, blisters on the small toes, blisters on the instep."

A mouthful of tomato basil soup squirted right past Tori's lips. "Oh, Zan, I love you!"

"And I love you with your pretty little blister-free feet more than anyone in the world, Tori. Did you know that I always turn blister cases over to Mattie? She does fine work with skin care!"

Alex popped the few remaining cherry tomatoes on his plate into his mouth, kissed Tori on her upturned nose and headed back across the street. Cate dropped into the chair he had vacated and stared out the window with Tori. "Looks like the two of you enjoyed your lunch," she said dryly.

"Cate, I love this town!" Tori flashed a wide smile. "Nothing beats real-life human comedy."

"Oh, we've got plenty of that, lately," Cate drawled. "I wake up every morning wondering what the day's hot topic will be. Personally, I'm ready for a whole new subject."

Helen's written record continued: *Monday—today it's a movie star from the '30s: sleek pageboy hairdo, rhinestone-rimmed glasses, ruby-red lips and nails, lacy white blouse and slim-line black skirt. Black pumps and, I can hardly believe this: black-seamed nylons. She's reading poetry aloud—with lots of inflection, and some of it in French, if Lou is to be believed.*

Tuesday, the Caravan Crew arrived. This brawny team had been the answer to small towns' prayers for nearly ten years. Any place with limited manpower for crowd control, heavy-duty labor, and jack-of-all-trades expertise needed these guys. This year, eight strapping young men fanned out across Prairie Rose, greeting old friends as they set up camp near the golf course.

Blyss watched the string of vehicles drive through town and followed them to City Park like a Swiss lass in pursuit of her sheep herd. The robust young men's eyes slid right past her rosy cheeks and shiny blonde plaits to zero in on the rows of Xs crisscrossing the mountain range that nearly burst free of her snowy white cotton blouse. These braided laces worked hard to join together the straining sides of her vest. Suddenly, the air in North Dakota felt very thin to the light-headed Crew. To a man, they gulped.

Ian, the Caravan Crew boss, assessed the situation immediately and called the men together to make work assignments, hoping to diffuse the highly volatile situation Blyss' appearance had nearly ignited.

Without an audience, Blyss eventually retreated to parts unknown. By nightfall, she was back at City Park, toting a boxed meal she had picked up at CATE'S CAFÉ. All that remained of her Swiss-look were rippling reminders of the braids. She propped a book before her on a picnic table, her unleashed hair falling around her glowing skin while she read and nibbled at her supper.

She had chosen a table close enough to the Caravan Crew's chuck wagon to hear every word—but far enough away to ensure a measure of privacy for anyone who might wish to saunter over. Somehow, even dressed in unremarkable jeans and a nondescript polo shirt she made male hearts do flip-flops. Maybe part of the enticement was the way one sandal dangled off her toes beneath the table—an innocent act for anyone else, a carefully plotted and alluring detail for Blyss.

Ian spoke loudly as he joked with his crew over their first-night supper. He blatantly made it his mission to let Blyss know each man on the crew was happily married:

"Hey, Kip, that's great news about *your wife's* new job—what a year for you two *newlyweds*, huh?"

"Yeah, we're pretty excited about moving here, too. I'm glad we're here in time for me to work with the crew again!"

"Pass those pictures down so Roberta can see them, too. Look at *Jeff's new son*, honey! Jeff, I've gotta tell you—this kid has your *wife's* good looks!"

Seemingly oblivious to all around her, Blyss read at her table until the light faded. Sauntering slowly across the grass, she took a long drink at the water fountain, turning even that into a seductive activity. Once the shadows had swallowed her from view, Ian heaved a sigh of relief. There had never been a serious threat to what he held dear—strong marriages. But this time, Ian admitted grimly to Roberta as they dished ice cream and sliced cake, "We've got a potential problem."

This weekend, no wives were expected. Roberta was the only woman on-board and she didn't have to ask her husband, *What problem?* While Blyss hadn't *done* one thing to merit their concern yet, she looked ready to do the unthinkable. Neither Ian nor Roberta wanted the men going home to their wives with nasty secrets—or even hints of such trouble.

"There are always flirts, Ian," Roberta said in a low voice. "Women and girls love to bat their eyelashes at the Crew and coo *You're so strong*—type messages. It just makes the guys work all the harder to show off."

Ian sniffed his disdain. "Maybe *some* females are innocent flirts; this one has nerve *up to here* and enticements *out to there.* She could be like the Pied Piper with a trail of googly eyed men following close behind."

"It will work out," Roberta said reassuringly, but even she wondered how.

Wednesday morning, Luke hooked CATE'S CANOPY CAFÉ to his pickup and hauled it into place at the City Park. The food wagon usually occupied a spot near the Meadowlark Trail where it did a steady business with Hawaiian Shave Ices, sloppy joes, and other eat-on-the-go favorites.

Mission accomplished, Luke took a moment to admire the refurbished Band Stand gleaming in the sunlight and ready for the Fourth of July concert. His dad had been practicing his saxophone for weeks.

The volunteer band, comprised both of members of the high school marching band and other citizens, like Tyler Larson, who dusted off their skills for this annual event, always gave a dress-rehearsal performance on the evening of the third.

The day sped by. The air crackled with excitement. Random firecrackers set dogs howling in sporadic concerts. The volunteer firemen hosed off the fire truck and gave fifty-cent rides around town. Father Casey O'Donovan set up a microphone on the front steps of his church and whistled Irish tunes for two hours—reaping enough spare change in the cap at his feet to paint the church kitchen. The Caravan Crew stationed sawhorses up and down Main Street in preparation for the parade, the street dance, and all other activities that required an empty street. The parking lot, which the Caravan Crew created annually from a field on the edge of town, filled steadily.

Finally, dusk fell. The Boy Scouts pulled wagons of chilled soft drinks through the crowd milling around City Park. Many visitors had learned it was worth coming early on the third of July. Not only was it easier to find a place to park an RV, but the day's entertainment made it worth the effort.

The band's discordant warm-up sounded the call to gather. Lawn chairs and blankets already dotted the park's grassy areas. RV owners opened their windows and doors and settled back to listen in comfort. Those with pickups had a birds-eye view from lawn chairs set up in the truck beds. Shouts and laughter mingled in the air together with the reminders of grilled dinners and the acrid odors of preliminary sparklers.

Band members gradually filled chairs on the stage. The bleats and toots and clangs and occasional scale-run from the instruments that gleamed beneath the domed lights added to the summer night's cacophony. The conductor's stand stood empty, waiting for Bob Marshall to mount the steps, raise his baton and cue the first notes.

Neighbors called to neighbors, teenage couples leaned against trees or lounged in their cars. Kids chased each other in last-minute games of tag. Two grade-school boys with squirt guns kept little girls squealing half-hearted protests. Bob observed all this from the sidelines. *Norman Rockwell could have painted a dandy portrayal of Americana tonight.*

He shifted his gaze to the band. *It's too bad Frank took off—we really need him on tuba. Jimmy's good—but he always seems to notice the crowd at the wrong time, or get nervous when he sees his girlfriend.* Bob looked over the crowd and groaned when he spotted Blyss, fully in white, like a bride awaiting her groom. Her clothing became all the more luminous as the evening shadows deepened. She appeared serene, sitting in what Bob could only suppose was a yoga position. His staccato version of *hmmm!* matched the disgusted expressions of townsfolk seated near her. City Park on the cusp of a band concert was hardly the place to seek serenity.

Bob looked at his watch and blocked Blyss from his mind: *It's show time—the* real *show people came to see.* He had walked only halfway to the steps when a joyous shriek sounded, rising high above the band's tuneless sounds. "Frankie!" A shimmer of white flew across the lawn, sidestepping blankets, dodging small children, practically airborne in a private flight pattern to the opposite side of the bandstand.

Frank Wilson braced himself against the corner of the stage as Blyss flung her arms around his neck and smothered his face with kisses. Except for a final *ta-da-boom* from the snare drum, an eerie silence descended as everyone absorbed the off-stage drama.

Slowly, details surfaced for the stunned audience. Blyss was doing all the hugging—even if Frank had been inclined to participate, he lacked the necessary appendages. One arm was encased in a bulky cast held firmly in place by a sling. A cast covered one leg from mid-foot to his knee, which left him hopping and leaning heavily on his crutch as he struggled to keep his stance in the onslaught of Blyss' affection. He looked like an escapee from a hospital ward in a Grade-B movie.

Pulling back slightly, Blyss looked closely at Frank. Her voice carried easily as she cried out, "Oh, Frankie! What savages did this to you? You're all black and blue and broken!" She spun around to face the crowd as if expecting the doers of such horrendous deeds to step forward. Then, she murmured something and gently took Frank's arm and the two of them disappeared behind the bandstand.

At first it was just a scraping chair on the stage, then a child's question rose from a blanket, and soon the evening air buzzed like a hornet's nest:

Did you see…?

Is that…?

What did she…?

What on earth…?

Was that Frank…?

Numbly, Bob climbed the steps and stood behind the conductor's podium. Notes blurred on the music before him. He blinked and looked up, uncertain and unnerved, letting his eyes roam over his band. In the trumpet section, Al sat like a zombie in first chair. *No help there.* Joy looked back at him from the clarinet section, her face a mirror of his thoughts. Helen clutched her French horn with white-knuckled concentration, her eyes glued to the spot off-stage where her husband had stood in Blyss' embrace.

Things weren't any better in the arcs of chairs than on the conductor's podium. Al felt his blood pounding in his veins and tried to remember the warning signs for a heart attack.

Joy sucked on her clarinet's reed and nearly bit it in two. *I suspected this concert would be hard for Helen, but I had no idea…* Then she heard a trumpet's lone note, like a foghorn sounding through an ocean's mist. Joy jerked her head toward Al.

He met her eyes in a private signal and pantomimed playing. *He's right—people came for a concert, not a sideshow.* Slowly, she ran a jerky scale, missing the sixth note entirely. One by one, the woodwinds and strings and brass sections revived and the percussionists added disjointed rhythms.

Bob Marshall picked up his baton and ran his fingers along its smooth length, his mind racing as the band warmed up again. He took a deep breath and looked down at his music. *We can do it; we must do it.*

The look he gave the musicians infused them with a sense of purpose. They played better than at any of their rehearsals. The swell of music rolled across the grassy park and drowned out the chatter. The night air pulsed with ragtime, jazz, marches, and blues—Big Band sounds reminiscent of Louis Armstrong, Fletcher Henderson, Duke Ellington, and Benny Goodman.

After a rollicking version of *Jeepers Creepers*, an out-of-town couple flew out of a camper and started dancing on the grass to *Don't Blame Me*. The band gave its heart and soul to *Blueberry Hill* and *Sugarfoot Stomp* and *Mood Indigo* and *Stardust*. If one French horn missed entire measures from time to time, the other musicians covered for it.

The park emptied slowly after the concert, and many lined up at Cate's food wagon for a late-night treat. Other townsfolk clustered around the senior Alexander Johanson—the returning retired physician who had served the community well for many years.

For Prairie Rose and the surrounding community, welcoming Doctor Alex to town two years earlier had been a cyclical event—they merely transferred their trust and affection from Alexander-the-grandfather to Alex-the-grandson. This year, two doctors Johanson would staff the First Aide booth, the elder one happily coming out of retirement to work beside his pride-and-joy replacement.

With so much attention on the physician-duo, Al and Joy and Helen relaxed in the knowledge something else now held center stage.

"Al, thanks for getting things rolling. I froze up there and you saved the day," Bob said in a low voice while the men stacked folding chairs against the wall in case of an overnight shower.

"No big deal. I didn't think the band walking off the stage without giving a concert would help, so I just…" Al shrugged and let his words fade as the two women joined them.

Helen said, "It's been quite the evening. I think I'll take off. See you all tomorrow."

"We're ready to go, too," Joy said quickly. "Right, Al?"

"Sure thing. G'night, Bob."

They gathered up their instrument cases and left the stage, passing by Rachel in her wheelchair. "If you don't need to talk with the doctors," Joy said, nodding at the men nearby, "we can help you get home through this crowd."

"Thanks, anyway, but Alexander has offered, as have Alex and Tori. I'm content until they're free. What a wonderful concert! This year's Grand Finale lived up to its name!"

After that brief encounter, it was a quiet trip from the park to Helen's apartment, hardly long enough to allow for much conversation and far too public for anything remotely personal to be said. Outside the back door to the D CURL, Helen said, "Try not to worry, Jenks. I know you will anyway, but I'll be fine. Really. The one you ought to be concerned about is Frank; I think he got the shock of his life tonight." Her laughter sounded hollow in the dimly lit alley. "See you tomorrow." She fumbled with her key in the shadows, her shaking hands the only indication of her emotional state.

"Here, let me," Al said gently. He unlocked the door, swung it open and reached inside to flick the light switch. "There you go, Helen. Be sure to lock up—lots of strangers in town tonight."

"Ain't that the truth?" Helen said wryly and stepped across the threshold. "G'night."

Al reached for Joy's hand and they took off toward home, unconsciously keeping step. With Main Street behind them, they slowed their pace. "If you had told me three months ago how today would turn out, I'd have asked what planet you were from," Joy said.

"What's wrong with Frank's head? Did he honestly think showing up at the band concert was a great idea?"

"I don't think anyone understands how Frank's mind is working these days, Al. Not even Frank."

"Let's sit out on the porch for a bit. My mind is racing and I need to wind down or I'll never get to sleep."

"Want anything?"

"Nah, I'm not hungry."

Joy's eyebrows arched in the darkness. *Al not hungry?* She dropped down beside him on the swing and scooted into her favorite position against his chest. They rocked, listening to the chain's squeak against the wood and the occasional *whoosh* of a bush brushing against the house. Al's heart pounded beneath Joy's ear.

When he spoke, she both felt and heard his voice. "Do you suppose Blyss has been right all along? Is it possible Frank has been hiding out in town somehow?"

"Highly unlikely. Remember, Sadie lives across the street from his house."

"How do you suppose he got so banged up? He looked worse than a run-over dog."

"Now *that's* a million-dollar question."

"With those wounds, maybe he's been to see Alex."

Joy tipped her head to look at Al. "You're dreaming if you think Alex would ever divulge patient information."

"Yeah, I know." He jiggled his knee hard, which jerked the swing. "Man, I hate this whole mess. It was bad enough when Frank up and left. In fact, then I thought we'd seen the worst." His laugh sounded harsh. "But here we are facing the town's busiest day of the year, all sorts of things need our attention and we really need our rest, and what happens? Frank limps back into town. That guy has a lot of nerve."

"Maybe he planned his return for this precise time, thinking it wouldn't attract as much attention with everything else going on," Joy suggested. "He seemed startled, to say the least, to see Blyss. He probably assumed she was still in California. She did say she was surprising him."

"You know what? The two of them can just take their little sex parade and march it out of town. They have no right to channel even one ounce of attention toward themselves."

"Maybe they'll just hole up somewhere. I imagine they're over at Frank and Helen's old house."

Al expelled a *Pfffft*. "Bet that place is a shock to Frank. He left a houseful of furniture and a loaded pantry. He comes back to echoing rooms and not a crumb in the kitchen. Serves him right. And while he's here, he better mow his own lawn," he added crossly.

"Yeah, that's gonna happen—a guy in his shape!"

"He can have Blyss Hathaway mow it, then."

"Hmm, I wonder what outfit she'd haul out to do yard work?"

Al snorted. "Actually, I take that back. I want Frank to boot Blyss out of town. Pronto. She needs to pack up her entourage of suitcases and go back home."

"It's really none of our business what Frank and Blyss do. Frank's made it very clear he wants nothing to do with us. We need to help Helen survive this as best we can, and do the jobs people are expecting from us tomorrow. Come on, Big Guy." Joy yawned and held out her hand.

Al stood and stretched, pulling Joy's hand in the air along with his own. "Right as rain, Joybells. Bed, it is."

They slid between the sheets. With a mere brush of Al's lips across Joy's forehead, they drifted into troubled dreams.

Chapter 7

In the early morning hours, Joy reached out and found the other half of the bed empty and cool; Al had not been there for a long time. Pulling on her robe, she made her way down the stairs in the dark. She sniffed the air. *Coffee?* She found Al leaning against the porch railing, perched on the top step. He gripped a half-full mug. *Yup, coffee.* "Hey," she said softly. "Your pillow is cold. I missed you."

"Yeah, I couldn't sleep so I came outside for some fresh air." He tugged her down beside him on the step. She tucked her hand around his arm and nestled in close.

Reaching for his cup, she took a sip and wrinkled her nose. "Yuck! Cold!"

"No doubt; I'll get you some hot stuff. Don't move." He pushed up and her arm fell free of his. She watched his hair-darkened muscular legs move him out of her view. He had pulled on a pair of walking shorts, but his torso and feet were bare. It was the body she saw in her dreams.

He was back in minutes, bringing her cup and the glass pot from the coffeemaker. He flung the cold coffee from his cup into the bushes and filled both cups, handing her one.

She took a swallow and stiffened. "When did you make this pot?"

"A while ago. Why?"

"It's on a par with Bob Marshall's idea of coffee!" She glanced at him when he didn't defend himself against her teasing. Lost in thought, Al downed coffee so potent he usually would have dumped it after the first swallow.

She slid her hand back into the crook of his elbow and rested her head against his shoulder. The trees and water tower poked the morning-gray sky, letting pockets of color push through the slits they made. A bird cooed overhead in a leafy hide-away. "You're awfully quiet, Al."

He lifted her hand and entwined their fingers. "I need to get away."

Joy's mouth went dry. "You mean, like Frank did?"

"Not like Frank in the reason *why*, but I'd sure like to forget about life for a while. Life's gone wacky."

"Hey, I know it's rough, but it's hard to believe there's someplace you'd rather be." She paused, waiting for the *You're right; I'm just disgusted* that never came. Hoping her voice held more confidence than she felt, she said, "I'm not sure how, but eventually this Frank-Helen-Blyss mess will sort itself out."

"It's not just that fiasco in the park last night, Joy. I've been thinking about this for some time."

"Have you thought about where you'd like to go?" It took all her willpower to quell the trepidation in her heart.

"No place special—just away."

"Two things pop to mind: first, there's the little matter of your job, and second, what about Dave?"

"I could walk away from that job in an instant," Al said with more passion than Joy had heard in weeks.

Her eyes widened. "Really?" An icy river washed over her. *What else could you walk away from without looking back?*

"And as far as Dave, that's something we'd have to work out. He's fine for a few days on his own."

Relief warmed her. "Oh, so you're saying you want a vacation. Whew! You had me worried for a minute. I thought you meant pitching the whole go-to-work-get-a-paycheck thing."

"If I never sold another postage stamp, it would be just fine with me."

Joy rubbed the back of her hand against Al's early-morning stubble. *Yikes, where have I been?* She heard a chipper voice float through the open window above the porch. "That'd be our clock radio. Rise and shine!" she said ironically.

Al gave no sign of hearing either her or the annoyingly cheerful morning announcer.

She jiggled his arm. "Hey, you've got today off from postage stamps and the town is full of people anticipating pancakes at the ballroom, so we'd better get a move on. You can shower first, if you'd like."

Al straightened and stretched, yawning widely. He stood beside her, turned and cupped her chin in his hand. He ran his thumb across her lips like a kiss. "Don't worry, J-bells. Unlike Frank, when I run, I'm taking my woman with me. You're the only thing that makes sense in my life."

Tears immediately clouded Joy's vision. As the door closed behind Al, she hugged her knees and let her thoughts skitter from one thing to another:

The hollow look in Al's eyes this morning and the rock-hard resolve in his voice when he talked about leaving—*I've never heard him talk like this before.*

The D CURL sign on Main Street—*It's like an inescapable reminder of a marriage gone sour.*

The startling note from Al's trumpet last night, guiding the band back from their shock even though it had hit him as hard as anyone. *We planned a funeral in our heart for someone missing in action, only to have the deceased show up at the service.*

Weighed down by troubling thoughts and images, she headed inside to prepare for the day. Freshly shaved and evidencing his usual post-shower wet-head look, Al had pulled on a sports shirt and khakis and was making the bed. "I won't be long, but if you need to get going, I understand."

"I'll wait," he said simply.

Within minutes, she had showered, applied minimal make-up and dressed in walking shorts and a blouse. Running a comb through her hair, she heard the pipes rattling and knew Dave was awake and showering. He, too, faced a busy day at the grocery store. She found Al in the kitchen, wiping off the counter, with clean coffee pot and cups dripping in the dish drainer.

"You look pretty," he said, looking over his shoulder.

She pirouetted. "Maybe you do need a vacation," she teased, "seeing as what you call pretty is a fifty-year-old woman with wet hair and wearing positively ancient shorts. But thanks, anyway. The look today is solely for comfort—I'm not entering any beauty contests." She stood on tiptoes to kiss him. "Come on; let's go feed the world."

From face painting to Rachel's recorded historical tour of town, from horseshoes in the park to a penny arcade in the Harmon's barn, from Harvey Thompson's museum of world-class headgear to the town's pride-and-joy Meadowlark Trail for hikers, bikers, and nature lovers—the day offered plenty of variety. "I find myself wondering just when Frank's going to pop up again," Al said glumly as he and Joy sat down for a late breakfast.

"He may not. Let's just put him out of our minds and try to enjoy the day."

Al arched his eyebrows above a humorless smile. "Isn't that kind of like 'Don't think about zebras' advice to say, 'Let's put Frank out of our minds'?"

"Maybe that's better advice: don't think about zebras. That will take your mind off Frank. And while you're at it, don't think about elephants, either."

"You're crazy, but you're my kind of crazy. I love you, Joybells," Al said, dipping a forkful of pancake into a puddle of syrup.

"Love you, too, Big Guy," Joy quickly blew her nose in a paper napkin.

"Are you crying?" Al asked incredulously.

"Nah, not me."

Al stared at her. "You're a pathetic liar; you know that, don't you?"

"A crazy emotional fibber," Joy admitted with a shrug. "Quite a package deal, huh?"

"Yup, and you're all mine."

"Maybe you're right—maybe we do need to get away if I'm sobbing over pancakes in a public place."

"Now you're singing my song."

Joy laughed through her tears. "You know something? We may be the only people in town today who are thinking about being some place else. The Fourth of July in Prairie Rose is usually where people make plans to be—not flee!"

"Hold that thought; tonight we'll plot out our escape."

A little girl pounded past their table in search of her mother who was on the clean-up brigade. "Mama! Pippi Longstocking is here! Really! She is—come see!" She latched on to her mother's hand and tugged the woman toward the door.

Joy's fork slid from her fingers and fell to the floor unheeded. "Oh, no! I know what's on the entertainment agenda, and there's No Pippi Longstocking on the master plan. Come on, Al. I'm afraid to look, but I just bet..."

Sure enough, it was Blyss-turned-Pippi. Anyone who had ever read or heard the classic tales—which included twenty-two years' worth of Joy Jenkins' first graders—recognized the character: A red wig sprouted two pigtails sticking straight out above each ear. A fringed white apron covered a faded jumper. One blue-and-yellow striped sock rolled short and an apple-green sock pulled high sprouted from scuffed hiking boots. Vivid freckles seemed in constant motion as Blyss smiled and chattered with the cluster of little children dancing around her. It was Pippi, right off the pages of Astrid Lindgren's storybooks.

Ignoring the excited squeals of delight and the ring-around-the-rosy hugs going on, Al said, "Wonder where Frank is?"

"He's probably home nursing his wounds. Maybe Blyss prefers make-believe stories to playing real-life nursemaid."

Al stiffened and turned on his heel, giving Joy a *Come on* jerk of his hand. "Let's go over to the Clinic; it's almost time for Lewis and Mitchell's big event."

On the sidewalk outside Alex's clinic, a small crowd gathered by a tarp–covered structure about the size of CATE'S CANOPY CAFÉ. "Doctor Alex is coming now," Lewis said excitedly. "So when he shows up, you all step back and let him stand right here when we whip the tarp off!" He took the good-natured teasing about his bossiness in stride, undaunted in his glee over pulling off such a great surprise.

Within minutes, Alex and Tori arrived and suddenly Lewis and Mitchell became crowd-conscious. "You take over, Justin," Mitchell muttered.

Justin took it all in stride and turned to Alex. "Mitchell and Lewis put their heads together to provide you with the ultimate birthday gift, Alex. I understand there's one thing you truly miss from your days in Rochester Minnesota. As you enjoy your favorite treat today, realize how much this town appreciates all you do for them. Happy Birthday!"

Lewis and Mitchell ceremoniously lifted the canvas. Alex stepped back a pace and read aloud from the sign attached to the trailer, "CARROLL'S CORN. I don't believe this! All that's missing is the popcorn!"

A car door swung open behind him and Pat Carroll stepped out. "I'll get right on that, Doctor!"

Alex whooped for joy and stepped off the curb to pump the man's hand. "What a day this is! Welcome to Prairie Rose!"

Pat laughed. "These guys didn't want any smells to give away anything, so now I've got to get busy."

"Stand back and let the man work," Alex commanded with a grin playing around his lips. "If anyone's injured today, you'll find me right here on the curb! I plan to be so full of popcorn, you'll have to wheel me home tonight."

"The first batch is for Doctor Alex," Pat announced to the gathering crowd as he stepped into the trailer and flipped the first switch to start the poppers, "and then, I'm open for business, thanks to Mitchell and Lewis who will help me. We'll move out to the golf course tonight during fireworks, but otherwise I'll be right here. So spread the word!"

"Actually, the smell of the popcorn will be your best advertisement!" Alex predicted.

While those enticing odors wafted along Main Street, the crew to prepare and sell boxed lunches replaced the folks who had flipped early-morning pancakes. Surges of visitors arriving in town moved from one feeding zone to the next, hitting LARSON'S GROCERY before heading for the Big Wheel races at the school. Craft-sale shoppers stopped by CATE'S CANOPY CAFÉ, balancing packages while they devoured mid-morning treats. The church-guild bake sales satisfied even the most desperate chocolate fixes. Throughout the day, the Boy Scouts pushed carts through town, picking up litter. The Caravan Crew worked diligently and kept things moving along.

But one unscheduled, unannounced event stole the show, upstaging even the high school drama club's street performances: Pippi Longstocking's appearance. Seemingly oblivious to anyone over four-feet tall, Blyss asked, "Who wants to hear a Pippi story?"

The enchanted children's shouts and clamoring "I do! I do!" drowned out all other noise in the town for a few seconds. Blyss smiled engagingly and lifted her hand; the din ceased. A swarm of eager children gathered around Blyss who sat on top of a picnic table, smiled broadly at her pint-sized audience and opened her book. Parents looked at each other in amazement as their rambunctious children gave full attention to the impromptu storyteller's tales of a goofy-looking little girl's antics.

Drawn back to Blyss despite her best intentions, Joy frowned on the fringes of the gathered adults and murmured to Al, "She's mesmerizing them. I don't like this one little bit."

"Don't let it get you down, Jinglebells. To them, she's just a storybook character. Look; isn't that Justin across the way with Gail?" Joy followed his gaze and nodded. Sure enough, in the middle of all the parents, there stood Justin Campbell-Lampman shoulder-to-shoulder with Gail Harker. Spotting Justin and his mother, little Alex left the story circle and ran straight into Justin's arms. "Look how happy that little boy is!" Al murmured.

"My, my," Joy said, forgetting Blyss for the moment.

"What?" Al asked.

Joy looked at him in amazement. "I mean, 'My, my, what do you suppose is going on between Justin and Gail?'—that's what."

"Huh?" Al asked, blankly.

"Come on, Big Guy," Joy said. *It's times like this I miss Helen most. She'd understand!*

The afternoon parade formed at the school grounds, with floats and candy-tossing clowns and show-class motorcyclists and high school marching bands mingling with a slow-moving procession of antique cars and tractors. The parade route circled through town, allowing everyone a chance to see from porches and lawn chairs stationed on nearly every yard. Enterprising kids hosted lemonade stands, and the ants enjoyed their own heyday following the sticky streams of sugary drinks from kitchens to curbs.

Even though the parade was a big hit, not everyone had time to enjoy it. The Evening Barbecue Committee gathered mid-afternoon at the golf course to set up for the day's focus: fireworks. Through it all, Joy was never far from Al. They always signed on as a couple to do many tasks and fulfill committee assignments. But today was different. As they worked together, Joy stepped back mentally and observed Al, as a stranger would do. What she saw scared her. His eyes seemed so distant his smile couldn't reach them. Even his posture and gait seemed changed. He engaged in conversations with coworkers and talked with visitors, but it all missed the heart-and-soul of Al Jenkins. He was a half-empty cup pretending to be full.

And she had to admit she wasn't much better. Tears lurked near the surface—tears she didn't understand and certainly couldn't predict.

She realized how closely her own happiness was linked to Al's. *We're like conjoined twins—our hearts beat as one.*

Finishing their duties at the barbeque ticket booth, Al and Joy made a quick stop back home to change clothes and gather up their instrument cases and packets of music. They wove their way between blankets and lawn chairs strategically placed to save spots in the park. Bob Marshall and a few band members had gathered and were setting up chairs in the bandstand.

"One more activity for you two," he called out, "and you can sit back and watch fireworks. You've had a busy day!"

"No worse than anyone else's," Al said. "The band concert is actually quite relaxing—we get to sit down!"

Trudy, Bob's wife, didn't play in the band but had a vital role: she provided cold beverages to the band. As each member straggled in, she took orders. When she handed Al and Joy their requested sodas, she said softly, "I hope tonight isn't as upsetting as last night was."

That's when Joy realized this was the first mention all day of the previous night's shock from anyone besides Al. Like a fearful mother hen, the townsfolk had tucked their wings around their own to protect them from unknown dangers. Not that Frank and Blyss deserved protection. But Helen did—and any airing of Frank's debauchery would splatter back on Helen. It helped that no one had seen Frank all day.

Helen came running across the grass, red-cheeked and animated. Joy smiled at her, trying to latch on to her mood but finding nothing solid to grab. Helen was a bundle of meaningless chatter. "Did you see the girls? They didn't get here until after the pancake breakfast—oh! You knew that! I was right beside you when you talked to them! They said traffic coming into town was worse this year than ever before! Oh, dear—did I not bring the right music? Oh, good, here it is! What a day, huh?"

"Hey, leave a few exclamation marks for the rest of us, Helen," Al protested mildly.

She laughed much too loudly. "I'm just so happy to see the girls, and delighted with how well everything went so far today—isn't that true? It's been such a good day, no accidents, no street fights, and such a positive experience for everyone, don't you think? And I had lots of fun at the face-painting booth—such darling little children!"

Joy stared at Helen, half expecting her to drop to the ground exhausted from all the energy her current level of excitement required. Joy wished she could either cover Helen's mouth or her own ears to dam up the flood of words.

Al shot Joy a questioning look. She nodded imperceptibly and said quietly, hoping to infuse Helen with a dose of calm, "I thought the parade was fantastic. It showed your touches. Everyone loved the clowns."

"Some of them were my summer interns, you know," Helen said giddily.

"That explains why some clowns knew people on the street, even though no one recognized them."

Helen finally ran out of steam and turned her back to the other band members, speaking so low only Joy could hear. "I'm a nervous wreck," she confessed.

"No kidding!" Joy teased gently. "Your motor is running at warp speed—take a few deep breaths, Helen, or I'm afraid you'll take off like a helium balloon. What can I do?"

"Nothing—unless you can guarantee Frank won't pull another stunt like he did last night."

"I think we're safe. I haven't seen him all day—have you?"

"No, and that's odd, don't you think? I mean, we both know there's nothing for him back at the house. What are they doing, anyhow?" As her own question registered, her cheeks burned. "No, don't answer. I can't even think about *that* happening in my old house."

"Helen, let's just play our hearts out at this concert. Al and I will walk past your old house on our way home to check for any signs of life there. Okay?"

"Thanks." Helen visibly relaxed. "I wanted to see for myself, but I didn't want to get caught snooping by Frank or you-know-who, or even the neighbors. I'm not sure how much more of a beating my pride can take."

The band shell had filled during their brief conversation and Joy didn't want to risk anyone overhearing Helen. She touched her friend's arm lightly. "Looks like we should be warming up. I'll grab a soft drink from Trudy for you while you get set up."

The concert went off without incident. The unanswerable question of *Will Frank return?* added a razor's edge to the program for the band members. Each note they played was crisp and clean. Bob Marshall's baton was a white blur in the evening shadows. Small children formed miniature parades on the grass and marched in time to the music, holding pint-sized flags aloft or forming horns with their clenched fists pressed against their lips. *Toot-ta-toot!* The program was the perfect launching pad for the much-anticipated spectacular fireworks.

Later that evening, with vehicles queued to leave town with the Caravan Crew acting as traffic patrols, Al and Joy walked home, barely able to lift their feet. Cars were parked along every street, so it wasn't the usual peaceful walk. The noise of car doors slamming, engines revving, and farewells wafting on the night air filled their ears.

"This ruckus just makes me want everyone to leave and let us get our small-town quiet back. Oh, look, Al," Joy blurted out, clutching his arm. "There's a light upstairs at Frank and Helen's."

Al sucked in his breath and looked across the street. "Make that two. One's in the bathroom, and there's another in the kitchen."

"Hey, it almost looks like someone's in the kitchen with a flashlight. Maybe it's prowlers, not Frank after all." Joy moaned. "I can't believe this. I had so hoped Frank had left town, but I guess I'd rather have it be Frank in there than some burglar."

"Helen didn't rent out the house over the Fourth, did she? I mean, they usually rent out the apartment, so maybe since she's living there, she switched over to renting out the house."

"If she did, she never said anything about it. Of course, it's not like we've had a meaningful conversation in weeks."

Al headed off across the street and circled back toward the garage with Joy following close behind. "It appears Frank has shifted stuff around in here, enough to get his truck inside, at least."

"Do you think he moved some things back into the house?"

"Must have, though that would have been tough to do with his injuries, even if Blyss helped. I do know there was no room in the garage before and that's definitely his truck in the garage. Come on," Al said.

"Where are you going?" Joy whispered loudly. "Al! You're not…" His actions answered her question.

Al pounded on the back door. Joy stood in the shadows and watched while fear marched along her spine. She clutched her stomach and looked around in the darkness. The lilac bushes would survive if she vomited on them—and that seemed like a good possibility, the way her stomach was churning.

After what seemed an interminable time, she heard the creak of an opening door. A hulking gray shadow filled the doorframe. Joy saw a flash of silver and cried out, "Al, run! He's got a gun!"

Al leaped off the back steps and flattened himself against the house. "Put the gun down, Frank," he said evenly. "It's just Al and Joy."

"*What* are you talking about? What gun?" Frank's voice rode the shadows. He flicked on a flashlight and swept its beam across the yard. "Where are you?"

Sheepishly, Joy and Al stepped into view. "Sorry about that gun comment. The moonlight made your flashlight look like a gun to me," she explained nervously.

"And why would I come to the door carrying a gun? No, don't answer that—from the welcome I've gotten here, maybe I should start toting a weapon. Seems like everyone's pretty much ready to shoot *me*. What do you guys want, anyway? It's kind of late to come calling." There was no hint of invitation in his voice.

"We saw lights in your place and thought we ought to check it out."

"Self-appointed house patrol, huh?" Frank jibed, pushed against the doorframe with both hands at shoulder-height. The cast on one arm offset his balance.

Al refused to rise to that baited hook. "Didn't want anyone trashing the place. Since we know it's you, we'll take off."

"Thanks for keeping an eye on the place," Frank said grudgingly.

"We didn't do it for you, Frank," Joy retorted.

"Never thought you did," he snapped. "Hey, Al, did you mow my lawn?"

Al stiffened. "Yeah, it was getting pretty bad. You better make arrangements for someone to do that before you leave town again. I don't plan to be your yardman."

"Who said anything about me leaving?"

"Frankie, who are you talking to?" Blyss tucked her head between Frank's arm and the door-jam and cozied up beside him. This was no storybook character—at least, not one from a children's book. Without the height usually added by shoes and hair, it was a shock to see that the top of her head barely reached Frank's chin.

Blyss circled Frank's waist with one arm, latching on to the waistband of the boxer shorts that were his only clothing. Playing with his chest hair with her other hand in a mesmerizing display of familiarity, she bumped hips with him. When Frank looked down at her, she puckered her lips and offered a blatant invitation of kissing noises.

Frank dropped one arm around her and moved his hand up and down beneath her armpit, her negligee alternately pulling taut on the downswings and pleating on the up-swings of his motions. Joy gasped soundlessly. Frank ducked his head and Blyss arched back in his arms. Their lips met like four metal arcs drawn together and held by powerful magnets.

Joy was very glad it was dark.

Al cleared his throat and Frank looked up as if surprised to see them. "Catch you guys later," he said with a chuckle, nuzzling Blyss' ear as he pulled her back into the darkness and closed the door.

Joy's heart pounded erratically. She closed her eyes for a moment and reeled in place as her mind replayed the horror of seeing Frank kissing anyone besides Helen. *But when did I last see that?*

Al stood beside her like a shell-shocked soldier. "Oh!" The single syllable came out in a shuddering sob and Joy instinctively moved closer. When she touched his arm, it was trembling. He fumbled for her hand and reeled her into his embrace like a drowning man clutching for a lifeline.

Without warning, Al began to weep. Quietly at first, but Joy felt the powerful agony churning within him. "Come on, Al, let's go home," she said, too alarmed to keep her voice calm. She entwined their fingers and pulled him along beside her.

Lingering strangers and neighbors alike looked quizzically in their direction as they stumbled by, but Joy ignored them all, glad the darkness masked their identities. Never had the two blocks separating the friends' homes seemed so long. Finally, they reached their own back door. She muddled through the infrequent task of unlocking the door. Al sank into a kitchen chair and dropped his head down on his arms even before Joy had closed the door behind them. In this safe place, Al set his sorrow free and great gulping cries echoed in the room.

Fear formed an iceberg in Joy's stomach, the tip scraping her heart. She rubbed Al's shuddering shoulders, wincing at the tension locked inside him. She thumb-massaged the knots in his back and murmured wordless sounds while she worked to penetrate both his muscles and his mind. "Do you want me to call Alex?" she asked, struggling to block the fright she felt from her voice.

Al's heart-wrenching sorrow seemed unstoppable. He couldn't speak, but shook his head *No*. Not a forbidding *no*, but one weighed down by futility: *What good would it do?* That evidence of despair terrified Joy even more than Al's tears. *Maybe we need Tori more than Alex—maybe we need prayers more than medicine.*

Joy worked steadily—massaging, caressing—until she finally felt him relax. Her knees shook as she held his head against her breasts. He hugged her close, resting his cheek against her body while tears still spurted, wetting her blouse.

Tenderly, she moved her fingers across his face, through his hair, along his neck. Cupping his chin in her palm, she tipped his head up and kissed him gently. First his brow, then each eyelid's glistening lashes, then along the edges of his trembling lips, to his full upper lip and its curved lower mate. Finally, lining the shape of his lips with her own, she poured out her love in one healing kiss. Gradually, his trembling stopped and his breathing steadied. Shifting his chair, he pulled her down to his lap.

She wrapped her arms around his neck and closed her eyes against her own tears. They soaked up comfort until, at last, she whispered, "It's pretty late, Al; I'm going to run you a bath."

He merely nodded, too spent to speak.

"Head on upstairs, Big Guy." Joy waited until Al left the kitchen and quickly dialed a familiar number. *One ring, two, three...where are those guys? They can't still be in the park.* Heart sinking, she hung up the phone. *You're on your own, Joy. Tori and Alex aren't around to give comfort and advice, so just follow your heart.*

Within minutes, the tub was full, the soothing scent of lavender wafted above the surface. Al climbed in and Joy knelt beside him on a folded mat. Using a time-softened cloth, she began to wash him. Reverting subconsciously to a habit borne long ago from bedtime baths for their son, she ministered loving touches to her husband and hummed spurts of Dave's favorite John Denver song...*like a storm in the desert...a walk in the rain...*

Al relaxed beneath her soothing touch...*like a sleepy blue ocean*...and murmured his response, "You fill up so much more than my senses, Joy."

"Shhhshhhshhh, no need to talk." She repositioned a rolled towel behind his neck and guided him back to it.

Just when she thought he was asleep, he opened his eyes. "I'm ready for bed—will you come now, too?"

"You dry off while I jump in the shower and I'll be right in," she promised, pushing up off the floor. "Be careful when you step out; it looks like we made waves."

"Nothing like the waves Frank is making, shacking up with Blyss." One long, lingering shudder ran through him.

She reached up and lightly tapped his lips with her finger. "Shush. No more talk about trouble tonight, okay?" She stepped out of her clothing and let it slide to the floor. "For tonight, our world consists of just you and me."

Al paused in the doorway and reached out tentatively as if seeing a mirage. He traced her silhouette from her nose to her chin, following an invisible line between the orbs of her breasts to the gentle tucks of her waist, stopping just short of the mysterious world known only to him. He whispered, "Will you make love with me tonight? I want to erase all we saw…" Seeing her nod, he let his words fade.

Joy showered quickly. Fervent, abbreviated prayers replaced her usual singing in the shower: *Oh, God, help us. Help us. Help us.* Wrapped in a towel, she stepped into the path of light from the bedside lamp and found Al sound asleep. He had made all the preparations for a night of loving, but her ministrations had worked their magic and sent him to a place where the day's troubles no longer reigned.

She turned out the light and crawled in beside her husband. Shaping herself against his familiar shape, she closed her eyes and rested her cheek against Al's back. Scattered words from an ancient hymn sprang to mind: *Abide with me…when other helpers fail and comforts flee…abide with me…* Slowly expelling a sigh that carried away her anxious thoughts, she drifted into a deep and dreamless sleep.

Perhaps it was the predawn calling of one bird to another outside the open window; perhaps it was habit that awakened Al and Joy together. Smiling across their pillows, they reached for each other's hands automatically. "G'morning. Did you rest well?" Al asked around a yawn.

Joy nodded and burrowed in beneath the sheet. "I wonder when Dave came home. I didn't hear him, did you?"

"No, but then I was being treated to the most marvelous spa. I hardly had room in my head for any other thoughts."

"That's good—that was my plan."

Al rolled to one side and supported his head on the tripod formed by his hand, his arm and the pillow. He traced the bumps and ridges of her shoulder. "I hope I didn't scare you when I lost control. So much has piled up and I'm not dealing with it very well. Seeing Frank with Blyss just pushed me over the edge. Thanks for being there to catch me."

Turning her head enough to meet his somber eyes, Joy said, "We both need a break from everything. I think your idea about getting away is perfect. Talk to Wendy today and see if she wants to be Postmistress for a few days."

"Really?" Al didn't even try to mask his surprise. "Where would you like to go?"

"Unless you have some place in mind, I'll work on it. You let me know what Wendy says."

"I'm sure she'll say yes; she's saving up for a big shindig for her parents' fiftieth wedding anniversary and would welcome the extra money. I can bring her in this afternoon and get her up to speed on the new postal rates, and maybe we can even take off today," he suggested hopefully.

Joy flung back the sheet and sprang into action. "Up and at-'em, then, Buster. The day's a-wastin' and you're still in bed!"

"I'll go talk to Dave and make sure he's okay with being alone for a few days."

Pulling on her own clothes, Joy listened to Al whistling and realized it was a sound she had not heard for many days. *We're getting away just in time—that near breakdown last night got our attention.*

Al's jubilant call to report, *Wendy said yes!* came while Joy peeled potatoes. Two hours later, she had chicken in the oven, which would feed Dave for several meals, and was frosting his favorite chocolate cake. Leaving Dave home alone wasn't a regular event, but providing him with ready-to-eat food guaranteed his contentment. She checked the refrigerator for his favorite pickles, sufficient breakfast supplies, and enough ice cream to last the weekend and crossed a few more lines off her impromptu To-Do list.

She headed outside to hang a second basket of laundry in the breeze. Hoping to cool down after her morning marathon, she was watering the geranium tubs when she heard "Hi, Missus Jenkins!" Petey squealed to a dramatic halt, gravel spitting out from beneath his bicycle tires.

"Hi, Petey! My goodness, you must have been working hard already today; you look pretty hot. Come up on the porch and have a glass of lemonade with me. I need to take a break, too."

"Okay. I'm sweating 'cuz I've been riding all over town. Everybody's got stuff they want me to take places," he said proudly, "and when I get to *those* people's houses, they've got other stuff for me to take somewhere else." He rolled his eyes dramatically. Then, his exuberance faded as he remembered something. "Missus Jenkins, do you ever give kids quizzes in the summertime so they can win prizes out of your basket?" His serious eyes met hers.

"I never have before, and my prize basket is pretty much…" She fell silent, seeing Petey's dejection.

"I know you're not my teacher anymore, but I haven't got a new one yet and I need to win a compass. I lost mine yesterday," he confessed dejectedly. "I'm just a little kid, you know. Sometimes I lose stuff."

Joy smothered a giggle. "How about if I give you a quiz while we drink our lemonade? You go wait on the porch swing and I'll be right back." She turned off the outdoor faucet and squirted the hose dry.

"Okay," Petey said, tossing his leg over his bicycle seat and bumping the kick stand into place.

When Joy returned with a plastic-wrapped compass in her pocket and two glasses of lemonade in hand, she bumped the screen door open with her hip. "Okay, here we..." but promptly let her words fade.

Petey had dozed off in the swing. *What is it with guys falling asleep on me?* A smile eased the worries from Joy's face as she watched him. He looked so utterly exhausted, so unerringly little-boyish, so trusting that her mind skimmed back across the years to when Dave had been Petey's age. She knew instantly what she wanted to do.

Placing the two glasses on the porch railing, she eased herself onto the swing and carefully lifted Petey's head to rest in her lap. The two of them rocked peacefully together.

She stared at the wispy tendrils of hair clinging to his dirt-streaked face and smiled. His T-shirt had a grape jelly stain on it, there was a scabbed-over mosquito bite on his arm, and his pocket bulged with lumpy boy-treasures. He clutched a zippered bag likely holding his stash of quarters. His leg twitched and he sighed, floating into a deeper layer of sleep while Joy kept the swing in motion.

She soon saw Al coming home for lunch and pointed at her lap, tapping her lips in the universal *Quiet!* signal. Al craned his neck to see and walked across the lawn. Quietly, he sank down on a chair near the swing; Joy motioned toward the glass on the railing. Al reached for it and drank deeply before asking in a low voice, "How'd this happen?" He nodded toward the sleeping boy.

Joy smiled. "It's hard work being a delivery guy," she said softly. "Would you please call June and Rusty and tell them he's here? They're probably expecting him for lunch and I don't want them to worry."

Al placed his glass back on the railing and walked toward the garden hose, pulling out his cell phone enroute. She wanted to tell him she had already watered, but didn't want to disturb Petey for something so inconsequential.

While he sprayed the side-yard flowerbed, Al talked to Petey's dad. Joy watched her husband, dismayed to see how very tense and tired he still looked. The past weeks had been rough on them and last night's debacle added nothing less than catastrophe to the mix, but still, to have missed noting the toll on Al alarmed Joy. She had thought she and Al were sensitive to each other's levels of endurance. *Have we been fooling ourselves? What is happening to us?*

Granted, she had commented occasionally about the dark circles under his eyes or when he seemed unusually quiet, and wondered what was up when he pushed his plate away without finishing a meal. But sitting in the swing with Petey sleeping on her lap, she sucked in her breath as she stared across the lawn. *He's different; something has changed inside Al.*

Over the summer, they worked together in the kitchen and garden, sat across the table from each other for countless meals, slept together every night. But when was the last time they had giggled together? When had they kissed each other just because it felt so good and was as natural as breathing? When had they stopped worrying that Dave might walk in on them, or realized the whole neighborhood could see their antics because they had been too lost in each other to realize the garage door was open or because they'd neglected to pull the living room drapes.

Joy hadn't really *looked* at Al in quite some time. What she saw now frightened her, but not nearly as much as acknowledging their intimacy level had plummeted. She missed having the bath water grow cold when they shared the tub. She longed for a mid-morning phone call from Al saying, *When I come home for lunch, let's skip lunch.* Joy suddenly realized something terrifying: Frank and Helen weren't the only ones destroyed by their personal storm; she and Al had sustained serious damage. *We've lost that loving feeling.*

Splinters of missed clues floated to mind: putting away a jigsaw puzzle before completing it—almost a sacrilege at the Jenkins' house, but it had happened just last week, nonetheless. Giving each other the silent treatment after a silly argument over a Scrabble word. Heading off to a ballgame together, but drifting apart to talk to others, or sitting together on the bleachers lost in silence. *Have we lost our ability—our need—to talk to each other, and to really listen?*

There was no wondering when it had all begun. Joy knew: the subtle downhill slide had begun on Memorial Day weekend. At first, they'd talked of little else than Frank and Helen. But at some point, it was as if they realized they were talking in circles and both retreated into their private fortresses.

It was time to lower the bridge across the moat. *We need to make time for us. This trip comes in the nick of time.*

Al returned to his chair. "Rusty just figured Petey was out taking care of business. He hadn't considered him missing yet." He chuckled softly, "With four kids and another on the way, Rusty and June are probably glad Petey's got this job to keep him busy. He probably doesn't get to fall asleep on June's lap too often."

Joy stroked Petey's forehead thoughtfully. "Then I'm glad he's here. As he reminded me, he's just a little kid, despite his busy days. By the way, when he wakes up, I need to give him a quiz so he can win a compass again. He lost his."

"Hey, can I take that quiz with Petey?"

"This contest will be rigged. I've only got one compass in my pocket and it goes to Petey."

"Shoot. How's a guy gonna find his way back home without a compass, huh, teacher?" Al's tone was light-hearted, but when he leaned back and closed his eyes, resting his head against the painted high-back chair's curved boards, Joy heard his all-too-serious underlying question.

"We'll find our way together," she said softly.

Al lifted his eyelids to half-mast and stared at her from beneath their eyelash fringe. "You lost, too, Jinglebells?"

"I feel like we're both floundering. I'm so glad we're getting away."

Al nodded and drummed his fingers on the chair in sync with the rhythmic beat of the porch swing in motion. *Squeak, tap-tap-tap, squeak, tap-tap-tap.*

As if sensing the presence of someone new, Petey stirred and when his foot bumped the swing, he awoke. He blinked several times, taking in his surroundings, and tipped his head towards Joy. "Did I fall off my bike and hit my head and get knocked out?" he asked hopefully, ever a boy in search of excitement.

"No, you just had a little snooze. Would you like some lemonade now, Petey?"

He nodded and sat up, a red mark on one cheek signaling how long he'd slept. Then he noticed Al sitting in the chair. "Hey, Mister Jenkins," he said by way of greeting.

"Hey, yourself, Petey." Al said. "I'll go get a lemonade for you since I drank yours."

Joy patted her pocket. "Guess what I've got in here!"

"A compass?"

Joy nodded. "Answer four questions correctly and it's yours."

"Wait for me—I want to hear this quiz-kid win the prize!" Al handed Joy her lemonade.

Petey shifted on the swing. "I'm gonna win, you know," he boasted and looked earnestly into Joy's face. "At least I hope so."

Al returned with the fresh glass of lemonade and handed it to Petey. "Thank you," the boy said politely. He took a noisy gulp, wiped his arm across his mouth. "Okay. Ready."

"First question: how do you spell Prairie Rose?"

Petey rolled his eyes and rattled off the eleven letters. "That's too easy. I spell those words right off the grain elevators every time I see them."

"Good. Now, question #2: how many blocks is it from your house to school?"

"Six," he said promptly. "Missus Jenkins, have you forgotten how to ask really hard questions?" he asked, leaning forward with a look of consternation.

Joy laughed. "I don't think so. Okay, two more questions, and I'll try to make them *very* hard. Tell me, using direction words, how to get from our house to your house."

"From the porch or from the driveway?" Petey asked gravely.

"From the driveway," Joy responded with equal seriousness.

He unfurled his legs, carefully placed his glass on the railing and stood beside the swing. "Turn right," his arm formed a bony 90-degree angle denoting a right turn "and go to the end of the block. Turn left," his arm shot straight out in the standard left-turn signal "and cross two streets. Then count to the third house on the left."

"Excellent!" Joy praised while Al applauded.

"That *still* wasn't very hard," Petey protested. "I do that kind of stuff all day long, you know, with my job. That's why I need a compass."

"One more question, and this compass is yours."

"Hey, may I ask the last question?" Al asked.

"What do you think, Petey? Shall we let him?"

"Okay." He eyed Al skeptically. "But if I get it wrong, I want *you* to ask me another question," he told Joy pointedly.

"Deal," Al said. "You'll do fine, I know. I'd like you to sing *My Little Compass* for me."

"Does that count as a question, Missus Jenkins?"

She nodded. "If you don't miss any words, it's like a test."

Petey puffed up his chest. "I won't miss a single word because I know this song by heart. My dad says it's like my commercial." He squinted and hummed a note, and said in an aside, "I always do that, just like your pitch-pipe, Missus Jenkins. Oops, now I gotta do it again; I forgot what note I hummed." He hit a close approximation of the same note and launched into a rapid rendition, complete with empty-handed gestures. Flopping back down on the swing, he looked at Joy expectantly.

"Well done, Petey!" Smiling broadly, she dropped the new compass into his hand.

"Thanks," he sighed with relief. "The song says, 'I pull it out,' and when I didn't have a compass, I couldn't pull it out, you see?"

"I see," Joy said solemnly.

"Ever since I won my first compass, I've only ever had one time when I didn't know where sumpthin' was. It was when that goofy lady who drives that red car and always looks like someone different every day asked me where Mister Wilson lives. I know where Mister and Missus Wilson *used to* live, but I don't know where Mister Wilson lives so I couldn't tell her nothing."

Al caught Joy's eye over the rim of his glass. "Even a compass wouldn't have made it any easier to answer, Petey."

"I better not lose this one." His brow furrowed in thought. "I know! I can put a chain around my waist and hook the chain to the bicycle. No, that wouldn't work..."

Al chuckled, "Come out to the garage with me, Petey. I've got just the thing for you."

When Al came into the kitchen a few minutes later, Joy eyed him quizzically. "Fancy key chain," he said succinctly. "Hooks to his belt-loop. Loaded with gimmicks only a little boy could love."

"And you, Mister Jenkins, are loaded with goodness that makes your wife love you from here to eternity and back. Thanks for being so nice to Petey."

"Hey, the kid worships the ground my wife walks on. Petey and I get along fine."

Joy hooked Al's waistband with her index finger and reeled him into her arms. Circling his neck with her clasped hands, she pulled his head down for a long and hungry kiss.

"Wow, if this is the reward for giving out key chains, I ought to warn you, I've got a boxful of them out in the garage!"

"That's only part of it. Mostly," she dropped a trail of kisses along his jaw line, "I'm just saying thanks for loving me."

"That's so easy to do, Jinglebells, I should hardly get credit for it."

"And thanks for not lusting after the Blyss Hathaways of the world. Ever. It's so wonderful to know I'm the one you love."

"Blyss may be poured out like a mile-wide lake of honey, but she's only an inch deep. A man could get hurt diving into that lake. With you, I have yet to find the bottom."

Joy promptly burst into tears.

"Whoa! I meant everything in a good way!"

"I know," Joy sobbed. "That's why I'm crying. And because it feels so good to kiss you. I miss kissing you."

The kitchen door opened and Dave entered. He stopped short in the doorway. "What's wrong?" he asked.

"Your mother is just…"

"…happy," Joy finished for him. "Your mother is the happiest person in the world, Davey."

Dave rolled his eyes and moved past them. "Girls are goofy, aren't they, Dad?"

"The best kind of goofy in the world, son. Now, when your mother dries her tears, I'm sure she's got some kitchen details to talk over with you."

"Where are you guys going?" Dave asked.

Al winked at Joy. "That's a good question, son. Your mom made all the plans so she's the one to ask."

"Al, you've got a little packing to do. I've laid out things on the bed, but didn't want to pack them until you look them over. So, why don't you pack while I talk to Dave?"

"Are you avoiding Dave's question?" Al teased.

"Bingo! I'll tell *Dave* everything he needs to know to find us if he needs to—but for *you*, it's one big surprise strictly on a need-to-know basis!"

Al left the kitchen and Joy settled Dave at the table with a sandwich and fruit for his lunch and pulled out her list. By the time Al came back downstairs carrying their suitcases, Dave had finished eating and tucked Joy's note into his shirt pocket. "Hey, Dad! You're going on vacation!"

"Sure enough, and you're in charge around here. You were half asleep when I asked you this morning, but now that you're awake, do you still feel comfortable being home alone?"

"Sure. I'm supposed to walk Cino and Cali every night for Doctor Alex and Pastor Tori. And I'll help Luke reshingle his garage on Saturday and eat dinner over there. And Aunt Helen wants me to come for Sunday dinner. I'll be busy, huh?"

Al caught Joy's eye and nodded his approval. *Good job.* "You sure will. The main thing is not to attempt to do anything weird or different than what you'd do if we were home. If anything goes wrong with something at the house—just call Luke, okay?"

"Or you can call us on our cell phone, too," Joy reminded him.

Dave patted his pocket. "Yup. That's what the note says."

"There's another copy of that note inside the kitchen cupboard in case you lose this one, and that list tells everything I fixed for you to eat."

"Oh, boy, I'm going to have fun! But I'll miss you," he added belatedly.

Al and Joy laughed and hugged their son before he headed back to work. Al looked around the kitchen. "What's this? Nothing for your hard-working husband for his lunch?"

"Nope. We're on vacation as of this minute. Let's finish loading the car and blow this pop stand!"

Al teased, "It's on-your-mark-get-set-go, huh?" Within half an hour, the car was packed, the final house-check was completed, and one last-minute note for Dave was propped against the sugar bowl. Al climbed into the driver's seat, and then paused for a moment and swung his legs back outside the car. Holding his feet above the ground, he cracked them together like cymbals.

"What on earth are you doing?" Joy asked, bemused.

"I don't want a single speck of our troubles to come with us—I'm just knocking the dust off my feet."

Joy promptly unhooked her seat belt, opened her door, swung her legs out and clapped her feet together in an exact reenactment of Al's performance. "There: we are one-hundred percent trouble-free. Now head 'em on up and roll on out of Dodge, cowboy."

CHAPTER 8

Passing by the seven landmark grain elevators, Joy and Al grinned at each other like two kids playing hooky. Even though there was a smattering of rain on the windshield when they finally headed their car south, they were almost giddy.

Just beyond the edge of town, Al said, "Sit back and enjoy my meager preparations for our big adventure. I may not be *strolling* these country roads, but I am definitely *rolling* along them with my baby." He pulled a tape out of his pocket and waved a Neil Sedaka tape in the air. "Pretty good, huh? I remembered to bring music!"

With each window rolled down a couple of inches, allowing a gentle mist to settle on their faces, they harmonized on *Laughter in the Rain.* "...Oooo, how I love the rainy days..." and reached automatically for each other's hands.

As other songs played, Al's smile grew until it erased each furrow from his brow. "Must say, you sang the words 'the happy way I feel' with special fervor!"

"Because it's true, Al. My cheeks are starting to ache from smiling. I'll bet I don't have to ask if you remember the last time we could have said we truly felt happy."

"Don't you dare wreck a good time even thinking about Frank. I'd just as soon not allow old F.W. to hitchhike on this ride. Let's talk about something else. How's this? Do you think it's fair our son knows all the details about where we're going and all I've been told is we're having dinner in Minot?" Al teased. "From the weight of our suitcases, I don't imagine we're heading back home tomorrow."

"Can't stand not knowing, can you?" She asked impishly. "I thought after an early dinner we would head to Bismarck, then we'll drive until we reach Minnesota. That may happen tonight, or maybe tomorrow, hey, it could even be Monday—we'll just pull over whenever we want. Out eventual destination is Rochester. And that's all the information you're going to worm out of me, buster!"

"Oh, you're a tough nut to crack, all right. Yup, I'm absolutely exhausted from having to try to trick you into spilling the beans!" Al chuckled.

She swatted at him, letting her hand rest on his arm. "Oh, I still have secrets! I've only told you enough to tantalize you."

"It worked, J-bells. I am one tantalized fella..." he wiggled his eyebrows suggestively.

"Whoa, there! First, we're doing lunch...you totally missed the fact there's a picnic cooler in the trunk. Then, we'll think dinner and we can contemplate...dessert!"

"Why is Minot suddenly so far away?" Al moaned, stepping on the gas. "Maybe we could just get a motel in Minot that offers room service?" he suggested hopefully.

"Only if you want to call Wendy and see how much of next week she can work," Joy teased. "We've got miles to go before we, uh, sleep."

"You, my merciless wife, are a cruel and heartless woman."

"Yup, that's me," Joy agreed cheerfully. "Rotten to the core. Hey, turn at the next corner and we'll get started with our picnic."

"Out here? All that's down this road is a deserted farmhouse and...oh, my-my-my, are you thinking the same R-rated stuff I am?"

She batted her eyelids innocently. "I'm just thinking about lunch. The fact I brought a blanket is purely coincidental."

Al stepped on the gas and created quite a dust storm on that country road. They left the car windows open for the music to form a cocoon around them. The introductory bars to a song by The Association stilled their conversation:...*ever come a time when you'll grow tired of me?...when you'll lose your desire for me?*

"Will there ever come such a time? Never, my love. When I promised to spend my whole life with you, I made an irrevocable vow." His lips ruffled her hair.

Joy forgot everything as she echoed the words of the song: "I've got nothing else to do, babe, but spend my life holding and loving you."

"I'm not sure who Al Green's talking about, but I know this, Joybells: I'm living for you." He held her hands close to his heart with one hand and tightened his grip with the other arm as the world retreated.

"This seems like a hallowed place," Joy murmured against his chest. She raised her lips to meet his and they entered the secret sanctuary of their love.

They ended up feeding much of their lunch to the birds and rabbits and squirrels. When they shook out the blanket several hours later, Al looked around and called out to the treetops, "And *that,* my feathered friends, was a lesson *for* the birds and the bees!"

Joy sported a sheen that spoke of happiness and a good deal of exercise. "So, how are you enjoying your summer vacation so far, Postmaster Jenkins?"

"It's beyond my wildest expectations, Missus Jenkins. You sure haven't lost your touch with planning lessons—I may have lost a bit of time in your classroom lately, but this session today brought me right back up to speed with the rest of the class!"

"There is no 'rest of the class,' Big Guy—you're it for me," Joy said with utter simplicity.

A gentle touch of fingertips to cheek, a brush of a hand across a curl, a light kiss on a nose, a bump, lowered eyes—and it was déjà vu with the soul-mining kisses.

"Keep this up," Al said, "and you might as well line up long-term care for me in Minot! I can barely walk! Thank goodness, you packed a lunch or they'd find us here in the spring, just two pathetic hollow shells."

"At least we'd be pathetic hollow shells with goofy grins on our faces!" Joy said as they walked slowly back to the car. "Hey, look; this place is for sale! We should buy it for a secret hide-away."

He studied the neglected landscape. "The house is in pretty good shape; it's the barn that's falling apart. But it is a good-sized property."

"We don't need much—just space to roll out our blanket, and big trees to hide what happens on that queen-sized piece of paradise!"

"You had fun planning this trip, didn't you?" Al backed the car around. "In just one afternoon, you've got your sparkle back."

"I didn't realize it had left."

"Oh, yeah; it pretty much deserted the premises. Every once in a while there has been a glint or a flash—kind of like a shooting star. But I've missed the day-to-day sunshine. So has Dave."

Joy's forehead furrowed. "Hmmm. I know Dave and I have missed *your* vigor and voom, but I wasn't thinking that *I* had changed."

"Dave has talked to you about me?"

She nodded slowly. "One day he asked me if you were sick. Another day he told me you were mad at him, even though I knew that wasn't the case. And just last week, he asked me if you were going to leave us like Frank left Helen."

Al moaned. "I've tried to act natural around him, but he always picks up on subtle things we're not aware of. I've had nearly identical conversations with him, except in my case, he asked if you were going to move into an apartment like Helen did—and where it would be since there isn't an apartment over the Post Office. The thinking that comment represents scared me."

"I guess we've changed more than we thought, Al. Usually, we would have told each other about these conversations with our son before the day ended."

"Yeah. If we've kept big things like Dave's worries to ourselves, we must have stored up tons of everyday chitchat."

"I vote we pull the plug and drown ourselves in everyday stuff again, okay, Big Guy? There's no time like the present."

Al reached up and crooked his finger midair. "Stand back!" He yanked an invisible plug.

Joy turned expectantly in her seat to face Al. She adjusted her seat-belt to a more comfortable position across her shoulder and focused on his profile.

"Where to start?" Al mused. He passed a slow-moving tractor, waving at the driver before pulling back into the lane. She could tell his mind was working, and waited patiently. Clearing his throat, he spoke thoughtfully, "J-bells, do we have enough compost to get us through this growing season, or should I buy some commercial-grade stuff?"

Joy blinked; she tipped her head; her lips twitched; she turned towards the window and bit a knuckle. But it was a lost cause; tears rolled down her face and she gasped for air around hoots of laughter.

Al glanced away from the road, staring at her in bewilderment. "What?" he asked. "What's so funny?"

Joy's shoulders shook as she attempted to speak. "It's just…I mean…I wasn't…"

"Thanks for clearing that up," Al said dryly.

She flopped back against the seat cushions and expelled a drawn-out breath. "Wow, that sure felt good." A stray giggle tumbled out. "I'm not laughing at you, Al. I'm laughing at the big picture."

"I don't even see the little picture, so fill me in."

"For the past five weeks, we haven't had a decent conversation that even skimmed the surface of our relationship, even though we've prided ourselves all these years in having open communication."

"Right," Al responded cautiously.

"So, when we start talking again, our first conversation is about compost!"

"Is that a bad thing?"

"Actually, it's exactly what I've missed—talking with you about things like compost. You know what? Drive a little faster. I'm kind of anxious to get dinner over, too!" She walked her fingers along his forearm, letting them dance in the curly hairs covering his tanned skin.

"Compost-talk gets your engine running, does it? If I'd known that, think of all the money I could have saved on romantic presents over the years," Al grumbled mildly.

"I love you, Big Guy." She leaned across the gearshift to rest her head on his shoulder. He put his arm around her and they drove for several miles in a contented stillness interrupted only by Joy's sporadic giggles.

The enticing steak-and-lobster odors emanating from Minot's famous Speedway Café always hooked a crowd. Those waiting in line couldn't help but notice one couple locking eyes and talking softly with the fervor of reunited lovers.

When it was Al and Joy's turn to enter, they did so in the utter silence that accompanied a Speedway Café tradition. They heard the bartender bawl out, "Phoooone caaall!" and saw him wave the receiver in the air. Al and Joy paused behind the hostess while the man called out a name. The recipient of the call stood up and walked to the bar through a tunnel of silence to accept his call. Only then did the diners resume their conversations.

Sitting so close together at their table that their thighs touched, it was easy for Joy to flick a piece of lint off Al's shoulder, or for Al to daub a bit of steak sauce off Joy's chin. Weeks of loneliness melted away when they leaned together until their foreheads touched, or splayed hands across the other's back like a branding iron that blazed *Mine* on their skin.

Topics roamed: trimming the lilac bushes; Joy's thoughts on Al taking piano lessons from Amber Larson; a cousin's upcoming wedding; Hal Harsted's plans to install a new garage door; the pros and cons of mail-order sweatshirts; Dave's wanting to learn to drive.

Joy sighed contentedly, "This is so wonderful. It's like I've been dehydrated and tonight I jumped in the ocean. I swear, no matter what you say, I soak it up!"

Cupping Joy's chin in his hand, Al looked intently into her upturned face and murmured, "Whatever I say, huh? How's this? A, B,

C, D, E, F, G, H, I, J, K...and wait—here comes my favorite part: L-M-N-O-P. Isn't that poetic? *Elemenopy.*"

Eyes twinkling, Joy replied, "Isn't that what Sherlock Holmes said? 'It's *l-m-n-o-p*, my dear Watson.'"

Al nodded sagely. "Yes, you're so right. Many think he said *elementary*, but whereas that sounds like a put-down, *elemenopy* implies heightened expectation. What Sherlock is really saying when Watson asks questions is 'This is just the beginning—we're really on to something now!'"

"I've always found *P-Q-R-S-T* intriguing," she whispered seductively. "Unfortunately, it means I can't spare the *P* for your word."

Al frowned. "How do I know your word merits one of my prized letters?"

"*Piquaresty* means freedom to investigate, as in it will require *piquaresty* to determine the spices in this steak marinade if you hope to duplicate it."

"Interesting; but I'm quite sure the *P* is silent, as in pneumonia. *Qu-ar-es-ty* is actually the correct pronunciation of your word. Thus, we can share the *P*. I'll use the sound, you use the letter itself."

"Just like always, we manage to work things out." Their playfulness stretched its toes and reached solid ground.

Al's voice cracked. "May I have *pquaresty* regarding how easily I can divest you of your clothes this evening, J-bells?"

"It's *elemenopy*, Big Guy. You know, we could invite Blyss Hathaway some evening for a rousing time of vocabulary exploration."

"I rather set fire to my shorts with me still in them."

"I guess I'd rather sleep on nails. Here's a better idea; let's leave heaps of money on this table and get out of here."

"Now you're talking a language I understand!"

Other diners watched in amazement as the couple who had barely touched a marvelous meal fled the restaurant. The waitress noted her substantial tip in addition to the payment and shrugged.

Al opened the car's back door. She looked at him quizzically and caught her breath. "Climb in, Joybells," he urged. "I'm sure Sadie's safely home by now."

Half an hour later, a busboy leaned against the wall smoking a cigarette in the darkness outside the café's delivery entrance. Hearing soft seductive laughter, he scanned the parking lot with growing curiosity. In the hazy glow of a streetlight, he saw two people climbing over a gearshift and twisted his face into a grimace. "That couple's as old as my parents—somebody ought to lock 'em up!"

As the car rolled slowly past him, the young man heard two voices belt out "*...we've got a thing called radar love...*" The parking lot lights picked up the glint of Joy's wedding ring and flung it from her hand to the busboy's eyes. His puzzlement increased. "Crazy old dudes," he scoffed and ground out his cigarette on the pavement.

At the counter of the first motel they spotted, Al and Joy fidgeted while the clerk processed the paperwork. If the woman thought it odd that the guest's driver's license gave Prairie Rose as his home address, she said nothing. But when the door closed behind them, she read the registry entry aloud: "Al and Joy Jenkins, huh? Yeah, right. Your spouses better not come disrupting any peace around here tonight."

Early the next morning, Al replaced their suitcases in the trunk and pulled Joy next to him. Standing hip-to-hip with his hand wedged in the waistband of her jeans, he gestured at the motel. "For as much sleep as we got, we could have stayed in the restaurant parking lot!"

"Oh, I don't know. I liked that bathtub, and the shower was, uh, refreshing!" Her face matched the red bands on the flag flying overhead.

Al kissed her neck. "We may be tired today, but no one can say we're not clean! How 'bout if we find some coffee and head on down the road?"

"Sounds good—especially since I want to be in Rochester tonight."

"Someone waiting for us?"

"You'll see," Joy said vaguely as she sashayed around the car.

* * * *

Had Al and Joy been home, they would have been caught in the web of phone calls that snared even the least inclined to gossip. Predictably, the rumor originated with Sadie.

It started when she was pouring boiling water on weeds in her driveway early Saturday morning. That's when her persistent guard duty paid off, big-time. Clutching her teakettle, she was the sole witness to a most amazing chapter in the Frank Wilson scandal.

If the weight on the back springs of Blyss' rental car was any indication, the trunk was packed full, as was the back seat. A slamming door alerted Sadie to action across the street. She puckered her lips into a disapproving frown as she watched *That Harlot* in lime-green stretch pants and a white eyelet cotton blouse and what appeared to be ballet slippers move from the steps to the driveway and climb into the car.

Frank stood on the steps, leaning on his crutch. Not a word was exchanged, not one speck of emotion was displayed between the players on this early morning stage. Blyss backed the car into the street where she paused briefly. She didn't wave, didn't toot the horn, and didn't smile—just halted, as if pulling up anchor. Frank didn't budge until Blyss had gone at least one block.

Then, he lifted his crutch as if in salute, pivoted on the ball of his foot, awkwardly opened the door and stepped back inside.

Sadie suddenly realized she was standing in a puddle of water and the teakettle was dry. She flew up the sidewalk to her own front door, her thoughts as wild and disjointed as her actions. She started a pan of oatmeal, unwittingly adding salt twice. She dialed Helen's phone number before realizing it was only 6:00 o'clock and hung up mid-ring, through this always riled her when it happened to her. She removed her wet footwear and tossed it all into the wastebasket, which would totally befuddle her when she searched later.

Startling her cat, who was unaccustomed to such commotion so early in the day, Sadie muttered and fussed, opening and closing drawers for no purpose. She wasted a great deal of electricity peering mindlessly into the refrigerator as she attempted to make sense of what she had just witnessed across the street.

"Did they have a fight?" she asked the cat who opened one eye and flicked her tail. "Or has Frank come to his senses? Will Helen take him back? Have we seen the last of Blyss Hathaway?" The cat stretched and yawned. "I simply must tell Helen—she'll be the first I talk to before going to the café and stopping by the grocery store." She frowned as she began eating her breakfast. "What on earth…this oatmeal tastes awful. Luke will have to refund my money."

At precisely 7:00 o'clock, Sadie called Helen and blurted out the news. "She's gone! I saw her leave myself, early this morning. It's quite possible they've had a disagreement of some sort, because neither said a word. And there was no display of affection, either. I thought you ought to know Frank's alone now."

"Thank you, Sadie," Helen said and disconnected.

"If that don't beat all!" Sadie huffed, plopping down on a kitchen chair. Her cat rolled over, stood up, arched her back and ambled toward the door. "Come back here!" Sadie ordered, to no avail. Following her cat into the living room, Sadie flicked her apron over lamps and knickknacks, creating a flurry of dust mites. "Helen must be in shock. I told her the facts and she needs time to think them through. I'll go give her moral support."

When the grandfather clock tolled eight o'clock, Sadie checked her purse for hanky, money and throat lozenges and snapped it shut. She followed the sidewalk to the corner and turned, coming to an abrupt stop. Half a block ahead of her, Frank hobbled toward Main Street. Sadie gasped and clutched her purse. Unconsciously mimicking her cat, she pursued him stealthily.

When Sadie realized she was tracking Frank to the very place she intended to go—the D CURL—she sucked in her breath. *Fiddle faddle!*

Petey's verbal "Toot, toot!" sliced the air behind Sadie as he jerked his bike around her frozen form. She was so captivated by Frank's actions that, much to Petey's amazement, she neglected to call the boy back for the dreaded lecture on bicycle safety every child in town could expect at least once.

Sadie watched Frank turn the doorknob, pull the door open and hop up the steps. Without realizing she was in motion, Sadie swiftly planted herself as close to the open window as the bushes would allow. She felt a heady mix of excitement and fear rush through her. Glaring at a passing car with a noisy muffler, Sadie strained her ears and managed to hear a rumble of voices inside the shop. Indistinguishable sounds soon became passionate syllables erupting like shots from a pellet gun:

"*...just what do...*"

"*...go...you slimy...*"

"*...how dare...*"

"*...listen, you...*"

Like a fly drawn to flypaper, Sadie separated the spiky bushes for a closer look. Inside, Helen waved a pair of scissors and Frank stood poised to strike out with his crutch. At that moment, Frank spotted Sadie and thundered sarcastically, "This is a personal conversation; do you mind?" Sadie jumped back and yelped.

"Leave her alone, Frank," Helen said coldly, her voice warming slightly when she called out, "Don't mind Frank, Sadie. He's just leaving."

"No, I'm not. If anyone should leave, it's Sadie. Go away, Sadie!"

"Sadie, you stay!" Helen spat out. "Sadie's done more for me in the past two months than you have."

Frank snorted and Sadie squinted through the window in time to see Frank heading to the barbershop side. "And just what do you think you're doing, Frank?" Helen demanded.

"Getting ready to open up. It's past 8:00 o'clock, you know."

"I'm fully aware of that. And equally aware that after two months of shacking up with that two-bit hussy, you stupidly assume you can just be-bop back in here and pick up your razor like nothing's happened. Ha! No way, no how. Get out of here. Now."

Frank shrugged. "I understand why you're upset, but I'm still part owner and I'm staying. The shop's name is still THE CLIP AND CURL. *I'm* the clip, *you're* the curl. Remember when we chose the name?" he asked, grasping at straws.

"I'll give you a clip and curl, Mister." No one could have misconstrued Helen's menacing words for a business proposition. "*I'm* the one who has kept this business going for two months—*you're* the one who jumped ship. Get out." Her stony gaze and chilly tone invited no discussion.

John Caston tapped Sadie on the shoulder and she jumped back, flinging her purse against his chest. "Stop that, you old fool! What…?" She watched him reach for the door handle. "Don't go in there—you'll die!" she warned in a choked whisper. John merely shrugged and stepped inside. Sadie shivered on the sidewalk as panic tiptoed down her spine. *Three people could die right before my eyes!*

Frank and Helen said in unison, "Have a seat, John." They were hardly an inviting pair. Frank was in the all-the-hues-of-the-rainbow stage of his injuries and gripped his crutch like the weapon it was; Helen clung to her scissors with all the grit so evident in her steely eyes and jutting chin. The air crackled with tension, mocking the WELCOME! mat out front.

John's eyes bulged. "Uh, I, um, I'll…back later…something…got to do…" He shot past Sadie with a speed that belied his age. Before the door could slam, Sadie grabbed it and crept inside. Neither Frank nor Helen paid her the slightest attention as she cowered in the corner.

"See? Even John Caston doesn't want the likes of you touching him," Helen taunted.

"I didn't see him climbing into your chair, either," Frank shot back.

"I've given him and every other man in town mighty fine haircuts for the past two months."

"What else have you given them?" Frank sneered.

Helen's screech terrified Sadie into a yelp of her own. Helen lunged at Frank. He knocked the scissors out of her hand with his crutch and slumped down on the barber chair, raising his arms to fend off her fists.

Sadie gathered enough air to produce a shuddering gasp. As she stumbled toward the door, one shoe deserted her like a traitor and skittered across the floor. She whimpered and limped outside to holler, "Help!"

Milt burst from the deserted building next to the D CURL. The door slammed behind him as he pounded along the sidewalk. "What's wrong, Sadie?" he demanded.

She could only point a wobbly finger into the shop and balance on one foot, clinging to the bushes for support.

Mildred had just parked her car outside the Clinic when, as she would report countless time over the next weeks, her life flashed before her, that's how terrified she was to hear Sadie's scream. But, she managed to gather her wits enough to join Sadie on the sidewalk, crossing right between two cars—another high point of her eventual account—without getting killed. "What's going on in there?" she asked Sadie in a voice riddled with excitement. "Where's your shoe?"

"Terrible things are happening! Frank's back and he may destroy my shoe in his fury!"

Mildred fanned her face furiously with her hankie. "Ooooo, mercy me!"

Both women flinched when Frank let out a blood-curdling wordless sound. It only took one look to communicate their thoughts; they promptly entered the D CURL, Sadie leaning heavily on Mildred's arm.

Milt stood between the two angry adults, his hands spread like a traffic cop to keep them behind an invisible line. "Shut up, Frank. Put the scissors down, Helen," he commanded in a no-nonsense tone.

"Not until that two-timing, lying, scheming snake gets out of my shop," Helen snapped, gripping her retrieved weapon all the tighter.

"*Your* shop?" Frank yelled. Mildred and Sadie clutched each other as he attempted to stand beside his chair. "I'll have you know…" Sadie eyed her shoe nervously; if Frank took one more step, his crutch would land right across the laces.

"Helen, if you'll go in back," Milt interrupted, waving toward the apartment, "I'll deal with Frank."

"I don't need *dealing with*. And I'm not going anywhere," Frank said. "I'm half-owner of this place."

"Fine time to remember that," Helen spit out.

"Helen…" Milt cautioned, jerking his head pointedly toward the door to the apartment.

"He'd better be gone when I come back—and he'd better stay gone. He's not welcome on these premises anymore." Helen spun around on her heels, flounced over to the cash register. She made a great show of gathering up a fistful of cash as if a marauding band of thieves lurked nearby, and strode to the door leading to her apartment. One hand on the knob, she looked back over her shoulder at Frank with narrowed eyes. "I mean it—he'd better be long gone, Milt."

Before the apartment door could slam shut, Mildred followed Helen into the hallway, torn between the need to comfort and the potential for gossip. Sadie, however, wasn't about to leave the scene of the near-crime—not with her shoe still at risk.

"Now, Frank," Milt began calmly, "Helen's made it perfectly clear she doesn't want you here."

"She has no right to kick me out of my own business," Frank sputtered. "Just let me talk some sense into her. You keep your nose out of this; this is between Helen and me."

"That may be true, but the way you two were taking after each other, somebody had to step in or Tina and Robyn would end up with two parents in prison, and as Mayor, I just appointed myself that somebody. You've been gone a while, and Helen's kept things running just fine in your absence. It will take some time for the two of you to work things out, but today may not be the day to start," Milt said reasonably.

"I figured if I tried to act normally, things would right themselves. You know—we'd work together and we'd go on home and..." Frank's plans fizzled along with his anger and he sank back against the vinyl cushion. "Oh, *man*..." he said morosely.

"Probably not the best way to orchestrate your return, fella. I think you better go on home to give you both some time to calm down. Just take it slow and easy, okay? We don't want to give Doctor Alex any stab-wound business. How'd you get here, anyway? I don't see your truck."

"Walked. Truck's wrecked."

That information launched a dozen questions, but Milt limited it to one: "Need a lift home?"

"Nah, I'll go," Frank said resignedly.

"Where's Blyss?"

Frank looked startled to hear his paramour's name coming from the Mayor's lips. "Uh, she's gone."

"Really?" Milt's tone showed genuine surprise, and he stared off into space as if contemplating the mysteries of the universe.

"Yeah." Frank sought a clue to Milt's preoccupation but found none.

Milt shook his head to escape a mental fog and sighed. "Get going, Frank. Folks have had enough of a show for one day. Think about the ramifications of anything you might do. We don't want to get our town on the nightly news because of any violence, okay?" He turned and saw a bug-eyed Sadie frozen in place on the beauty shop side and grimaced. "Sadie, you've seen and heard a bit too much today. Do Helen a favor and keep it under your hat, okay?"

Sadie bristled. "Helen is my dear friend—I wouldn't do anything to betray her trust."

A choked sound from Frank made Milt turn back to him. "Things have changed while you've been gone, Frank," he said. "You've got to watch your step. This isn't the same place you left."

Frank pushed forward in the chair, positioned his crutch and hefted his body into position above it. Tottering for a moment, he waited until he regained his equilibrium. The soft tap-brush of his crutch and adjusted gait were the only sounds in the room. He reached the door and pushed it open with his crutch and hopped down the steps.

Milt looked at Sadie for a moment and said succinctly, "Tell Helen he's gone," and followed Frank outside.

Sadie nodded at Milt's disappearing back and took a shuddering breath. With the excitement over, she felt weak-kneed. She hobbled over to retrieve her shoe, sank down in the nearest chair and noticed a most interesting detail. In his haste to come between Frank and Helen, Milt had dropped his clipboard there. Picking it up, she glanced at the hand-scrawled details on the top sheet and felt a pinprick of exhilaration. *Well, well, well!* Without an ounce of guilt over snooping, she lifted the page and found a completed form beneath it that floored her with the implications of its contents.

Milt only told me to keep quiet about what happened in here this morning—that has nothing to do with what's written on these papers. Sadie pursed her lips thoughtfully and tapped her index finger on the clipboard. *Milt could just as easily have left this on a table at the café and if he had, you can bet your bottom dollar no one else would have kept quiet about this.*

She nodded her head briskly, replaced the clipboard on the chair, bent to retie her shoe and stood before the mirror to position her face into a vague expression. In response to Sadie's knock, Helen called out, "Come in." A noise in the shop distracted her and she halted; surreptitiously she watched Milt open the front door, spot the clipboard across the room and nod with relief. He left again, unaware that the town's worst gossip possessed a potentially volatile bit of news.

Sadie eased the door shut. *So, Milt, for all your pretty speeches to Frank, you're not exactly helping him and Helen get back to normal, are you?* Straightening her shoulders, she made her way into the living room where a nervous Mildred and a flushed Helen awaited her. "They're gone," she said succinctly. "Milt sent him home."

"I can't believe Frank's nerve, waltzing on in here like he'd never been gone," Helen sputtered, her color high and her voice shrill.

"...waltzing in..." echoed Mildred. "Helen's so upset!"

"Of course she is," Sadie snorted. "But Frank will think twice before he comes back to bother her. Milt gave him quite the lecture."

"I don't know, Sadie," Helen said morosely. "He's gone now, but I'm sure he's going to put up a fight. I'd better get out there and run the show." She sighed and gathered up the cash again. "Do you ladies want to go out the front door, or let yourselves out the back?"

Shocked by Helen's abruptness, Mildred said, "We'll go out the front with you. Come along, Sadie."

And so it was, Sadie hit Main Street with the skeletal details of a powerful enigma.

Chapter 9

Driving south on Highway 83 on Saturday morning, it was as if the Jenkins' car were the shank of a zipper and the road's yellow centerlines were the cogs. With each passing mile, the zipper loosened a bit more, allowing the release of pent-up thoughts and emotions.

"We need to talk about Frank," Al said abruptly when they had merged onto the eastbound lane of Interstate 94.

"If you'd like…" Joy's heart pounded. "Do you want me to drive for a while?"

"No, I'll be fine, Joybells," he said softly. "I can think about Frank now without falling apart. I didn't mean to scare you last night."

"I didn't think of it as falling apart, Big Guy. I just didn't know if a back rub and hot bath were enough, or if you needed more serious help. It felt like telling someone with all the signs of a heart attack to sit down and think good thoughts and everything will be fine. I was afraid I wasn't doing the right thing."

"What you did was perfect. It was just a case of this ol' camel buckling under the final straw. Seeing Frank kiss Blyss pushed me over the edge."

"When was the last time we saw Frank and Helen kiss?"

"It's been a while, hasn't it? Not to say every couple who doesn't smooch in public is heading for divorce court, but there has really been very little evidence of love or caring between them lately. What did we miss?"

"In a small town, people keep a lid on their personal lives. Everyone knows enough, as it is. Look at what happened when the furniture store delivered twin beds to Leola and Buster's house and hauled away their double bed? The whole town watched them like hawks for weeks."

Al chuckled at the memory, but turned serious again. "Can a person fall out of love? I mean, do you think Frank ever really loved Helen?"

Joy caught her breath. This question ventured into places she and Al rarely strayed. "Do you really want to talk about that, Al?" she asked softly.

"Yes, I do," he said firmly. "I hope you believe you're the one and only woman I love."

"I know you love me with every fiber of my being," Joy said. "I would never have married you if I thought," she paused to form the words she had never said aloud, "you still loved Helen."

"I doubt I ever did love Helen. Now, I love her like a sister, but back in college when Frank brought me home with him and I met the two of you, it wasn't love between Helen and me. Not compared to what you and I have together. At the time, Frank was trying to hook me up with Helen, so at first, I paid more attention to her than to you. That was before I knew about their history."

"She and Frank were an item in high school, and when he went away to college, she didn't get over him. She was very confused when she picked up vibes that it was okay with him if she went out with you. She's been in love—until this mess, anyway—with Frank since Junior High."

"And Frank?"

"I always thought the relationship tilted more in Helen's direction than Frank's. He liked having a pretty girl like her interested in him, but I wonder how it would have turned out if Helen hadn't been quite so interested in him. Once he saw her with you, though, jealousy—more than love—motivated him. Originally, he wanted you to help free him to pursue other girls. But when he actually saw Helen with another guy—and his good friend, at that—he wanted her back. What a terrible thing to realize this late in the game."

"Jealousy is a pretty thin plank on which to build a marriage."

Joy stared out the window at the passing landscape. Tears welled up in her eyes. "I've never asked you this, maybe because I was afraid of what the answer could be..."

"Sounds serious, Jinglebells." When she didn't respond immediately, he glanced over and quickly said, "Hey! It's me over here, the guy you've lived with all these years—nothing can be that hard to ask, can it?"

So softly that passing traffic nearly muffled her words, Joy asked, "Did you pick me on the rebound? I mean, if we had met on our own without the Frank-and-Helen connection, do you think you would have picked me?"

Al pulled off the road and turned the key. "Look at me, please. The answer to your dreaded question is an unequivocal *yes:* Y.E.S. Got that? I picked you because I looked away from the flash-in-the-pan that was Helen and saw the true pure light from the lighthouse that was—*is*—you."

"Wow." Joy breathed deeply. "I know you love me, but I still had to ask. That's how rattled this whole thing has gotten me—it's got me doubting something as unshakeable as our love."

"Come here," Al said gently. Their lips met across the gearshift. First a fly-by kiss, then a coming-in-for-a landing kiss, then a wing-tilting heart-stopping kiss that made Joy reach out for safety, finding it against Al's shoulder. "I love you, you silly goose," he whispered in her ear.

They rode in contemplative and comfortable silence for nearly a mile. Al cleared his throat. "I, uh, owe a lot to Frank. It's because of him I met you. Otherwise, our paths would never have crossed. Frank got me to the same square acre with you."

"Oh, I don't know. Helen and I would have probably stayed friends and she'd have married Frank, and if you and Frank had stayed friends, you and I would have met each other through them, I suppose. Even if only socially."

"Yeah, I would have been this miserable bachelor meeting a gorgeous woman married to some other lucky guy and thinking *Now why do you suppose Frank never told me about his wife's best friend?*"

"No, I would have been a sad spinster pining away after love that never came my way—and you would show up with a drop-dead beautiful wife and a boatload of kids and I would have wept quietly into my pillow every night for years, despondent over what might have been!"

"A boatload of kids, huh? Now there's an image!" They laughed easily.

"Thank God, none of that happened. We have each other. And we have Dave," Joy mused.

"That's one change for the good since Frank defected. I've spent more time with Dave. I never realized it, but subconsciously, I let Frank take time away from my son over the years."

"You and Dave have hung around more lately. He likes it."

"You mean, he's noticed a difference?" They both jumped at the sound of a semi's horn behind them. Al pulled securely back into their lane even as he waited for Joy's response.

"I don't think he thinks of it comparatively—like *before Frank left, Dad didn't hang around with me, but now he does.* Did you know he asked me for a calendar so he could mark the things you plan to do together? He's real excited about going to the State Fair. 'Just me and Dad!' is how he put it and I was so happy for him, I didn't even correct his grammar!"

"We'll take you along, too, Joybells, though I did remind him some shows are of more interest to guys."

"He rattled off a host of things you had found on the Fair's Internet site: the K-9 Comets with their Frisbees, and the Paul Bunyan Lumberjack Show—that's one you two can hit together and leave me with the 4-H-ers!"

"Don't want woodchips in your hair, huh?" Al teased. "I'm glad he's looking forward to it, because I am, too."

"He's gained a lot of self-confidence working with Luke. And being home by himself for these few days we're gone is good for him, too."

"Over the summer without Frank around, I see what I've missed by not spending more time with Dave—quality time, I mean. Dave and I have done stuff together, but I've held the best parts of me in reserve for Frank. Since he didn't have sons, we subconsciously justified spending so much time together. Apparently, Frank was using me to avoid Helen and I used him to avoid dealing with the fact my son wasn't like other sons."

"You're a good father, Al," Joy said, gently.

"But not the best dad I could be. It took this mess with Frank to make me face up to that."

"What was it at the very beginning of this mess that hit you so hard? I was afraid you were so upset that your old-time feelings for Helen surfaced again. I even imagined you telling Frank *How dare you leave such a wonderful woman as Helen, you jerk!*"

"Trust me; I have no left-over feelings for Helen. The sum total of anything between Helen and me began and ended that summer. It was obvious Frank was her only interest. An effective way to turn a guy away is to spend every date talking about how wonderful another guy is!"

"What caused you and me to drift apart this summer?" Joy asked, worry still pricking holes in the relief she felt.

"I felt betrayed. It was like learning someone is in the witness protection program and everything you thought you knew is a lie. It's hard to trust anyone anymore, and I even pulled back from you. Every day I went to work and saw people hanging around like vultures waiting for some new scandal to devour."

"Do you really hate your job, Al?"

His lips tightened. "I really do. Some days when I walk up the loading dock steps, I'd like nothing more than to fast-pitch that government-issued key at the Post Office door and never return. Those four walls get tighter every day until I feel like I'm suffocating."

"Why haven't you said anything to me about this?"

"I knew you wanted to retire," Al said matter-of-factly, "and you've worked so hard and so long. You deserve to be a stay-at-home gal. But one of us needs to keep working for a while; fifty *is* a bit young for me to ditch the working life. I don't think I could stand to be retired for forty years. We Jenkins men last a long time. Look at dad—he's going strong at eighty!"

"So you kept your mouth shut about hating a job so I could achieve my dream?"

"Don't make me out to be any big-time hero."

"You are, in my book." She bit her lip thoughtfully. "Maybe there's some way we can both be happy."

"We've got Dave to consider, too."

"I'm not suggesting we turn him out to pasture! But if we think about us first and make sure we're happy, Dave will be happy. Meanwhile, if you see a truck-stop or something, I need a bathroom break."

"How about this for good timing? Would an official government-authorized rest-stop suit you?"

"Perfectly."

Al flicked on the turn signal. "Don't get all freaked out by all this, Joy. We haven't been talking like we're used to on a daily basis and, if you think about it, we've also lost that regular Friday night conversational bonanza with Frank and Helen. Now, you're getting a whole barrelful instead of spoonfuls of everything bottled up inside me."

"Yeah, we have covered a lot of topics on Friday nights over the years, haven't we?"

Al nodded. "Before you run to the restroom, I've got one more thing to say: I'm willing to work at the Post Office for the next fifty years if it will give you a settled life and a sense of being loved and cherished. I just think we could explore some options to life in Prairie Rose."

"I've always liked our lives and I thought you did, too. I know it's not your home town, but you seemed to have settled in over the years."

"It is a good place to live. But that doesn't mean we have to stay there forever, does it?" He turned off the engine and the car grew silent, inside and out.

Joy shook her head slowly, one hand on the door handle. "Of course not. Can you picture me sitting at home being loved and cherished by a man who is miserable, but goes to work everyday at a job he hates? That's not a happy retirement."

"Precisely why I haven't talked about not liking my job. I knew you would be upset. Especially lately with Frank and Helen, and Blyss showing up, and all."

"Oh, boy. Now *there's* our topic of conversation when we're back on the road! Little Miss Blyss." Joy pushed open the door. "See you in a few minutes."

Exiting the women's restroom a few minutes later, Joy was surprised that Al wasn't waiting in the car. She scanned the grassy expanse and spotted him in the large-vehicle parking area talking to a man by a recreational vehicle. She quickly criss-crossed the lawn to join them.

"Hey, here she is!" Al said with more genuine enthusiasm than Joy had heard in weeks. "Joy, this is Chet Neal. He and his wife are full-time RVers!"

Joy gathered her wits and greeted the man, surprised to have Al so enthused about anything and mildly amused at Al taking time for introductions to folks they would never see again.

A pleasant-looking woman came out of the RV carrying a plastic watering jug. Puzzled, Joy looked around and saw a bright-colored pot on the ground outside the rig's door "What healthy pansies!"

"Hello. I'm Myrna Neal. You must love flowers as much as I do."

"Passionately! I'm Joy Jenkins, and this is my husband, Al." Suddenly, introductions seemed the most natural thing in the world.

Al dropped an arm across Joy's shoulders, just like old times. "I see by your license plates you're from South Dakota."

"Actually, we hail from New Mexico, but we live in the permanent state of contentment!" Chet said.

"Oh, Chet, that old joke!" Myrna scolded playfully. "Actually, we're full-timers and made South Dakota our new home state for a variety of reasons we won't bore you with."

"Are you delivering this flowerpot to someone?" Joy asked.

"No, it travels with us. Chet calls these flowers my grandchildren, given how I pamper them. They ride right inside when we're driving along!"

Chet interjected, "That's not all she's got. I was just about to climb up to Myrna's Freeway Greenhouse!" He pointed toward the roof where Joy now noticed a low-profile curved cover with mesh for protection against the wind and sun. "Cherry tomatoes and pepper plants. Plus, a row of lettuce. The radishes are done, but soon we'll have carrots."

"This I've got to see," Al said. "May I take a look?"

"Help yourself," Chet said. "You, too, Joy. It's quite the sight up there on the roof!"

Where other people might store bicycles or canoes or anchor lawn chairs, Chet and Myrna had constructed a compact portable garden. Each segment could be lifted out to carry down the ladder, if needed, but all were secured together and fastened to the RV's frame. A special cover let rainwater in and yet prevented wind damage while allowing good air circulation.

"What beautiful tomatoes, Myrna! Where did you get these long, low plastic containers your lettuce is growing in?" Joy exclaimed, peering over the edge at the beaming gardener.

"They're a carry-over from our old life—it's a good use for wallpaper tubs. We retired from the paint and wallpaper business. And let me tell you, I enjoy pulling lettuce out of them a lot more than sopping wet wallpaper!"

"That's quite a garden," Al praised as he led the way down the ladder. "How long have you been full-timers?"

"Ten years. Best days of our lives," Chet crowed. "Our kids thought we were trying to destroy their inheritance, our bosses thought we were deranged, and our neighbors told us we'd regret selling our cute little colonial, but we followed our hearts and are loving every minute."

That's the guy's perspective. "How 'bout you, Myrna?" Joy asked nonchalantly.

"I'd put heel marks in the sand if Chet tried to drag me back to suburbia just yet!" Myrna said with a contagious chuckle. "At first, all I could think about was what I'd have to give up—but it didn't take long for me to realize you carry most of what's important for a good life right inside yourself. Two things I wouldn't bend on were gardening and hanging clothes on a line, and Chet has been very understanding about helping me keep a garden even on the road. Plus, we hook up a clothesline right here whenever I need one." She walked over and tapped an eyehook bolted to the RV's frame. "We tie one end here and one line to a tree and I'm in business."

"Flowers keep her happy, veggies keep us both healthy, and the clotheslines save us money—it's all my gain," Chet said cheerfully. "Besides, even on the road you need to have a hobby, and Myrna's gardening hobby fits in fine."

"What's your hobby, Chet?" Al asked.

"I write." Chet winked at Myrna.

"Travel books?" Al guessed, wondering what secret this delightful couple shared.

"Have you ever read anything by Raquel LeBeau?" Myrna asked.

Al shook his head *no*, but Joy nodded *yes* just as Myrna broke out in laughter. "I go to bed every night with that award-winning author!" She reached for Chet's hand and grinned from ear to ear. "I'd like to tell you I'm the inspiration for all those bright and gorgeous heroines, but you've already met me! My dear husband just has an overly active imagination."

"Raquel LeBeau is a man?" Joy asked incredulously. "I haven't read all your books, but my goodness, you surely do understand human nature and a woman's heart."

Chet bowed. "Thank you. That part you do owe to Myrna. She's my number-one fan and keeps me in line. Until she signs off on a book, it doesn't go to my agent. She's also the photographer for the covers."

"Living on the road sounds like the perfect deal for both of you," Al said.

"We do miss our kids—but they had moved all around the country, so it's not like we were in each other's back pockets even when we lived in one place. We can always plan to roll into the towns where they live in time for any big events in their lives," Myrna said.

"When we were both working full-time at the paint and wallpaper store, we were slaves to the front door. If it was open, we had to be there; if it was shut, we weren't making any money," Chet said.

"Would you like to see our place?" Myrna offered. "I've noticed you eyeing it, Joy. Come on in, both of you."

Inside, Al and Joy looked around in undisguised astonishment. The compact quarters were neat and decorated with flair. All the comforts of home were in evidence: a microwave, stovetop, oven and refrigerator completed the kitchen. A couch and matching armchair, a small desk and a self-contained bathroom just outside the bedroom filled in the space behind comfortable front seats that gave a birds-eye view. "Look at all the storage, plus there's much more underneath!" Chet said enthusiastically, opening cabinets full of dishes, books, games, and carefully marked boxes. Efficient pantry shelves held an amazing amount of canned goods and packaged foods.

"I had no idea these units were so complete." Joy said. "It's like a little cabin! And you've wallpapered it so beautifully!"

"Of course! We had all those skills, so we decided to reap the benefits ourselves. Besides, it makes it homier for us than the look right off the showroom floor. If you're thinking about getting one, you'll want to check out lots of models—all are different, which is a good thing since everyone's requirements for happiness on the road vary as much as their budgets. I'm glad you could see our rig. Most RV owners will happily show you their homes. It doesn't hurt to ask!" Chet said.

"Hey," Al checked his watch, "we need to get going ourselves. This has been most interesting. Thank you!" They shook hands with Chet and Myrna, casting lingering looks around in hopes of retaining all they had seen.

"It rarely fails; we pull over as rest stops and usually get to meet people like yourselves while we water plants and walk around. After all, the beauty of life on the road is no schedule to keep!"

"Just heart-warming stories to write!" Joy said. "It has been delightful meeting you."

Back on the highway, Al chuckled. "Weren't they something? What did you think?"

"I'm operating on sensory overload right now. Wow—this is just not our normal day!"

"Our lives could be like that—something new every day. We could get an RV and head off into the sunset."

Joy's eyebrows shot straight up. "Whoa, fella! What's going on here? After meeting one happy couple in a parking lot, you've already got a whole scenario developed?"

"It's just an idea that's been rumbling around in my head for a few weeks. Doesn't it sound exciting?"

"Exciting? Do you know how much those rigs cost?"

"Yeah, actually I do. I talked with several RV owners over the Fourth. You can get a good quality used one for about the same price as a new car."

Joy frowned. "What kind of new car are you talking about, anyway? We don't usually car-shop for new Rolls Royces!"

"Okay," Al shrugged sheepishly, "maybe not a typical new car—but if we sold everything and traded in our two vehicles now, we'd have more than enough to buy a nice RV and live the life of vagabonds for several years."

"And this idea appeals to you because..."

"Think about it. We could go to warm places when it's cold here and nice cool places when it gets hot and sticky. Like Chet said, we would meet new people and see new places. And all the while, we're free of boring day-to-day jobs."

"What do we live on? It's not cheap to drive those things, you know. And even buying one would take more money than we've ever spent on anything in our lives. And what about mail and e-mail and telephone service? What about health insurance?"

"I didn't say I've worked out all the details yet. I ordered a book about full-timing in an RV—that's what they call it: full-timing—and I'm sure it will answer all or most of our questions. I have zillions of questions, just like you do."

"You've already ordered a book? Good grief, Al! When were you planning to talk to me about this?"

"Hey, hey, hey, Jinglebells! It's just how I've been keeping myself sane at work, thinking about things I could do instead of filling out hundreds of government forms every month and having the same conversations over and over again with the same people, day in, day out. The Post Office owns my body from 8:00 to 5:00, but my mind is free to roam as long as the work gets done. Some days there's so little stimulation I want to tear my hair out—that's when I put my mind on auto-pilot and dream big dreams."

"I didn't mean to attack you. I'm just sorry I haven't picked up on how miserable you've been."

Al shrugged. "Most people hate their jobs at some point, Joy, or at least are bored out of their skulls by them. It's a fact of life. We have to work to live, and it's good to work so we keep our minds sharp and contribute to society—but most work is not in the pleasure-giving category. For some people, it's meetings, meetings, meetings. For others, it's impossible deadlines. For still others, it's dysfunctional work environments or lazy co-workers. It's a rare person who bounds out of bed every morning and races off to work with an ear-to-ear smile. Many people are just counting the hours until the quitting bell rings."

"Then you definitely need to resign, Al. Life's too short to hold down a job that pushes you to the edge of your wits. There's got to be something out there to make you want to get out of bed in the morning. I can guarantee it won't be perfect, but you need to find something different. I'm just not sure living on the road is the way to go."

"You must have felt it, too, Joy, when you started thinking about retirement. Did you really find teaching all that wonderful every single day?"

"I like teaching, I love kids—and I enjoyed most of my co-workers. It's just that I didn't feel as sharp anymore. A teacher has to be in top form. Teaching is a younger person's world these days. When I met Amy Carter, it was like meeting myself years ago and seeing the same unquenchable spark in her eyes I once had. She's cutting-edge and will be for years to come. She's what the kids deserve. They are heading into a world more closely aligned with Amy Carter's world—and she's the person to lead them into it."

"You're hardly ready for the rocking chair, J-bells."

"I know. But on a line between cradle and rocker, I'm much closer to the rocking chair end of things."

"So, what could the two of us old duffs do? Doesn't the RV idea have any appeal to you?"

Joy sighed. "If you hadn't said *sell everything,* I might not have jumped down your throat as fast about an RV. I do like the ideas about new places and new faces—but I need roots, too. If we sold everything, we'd be rootless."

"Potted plants have roots. But pots can be moved around. An RV is like a giant flower pot."

"Think of *my* RV as a giant flower pot with a zillion wires holding it to the ground. One for phone, one for insurance, one for mail, one or two for family...not a very mobile image, is it?"

"We would just have to investigate those things."

"But what about Dave? Do you think he'd do okay living on the road?" Joy asked dubiously.

"I don't know. Do you think he'd do okay living by himself?"

"No, I don't," she said firmly. "There are too many things that could go wrong and he wouldn't know how to deal with them. And it's asking too much of our friends for them to keep track of him like they are during this trip."

"What if he lived in special housing?"

"You've been doing some thinking about this, haven't you?" Joy asked with undisguised surprise.

"Some. But some is also off the top of my head."

She bit her lip and watched a semi-truck pass them. "I think if we moved Dave to another town at the same time we took off, it would be very unsettling for him."

"He could come along with us."

"He does best with routines. Life on the road hardly fits that description."

"It could. It would just be a different routine for all of us to get used to. There is a definite process to setting up camp—he'd like that."

"Before Frank took off, had you ever thought about quitting your job?"

"Not seriously. I envied Frank that aspect of his abrupt departure. I mean, the guy pitched his whole life and started over. I'm not condoning what he did, but you have to agree, it took guts."

"Guts, maybe, but look how his grand plan turned out. I wonder how he got so beat up?" Joy mused. "He's not exactly a poster boy for successful mid-life adventures in the shape he's in."

"Maybe Blyss has a husband somewhere—a big dude who doesn't like old guys like Frank coming along and stealing his woman."

"You know, having seen Blyss and knowing Frank like we do, isn't it amazing he could inspire the kind of devotion she has shown him? I mean, the girl followed him across the country, for crying out loud. We *know* Frank—he's not a Babe Magnet."

"We thought we knew Frank. Obviously, there was a layer to him none of us had ever explored. And now he's back. I am so glad to get out of town. I feel sorry for Helen having to see him and Blyss together, but I leaped at the chance to get away. Thanks for saving my sanity, Joybells."

"It's a selfish measure, all the way through. I just wanted my guy back—all of him. I've got nearly thirty years invested in you. I'm not going to give you up without a fight."

"That's what's really sad about Frank and Helen. All those years together, and for what? A lot of heartache for Helen, especially. A little bit of excitement for Frank, maybe, but can that last?"

"Only time will tell. I can't imagine he'll stay around. Blyss showing up has pretty much ensured that. He's most likely going to get his business over and done with, and hightail it out of town. Unfortunately, that business includes making a decision about his marriage and his half of the business," Joy said.

"Before Blyss showed up, Frank might have had a chance at getting reinstated in Prairie Rose, but now that people have seen her, every time we look at Frank, we'll be wondering *Why?* Frank and Blyss hardly seem like a match made in heaven. Even if Frank and Helen aren't a perfect couple, at least they appear to belong together."

"I don't know what to think. I never dreamed Helen would up and move out of their house. If anything, I'd have bet she would dig in and refuse to budge an inch. She really liked her home and her garden and her birds."

"Go figure," Al said. "You getting hungry?"

"We can start looking for a place to pull over. I'm still tossing around something you said many miles back, the thing about does love ever die. To all outward appearances, Helen has fallen out of love with Frank. But you know what? I think what we're seeing now, in her case, is badly bruised love. I'm not sure those bruises can heal, but I think there really was love on her part."

"How about Frank?"

"I'm sure he'd say he loves, or at least used to love Helen. I guess love can change levels. Maybe his never left the stage closest to infatuation, which is easily dislodged. Love needs to dig down deep to withstand all the storms we can face in life."

"Frank and Helen really haven't had that many disasters in their lives, Joy. I mean, both their girls are bright and happy and successful—no problems there. Their business has beaten the odds for survival in a small town, which is pretty amazing and extremely risky since it has been the sole employer for both of them since day one."

"They've lived simply, just like the rest of us, and the girls earned good scholarships and got decent inheritances when Frank's dad died. And it helps that Frank and Helen are very good at what they do. Plus, they've got a faithful clientele, and not just from Prairie Rose."

"But even with what appears to be a good life, Frank looked outside his marriage for a thrill."

"That's the problem with thrill-seeking. It makes the everyday look blah when actually, the everyday is full of wonder and amazement."

"Somehow, I wish we'd had this conversation about a year ago—and with Frank and Helen."

"A year ago, Frank was as appalled as we are about anyone having an affair," Joy said. "At least at the time I would have said he was. Now I wonder."

"Do you remember about three years ago when the four of us went to see some movie where the hero had a secret life? On the way home, Frank said something about how it takes a special kind of talent to live one kind of life and appear to live another. Afterwards, you asked me if I thought Frank was happy with his life."

"Yeah, I remember now that you mention it. And as I recall, your answer was a very confident *Sure*. Are you doubting now?"

"It's just interesting."

"I'm going to say something pretty radical, Al. Please hear me out. We have a friend who appears to be floundering in deep seas and we want to help. But a vital lesson they teach lifeguards is that a drowning man can drag a rescuer down pretty fast. It takes a very strong and smart rescuer to keep from drowning, too. That's why tossing a lifeline in the water makes sense—it gives the drowning man something to hang on to and lets the rescuer do his work without putting himself in danger, too."

"So what's this lifeline we're supposed to toss out to Frank?"

"Hey, I just come up with the illustrations—I shouldn't have to do the applications, too! Seriously, I just want to make sure we don't get dragged down ourselves. They are our closest friends, but we made vows to each other, not to them. Our first concern is keeping *our* marriage afloat. It sounds selfish, but we're of no use to them if they pull us under, too."

Al twisted his lips. "I think I'm water-logged already."

"You've been a good friend to Frank, Al. But he's got big problems. Possibly so big, neither of us is equipped to help him."

"So we just let him drown?"

"No, not at all. But maybe we need to call for help—we can't do the rescue on our own. I mean, look at how we're dealing with it so far—I've swatted the guy, you're about ready to punch out his lights. Neither one are probably standard counseling procedures! I think we're too much in the storm path ourselves to be much help as rescuers."

"I've felt horrible about failing Frank. But on a subconscious level, I've known I couldn't bring him back."

"That would be hard to live with even if the guy in trouble were a total stranger—but to have it be such a good friend makes it almost unbearable."

"So who's going to save Frank? Blyss?" Al scoffed. "If Helen were to toss him anything, it would be solid steel, which would take him down to the bottom mighty fast."

"You're right. I just wish Helen would talk to someone—she's withdrawn from all of us. She works like a dog to keep the shop going, but it's growing harder and harder to reach her."

"Seems to me, Pastor Tori could step in."

"I don't think she's ignoring the situation, but even Tori can only do what Helen allows. If Helen's putting up road blocks, they're holding Tori back, too."

By unspoken agreement, they halted their conversation during lunch at a sandwich shop and simply enjoyed watching people, listening to disjointed conversations, and participating in the idle chitchat their waitress offered. Outside again, they held hands and walked a block in either direction, window-shopping and reveling in each other's company.

Joy climbed behind the wheel when they returned to the car and put Al in charge of navigation on Minnesota roads. "How can I do that if I don't know where we're going?"

"Rochester. Keep us on the most direct route to Rochester. That's all the instructions you need!"

"You're really getting into this life-of-mystery business, aren't you? Don't you know you're already a heap of intrigue to me? The way you keep things moving so smoothly at home, especially when you've worked full-time for years. And how you help Dave live such a normal life. And how you never complain about things like nothing to do in town, or our not taking fancy trips like your cousins whose Christmas letters are more like an itinerary than news."

"And this all has to do with me not telling you why we're going to Rochester?"

"I thought I knew all about you, but up pops Joy, the Woman of Intrigue."

"Tell me what you do know about me."

"You're kidding, right?"

"Nope. How would you describe me to someone who had never met me?"

"Physically?"

"Sure," Joy said, "As long as you're kind! Close your eyes—no fair describing what you see."

"I see you in my dreams, so this won't be hard. You're the right height to fit beneath my chin—which is important because I love the way your hair smells. Your hair is long enough to hide my hands when I pull you in for a kiss and the right color to pick up all the glints of candlelight when we're making love. Your curves come at all the right places and in all the right sizes to fit perfectly against me. Your eyes are the seat of your soul—dark when you're troubled, glistening when you're happy, bright when you're curious. Your hands can massage the most troubling thoughts right out of existence, or create a beautiful garden from a heap of dirt, or bring music from black notes on a white page. What are you doing?"

Joy blindly clutched the wheel as tears welled up in her eyes. "Oh, Al!" she blubbered, wiping her cheeks with the back of her hand and blinking rapidly to see the road.

Al quickly grabbed for the steering wheel and kept the car steady. "What'd I say? Joy, talk to me! What's wrong?" The blast of a siren scared them both and Joy yelped.

A Highway Patrol car edged up next to them. His car-top speaker blasted them: "Pull over, please!" He moved ahead of them into their lane and eased off onto the shoulder where he parked several car lengths away from them. The door opened and a trim, gun-toting officer in a Smokey-the-Bear hat approached their vehicle.

"Roll down your window, Joy. He's coming to talk to us," Al prompted.

Still sniffling, Joy lowered her window to half-mast and fumbled in her purse for a tissue.

"Hello, folks. Having some trouble?" The man peered in through the driver's side window, glancing at Al in the passenger seat and coming back to rest on Joy's tear-stained face. "Everything okay, Ma'am?"

Joy caught a glimpse of herself in the rearview mirror and nodded, even though she now realized she looked more like a raccoon than a traveler with her smudged eye makeup. She blew her nose loudly.

"You seem upset. Has your passenger endangered you in any way?"

Joy looked at him blankly. *Endangered?* Quickly, almost too quickly, she shook her head and glanced at Al who sat in numb confusion beside her.

"I'd like to see some identification from both of you, please." The officer pulled out a notebook and waited while Al and Joy extracted licenses and handed them over. He recorded their names, walked behind the car to copy their license number into his book, came back and bent at the waist to say, "I'm going to keep your licenses while I call in your plates. Please wait right here."

Joy watched him walk back to his car and whispered, "Was I speeding? What's this about?" She reached for Al's hand and clung to it with both hands, the right hand tucked into his grasp, the left hand nervously rubbing his knuckles.

"I don't know. Maybe a car like ours has been reported stolen or something." Hearts pounding, they stared at the mesmerizing flashing light in front of them. Then the patrolman stepped out of his car again. "Shhh, here he comes," Al said.

"Okay, you're free to go. Drive safely and have a good day," the man said pleasantly.

"Uh, did we do something wrong, officer?" Joy asked.

He appeared surprised at her question. "No, but when I came up along side your vehicle, you were crying quite hard and I thought perhaps you were being held against your will."

"Oh, no—not at all! This is my husband, and he had just said…" The memory of Al's words juxtaposed against this startling encounter triggered a resurgence of tears. Joy's lower lip trembled and suddenly, the lump in her throat blocked her words.

"What had you said, Mister Jenkins?" The voice allowed for no frivolous response.

Red-faced and nervous, Al replied, "I said she's a good height and I like her shape and she has nice hair and eyes."

"And that made her cry? You reciting her vital statistics?" The officer looked at Joy skeptically. "Is that correct, Ma'am?"

Joy nodded sheepishly, "It sounded much prettier when he actually said it to me. He gave you a much-abridged version. Does this mean we have a police record now?"

"No. If you were in any danger, I just wanted to give you a chance to get away from him." He leaned over to catch Al's eye. "As for you, Sir, watch that sweet-talking when the lady's driving, okay? People have accidents when they can't see the road." A hint of a smile twitched his cheek.

Al heaved a sigh. "Summer vacations surely are educational."

"Ain't that the truth?" Joy said ruefully. "I love you, Al. Sorry about all this."

"If I tell you I love you, it won't make you cry again, will it?"

"Nope—I don't know what came over me. Must be hormonal, huh? That's what you get when you live with a retired lady, Big Guy. You're facing years of tears without warning."

Al selected another tape and they rode along as the sounds from their past filled their ears and mapped their conversation:

Three Dog Night sang "Sure As I'm Sittin' Here" with its poignant words *You get the truth, ya get a lie... 'nough to make a grown man cry...*

"Do you think Frank would try to get back with Helen, assuming his relationship with Blyss can't last forever?" Joy asked. "Or do you think he'll just find another Blyss?"

"He and Blyss are from such different worlds—shaped by different decades, different locales. It's hard to imagine they could maintain much of a long-term relationship."

"You'd hope the old saying 'once burned, twice shy' would be true, but it may be hard for him to swallow his pride enough to come back to Helen."

Al whistled along with "Help Me," breaking into words for...*hot, hot blazes come down to smoke and ash...*When the song ended, he mused, "Frank must have shown Blyss some pretty hot blazes. If he brought that same passion back to Helen, couldn't it work out?"

"Like Joni Mitchell sang, I guess a person can hope for the future at the same time they're worrying about the past."

"I've got a question for you, Jinglebells. Why, when I described you, did you cry, and when we said our vows you made it through without a tear? Are hormones that selective?"

Joy pondered his question for a moment. "I think it's because I cry vicariously—when you started telling me how you think *about* me, it was like I was hearing someone else described and I couldn't help but cry. Kind of like why I cry at movies. But at our wedding, both words and tears were inadequate. My heart says *Me? Me!* and all I want to do is make love to you."

Al shook his head ruefully. "That's got to be a woman-thing. Just thinking about you and looking across the car at you right before that patrolman pulled us over made me want you right then-and-there."

"Even with mascara running down to my chin?" Joy teased.

"Believe me, I wasn't looking at your chin, Jinglebells!" Al said with a sensuous chuckle.

"Whew, we'd better change topics or we'll never make Rochester today!"

"That's important to do, huh?" Al teased.

"Sure is," Joy agreed amiably.

"Not giving a single clue, are you?"

"Nope."

"Let me get this right. No sex talk, no clues about Rochester, you laughed when I mentioned compost, and I'm sick of talking about Frank and his debacle. Whatever shall we talk about?"

"How about retirement? We just made promises to love each other forever and ever, Amen. So, what are we going to do to make our golden years shine?"

"One thing we have to decide first is when do those golden years begin?"

"I'd always assumed much later than this, but I gather you're think more in the one-digit numbers."

"Actually, how does next Tuesday sound?"

"What! You're kidding, right?"

"Just thinking outside the box, J-bells! Hold on."

"I'm holding."

"Okay, what's your number-one concern about me retiring early?"

"Health insurance."

"Wow. That didn't take you long." He sighed. "You're probably right. That's the primary thing that keeps the whole generation of baby boomers from walking away from their jobs."

"Without a job that offers insurance, I can't imagine being able to afford it."

"Okay, if we were able to figure that out, would you be afraid of me quitting the Post Office?"

"We do have our inheritance from when our folks sold their farms," Joy said slowly, "but how long could we live on that?"

"It could be our fall-back plan. We could both get part-time jobs and use the farm-sale money only for emergencies. If we sold our house, we'd have even more money."

"But then, where would we live? Living in an RV sounds romantic, but we're hardly the type driven by wanderlust. You'd think if we really wanted to travel, we would have managed to take more trips by this time in our lives."

"I really don't know what to tell you. All I know is I can't take much more of my job right now, and there aren't a lot of local options."

"Then, there's Dave. Which reminds me, I'm going to call to see how he's doing. It's weird he hasn't called us yet."

"He's probably enjoying a new level of independence. After all, he is twenty-six."

"It's ringing." Joy tucked the phone under her chin as she adjusted her seat. "Hey, Dave! It's Mom. I'm surprised you're home! Thought I'd have to leave you a message, but this is much better. How are you doing?"

Dave's excited voice came through loud and clear and Joy held the phone away from her ear so Al could listen, too. "I came home to change shirts. I got all sweaty at Luke's 'cuz we're shingling and it's real hot. I'm doing a good job, Luke says."

"That's great, Dave. Which reminds me; when you get home tonight, would you put the sprinkler on my garden? I don't want my plants to die. Just set the egg timer for an hour."

"Okay, Mom. Is Dad there?"

"Yes, but he's driving, and you know the rules: no driving and talking on the cell phone!"

"Okay, but will you give him a message? Tell him Frank wants to see him."

"Oh? When did you see Frank?" Joy asked, turning to Al with a worried look.

"I didn't see him. He called the house phone and left a message and I just listened to it. I was real careful not to erase it, too."

"Good, son. Did he say anything else?"

"Uh, let's see. He said, 'Hello, Al. This is Frank. I need to talk to you. Blyss is gone.' That's what he said."

"Okaaaay," Joy said, noting Al's tightening jaw.

"Gotta get back to work, Mom. Luke said come back in half an hour and it's time."

"Okay, Bye, son. We love you. Be careful on the roof!" She disconnected and stared at Al, shaking her head slowly. "So Blyss is gone. Wow."

"That's not as hard to believe as Frank wanting to talk to me."

"He can just cool his heels for a few days," Joy muttered. "We're unavailable." She tucked the cell phone back into her purse. "He had plenty of opportunities before; we're not going to go running back now just because poor Frankie has lost his Blyss."

Al drummed his fingers on the steering wheel. "Don't worry; I'm not all that eager to talk to Frank. I know exactly how the conversation would go; he'd try to defend his actions and I'd just get angry, and we'd both say things we shouldn't. Such a non-productive conversation is hardly worth wrecking our time together, so no, I don't want to talk to Frank."

They rode for several miles in a silence that could have lasted indefinitely had they not been jolted out of their reveries by the cell phone ringing. "Do you think it's Dave?" Al asked while Joy fumbled for the phone.

"Could be; after talking to us, he probably remembered something else."

"Hello," she said brightly.

"Joy, this is Frank. Could I speak to Al, please?"

Dumbfounded, Joy clutched the phone and buried it against her breast. "It's Frank. For you." Her eyes grew round with indecision and narrowed with resolve. She held up her hand to halt Al's words and returned the phone to her ear. "No, you may not speak to Al. He's driving."

"Wait, Joy! Don't hang up!" Frank pleaded. "I need to talk to him."

Joy's lips tightened and she looked questioningly at Al. "He's not taking *no* for an answer. What should we do?"

Al flipped on the turn signal and pulled off the road, turning his flashers on. The annoying click filled their heads like a metronome gone crazy. He leaned back against the seat, closed his eyes for a moment, and reached for the phone. He held it against his ear for several seconds before saying woodenly, "Al, here."

Joy chewed her bottom lip nervously and watched traffic zoom past them. During the quiet pockets of time when traffic was light, she could hear the low drone of Frank's voice, though no words were distinct. Just as a trio of trucks thundered by, Al spoke his first words. "Did you really think it would last, Frank?"

More traffic, more muffled words from Frank, more silence from Al. Finally, Al said grimly, "You can't whip through town like a tornado and then expect that nothing's changed."

An interminable silence followed on Al's part. Then, he simply said, "Goodbye, Frank," and hung up.

Joy glanced automatically at the call-timer when Al handed her the phone. *Nine minutes and eleven seconds. And not even two-dozen words from Al.* She looked around them and noted a sign for a restaurant. "Let's stretch our legs, Al; have dessert." Her voice prodded him back to the present and he went through the motions of turning the ignition key, signaling his return to traffic, and easing into the flow on the road again. "Here; this exit. Two blocks to the right it said. That will be easy to get back on the road again." She talked steadily, hoping to wedge Frank out and herself into Al's consciousness.

They parked, entered the small Mom-and-Pop café, found a table, and ordered dessert. "What did Frank say?" Joy asked impatiently when it became clear Al wasn't volunteering information. "Talk to me."

"Same old, same old. No repentance, no sorrow over any misery he caused. Just a sob story about how Helen won't have anything to do with him, the girls aren't talking to him, how he's running low on money, and how he's all alone and feeling blue."

"Is Blyss really gone?"

"Apparently. He wanted me to talk to Helen to convince her to allow him to come back to the shop."

"Pfffft. *That* ain't gonna happen. Not unless he comes crawling back with a whole lot of remorse and even then…"

"He said Helen tried to kill him."

"What?" All sorts of commotion around them stopped as all eyes turned toward their table. Joy flushed and lowered her voice. "*Helen*? I don't believe that."

Al nodded. "Said she took after him with a pair of scissors and would have stabbed him without blinking an eye if Milt hadn't intervened."

Joy flopped back against the booth. "Is she in jail?"

"I don't think so. Remember, this is only Frank's version. Besides, we just talked to Dave and he surely would have mentioned if anything that dramatic had happened to Helen. Or we'd have heard from someone else by now."

Joy contemplated the remaining chocolate cake before her, the rest of which she had not tasted. "So, why exactly did Frank call you?"

"Oh, he hemmed and hawed about having blown us off that day in the bedroom, but never really turned it into a true apology. Said it was all because he was stressed out from Helen ragging on him."

"Poor baby," Joy said sarcastically. "I want to talk to Helen about the scissors story before you talk to Frank again."

"What makes you think I plan to talk to Frank?"

Joy stared at Al. "You don't?"

"After hearing him whine in my ear about what a rough deal he's gotten, I have no desire to waste any more of my time on him. If I see some radical evidence of a change in him, then I'll reconsider. There's no way he and I could still have a friendship, so what's the use?"

"None," Joy said slowly, "unless you were able to talk some sense into him."

"His head is so filled with self-pity and indignation over how everyone is against him, I don't think there's any room for sense between his ears." He glanced at his watch. "We'd better move along."

Several hours later, coming into Rochester from the north, they noticed two large construction cranes piercing the evening sky. Since Joy was driving, she pulled into a gas station on the edge of town and used a pay phone to make a call away from Al's hearing. "Okay! Ready?" she asked, coming back to the car.

"How do I know if I'm ready when I don't know what I'm to be ready for?"

Joy laughed and dodged his question. "I found out precise directions—we're just supposed to keep our eyes on the cranes and they'll lead us right to the spot we need to be."

"Kind of like Petey's compass, huh?"

"Absolutely. Except for the fact we're heading south, think of the cranes as the point that never moves. When we're at the base of them, we look for a park across the street from a high-rise."

A couple blocks from the Mayo Clinic, Joy found an open space near a towering building in the crane's shadow and parallel-parked the car. Al tilted his head to get the full view. "You know someone who lives here?"

"We both know someone who lives here. Come on. They're waiting for us."

"*They*, huh? So *two* people we know live here."

"Now you're getting technical," she chided, poking his ribs. She shielded the building roster from his view, punched a button for admittance and, when a buzzer sounded, grabbed the door open for them to enter. After a short elevator ride to the eighth floor, Joy led the way down a carpeted hall to an end unit. Spotting a brass nameplate beside the door, Joy quickly planted herself in front of it and motioned for Al to ring the bell.

One short ring and the door swung open. "Hello! Come in, come in."

Al stared at a trim, silver-haired man with a tan that hinted of golf courses. "Doc!" The word was wrapped in delight. "Joy, it's Doc!"

"Duh!" She gently pushed Al into the hallway. "I planned this trip, remember?"

The man greeting them was none other than the senior Doctor Alexander Johanson—the man who had first hung his shingle in Prairie Rose many years ago. "We just saw you over the Fourth of July—but I'm sure no one mentioned that you live in Rochester now."

"I moved here in January, or moved back here, I should say." He ushered them into the apartment, talking as he led the way to the living room. "Years ago, when I was in residency at the Mayo Clinic before I ever came to Prairie Rose, I always thought Rochester might be a place to live when I truly retired. And when an apartment opened up here, I leaped at the chance." He bowed and directed his guests into a tastefully decorated living room.

"This is great, Doc! All Joy would tell me about this trip was we were coming to Rochester and I would like what we found here. Nothing could please me more than to find you here." Al paused as he caught an enigmatic smile pass between Doc and Joy. "What? There's more?"

"Oh, you might say that," Joy teased. "Actually, I only know part of it and I've been bursting at the seams ever since I heard even the bits and pieces. Doc knows the full story—when can we hear the rest, Doc?"

"Quite soon, in fact, very soon." The older man looked beyond them to an inner hallway. In the distance, they heard a door open, followed by an almost familiar noise. Doc stood immediately. "Excuse me; I'll be right back."

"So, how are you enjoying your vacation?" Joy asked, her face glowing.

Al scooted closer on the love seat and kissed her forehead. "Rochester's great, but you—you're the best! I didn't know you had it in you to keep a secret of this magnitude."

"You just wait—you ain't seen nuttin' yet, Big Guy!"

"Hello, Joy and Al," a soft voice said. Both turned and Al jumped to his feet.

"Rachel Lindquist! What on earth are you doing in..." Al's eyes lit on Doc's hand clasping Rachel's shoulder. "Oh, my goodness! Is there romance in the air?"

"Probably not so romantic by some standards, but almost more than a couple of senior citizens like ourselves can handle!" Doc said with a chuckle, meeting Rachel's sparkling eyes as her hand crept up to cover his.

"What a fabulous surprise!" Al exclaimed and bent to kiss Rachel's cheek. "How did this all come about?"

"I've been in touch with Rachel ever since we spent a little more time than usual together during the Meadowlark Trail's Grand Opening several years ago," Doc explained as he moved Rachel's chair across the room. "We found it very easy to renew a friendship that has spanned many, many years."

"Randolph and I counted Alexander and Charlotte among our dearest friends," Rachel said. "And Alexander and I knew each other even before we married our long-time partners." Her eyes glistened. "To think, after all these years, the dear Lord would bring us together again!"

"As you may have noticed, Rachel's symptoms of multiple sclerosis are advancing, and so I suggested she might want to come down to Rochester and go through the Mayo Clinic for a thorough check-up."

"Alex, the younger Alex, that is," Rachel said with a rolling chuckle, "has been trying to convince me to do that for months, but I've been quite stubborn, I'm sorry to say."

"Once she agreed to come to Rochester, we decided to ratchet it up a notch and add a level of romance to the mix."

Rachel laughed and looked up over her shoulder at Doc. "The way he tells the story, it all sounds very calculating! In reality, we've both been bowled over by love. It's extremely exhilarating!"

"Who knows you're here, Rachel?" Al asked.

"Only Alex and Tori and your wife. When Joy talked to Alexander about coming to visit, we thought we ought to let her know I'd be here, too."

"How did you know where Doc was, Joy?" Al asked, shaking his head to dislodge the fog.

"While you're answering that question, Joy, fill us in on what brings you here," Alexander said.

"The stories combine nicely," Joy said. "Al and I have been going through some hard times, "she slid her fingers into his hand as she spoke. "As Rachel may already have told you, Doc, Frank and Helen's marriage is in rough shape."

Rachel nodded sadly. "I know this has been very difficult. I'm on the outer fringe, so to speak, but it must be devastating for you. Your lives have been so intertwined with Frank and Helen and the girls."

Al shifted beside Joy. "If we'd had any clues—or, should I say, been more alert to the clues that must have been there, it may not have been as upsetting. At least we could have tried to help before things got so bad."

"And that's why we're here, Doc," Joy said. "Not only did the Wilson's marriage fall apart, but we were starting to see cracks in ours. I got scared—and you're the person I thought of right away. For all my growing-up years, you were the town doctor and the town's best counselor. I'm sure you've heard countless stories from dozens of desperate people—and sent them on their way feeling much better. Somehow, you pulled folks through their traumas and troubles."

Rachel smiled sweetly at Alexander. "He does have a way about him, doesn't he?"

Joy nodded. "When I got scared at how this was affecting us, it came to me like a bolt out of the blue—we need to talk to Doc. I called the Rectory, thinking you might still be there since we'd just seen you the day before. I was surprised when Alex said you were already gone, and he seemed hesitant when I asked him where you were living these days. But I was pretty persistent, and here we are!"

"Rachel, seeing you here amazes me. Being the postmaster, I usually know who is going where. I knew you were out of town, but all you had said was that you were visiting friends, and seeing you over the Fourth, I assumed you were back home."

Rachel laughed. "Tori and Alex took over collecting my mail so you haven't noticed my box overflowing—and since I don't get out and about as much as others, you probably didn't even think twice about not seeing me around town lately."

Al shook his head ruefully. "I'm just glad everything has turned out so well." He couldn't help but notice that Rachel and Doc held hands with almost adolescent abandon. "Rachel Lindquist, you amaze me."

Rachel smiled at Alexander and, seeing his slight nod, said, "I must correct you on one important detail. Thanks to Pastor Tori, I'm now Rachel Johanson. When the fireworks were bursting-in-air, Alexander and I were married in the Rectory living room!"

It was Joy's turn to sputter. Recovering quickly, she rushed to fling her arms around the older woman. "Oh, Rachel! You got married! I'm so happy for you!"

"Congratulations to both of you! I can't think of a more perfect match. But does this mean you're not coming back to Prairie Rose, Rachel?" Al asked in amazement.

"Oh, we can't give up Prairie Rose. I plan to keep my house. Having Alex and Tori in town ensures we'll return frequently for visits, and having a place to call our own will make each trip back so much easier," Rachel hastened to explain.

"So we're interrupting your honeymoon," Joy said.

"Don't fret about that. We plan to extend our honeymoon for the rest of our lives. We moved quickly on this once we realized we love each other," Alexander said. "And even though Rachel could have stayed in a neighbor's apartment at first, I knew those folks would return soon from their European trip which meant we'd need to make other plans. Marrying the woman I cherish was what made the most sense."

"...love, honor, and cherish..." Al mused. "Doc and Rachel, it's refreshing to see you so obviously in love and hear you talking about old-fashioned values. We're about up to here," he tapped the back of his hand on the underside of his chin, "with one particular marriage gone wrong."

"The most important thing is not to lose your way," Alexander said thoughtfully.

Al arched an eyebrow in Joy's direction. "Looks like your first graders got it right," he said softly.

Joy nodded and turned to their host and hostess. "Did you ever hear the song my last class wrote, Rachel? The one called *My Little Compass*?"

"Yes, it was on a sermon tape from when the first graders who attend our church sang it earlier this summer."

"I forgot it would have been taped. Her sermon was about finding shelter in a storm. The kids' song has the line *Remember, north never moves*. Tori has a gift for linking everyday problems with spiritual solutions. Coming when it did, that sermon was very encouraging." She turned to Doc. "You weren't in town long, but you probably heard enough to realize everyone got pretty rattled when Blyss—that's Frank's girl friend, Blyss Hathaway—appeared. Then, Frank came back, as you saw at the concert on the third. Now we learn, Blyss is gone."

"That's a blessing for Helen," Rachel said.

Al's jaw tightened. "I'm glad Blyss is gone, but it's unlikely Helen will welcome Frank home. She's pretty steamed."

"It's a big mess," Alexander sighed, stretching his legs out. "Alex mentioned that people are reporting they can't sleep, or they're feeling out of sorts. Emotional upheavals affect us in many ways."

"Doc..." Al cleared his throat. "I'm one of the affected ones; I didn't go see Alex, though I probably should have, but my whole world went topsy-turvy when we first heard about Frank's affair. Joy and I..." He swallowed hard, "I, uh, got so unglued that I've neglected her. I haven't been much fun to live with lately."

"I'm not much better," Joy interjected. "It's amazing how easy it is to let a relationship slide. Even a good marriage like ours isn't immune."

Alexander nodded. "People are an interesting package. There's the physical side—the most obvious. And the emotional side—the most fragile. And the spiritual side—the most often neglected. Picture a three-legged stool. If a rodent gnaws away at one leg, the stool will soon totter. The way we compensate is to chop off the other legs to make it level. What we really should do is repair the leg that's in trouble. Otherwise we'll end up with a very short stool," he ended with an ironic smile.

Rachel spoke softly. "You have been trying to keep Frank and Helen from tottering, but at the same time you've had a nasty rodent, as it were, nipping at your marriage. I think you've held up amazingly well under dreadful conditions."

"We've learned a lot this summer," Al said. "Mostly about ourselves. It's been a good heads-up for us."

"We've had a lonesome summer. At first I thought it was because we lost two friends, but after spending the time on this trip alone with Al, I know my loneliness is because I've missed *us*. It's staggering how isolating pain can be."

Al stroked Joy's hair. "It's too bad the two of you haven't been in Prairie Rose—the whole town could use a dose of your contagious loving!"

The older couple smiled at each other and Rachel said, "Even though Alexander and I have only been married a few days, we each had a long happy marriage on which to pattern our new life together. We know storms will come. After all, Alexander married a woman in the advanced stages of multiple sclerosis."

"And Rachel got a fellow who regularly loses his reading glasses, and who goes into an dismal funk if he does poorly on a crossword puzzle! But seriously, storms have a way of either knocking us down, or making us stronger. Rachel and I will buttress each other against the worst life can toss at us. Hey, enough serious talk for the moment; let's have wedding cake!"

"Sounds good. How about going out for breakfast tomorrow? Our treat," Al suggested as they followed Rachel's wheelchair into the kitchen. "All Joy told me about this trip would fit in a teaspoon, but surely I can make breakfast plans!"

"Let me fill in a few gaps," Alexander said. "When Joy contacted us about coming down, we reserved the building's guest apartment. As for breakfast, your offer is accepted. Rachel and I require a bit more get-up-and-go time in the mornings than you young folks do, so breakfast out is always a perfect suggestion."

Seated around the kitchen table, they reminisced while time sped by. Joy was surprised to see a familiar teapot on the table. "I packed pretty quickly, but remembered several treasures from my house in Prairie Rose!" Rachel said with a twinkle in her eye. "This teapot is special—it was a gift from Charlotte and Alexander when Randolph and I married. I thought it fitting to grace our table here."

"And you're sitting beneath one of Rachel's embroidered pieces—the Lindquist's gift to Charlotte and me when our son, Charles, was born." Al and Joy looked at the framed linen piecework hanging on the wall above Joy's head: *Love forms the truest foundation, the strongest walls, the safest roof, and the widest door—turning a house into a home.*

"You made one for Alex and Tori, didn't you, Rachel?" Joy asked. "I've seen it in the Rectory."

"Yes, I gave one to Charles and Jessica for a wedding gift, and they not only kept it all these years, but asked me to continue the tradition for Alex and Tori."

The teakettle's whistle intruded, and the conversation shifted topics. Rachel mentioned Joy's retirement, and Alexander asked Al, "How's that going to feel in September when Joy stays home and sends you off to work?"

"Maybe she won't be sending me anywhere. I'm giving serious thought to quitting at the Post Office, though it's not something I've announced yet."

Doc nodded thoughtfully. "Understood. Interesting that you bring it up; Rachel and I have talked about you in that regard, Al."

"You have?"

Rachel replied, "One day we were analyzing how people in Prairie Rose got into their current jobs. Hal Harsted's dad passed

THE GENERAL STORE on to him, the same with LARSON'S GROCERY and for several other businesses. I think what got us started was talking about how gratifying it is that Alexander's clinic has reopened with his grandson at the helm, even though Charles chose another career path."

"Then, we got around to the Post Office on our mental tour of Main Street and remembered that you, Al, had come to Prairie Rose frequently on trips home from college with Frank. We commented how remarkable it was you were interested in the position in the first place and that you've held the position as long as you have. What did you study in college, Al? I'm sorry I don't recall."

"I graduated from NDSU with a business degree. Many years ago, now."

The older man's eyes brightened. "What a marvelously adaptable degree! Think of the things you can do with it."

"You and Joy are at such an exciting time of life..." Rachel leaned forward, "...still young enough for adventure, and not too old for change!"

Joy smiled. "You model perfectly how that stage of life can go on for a long time."

"Rachel and I think young," Alexander said. "This reminds me of something from Tori's wedding homily. She told us, 'Even if your bodies need a rocking chair or a wheelchair, never clip the wings on your love—let it soar!' And that's what we plan to do. That's what your career-change plans could do—allow you to soar together."

"Everything you say makes perfect sense—it's just a little scary," Joy mused and then shook off those thoughts and continued, "It's wonderful Tori performed your wedding ceremony. She has always loved you, Rachel, and now you're her grandmother-in-law!"

"I'm delighted to gain such wonderful grandchildren," Rachel beamed. "Randolph and I had many children-of-the-heart over the years, but this is one step better."

"Everyone will be so jazzed about your marriage!" Al said. "When will you let the word out?"

"Alex and Tori want to host a reception when we come back in September since we insisted on keeping our wedding a private affair. Only Alex's family was present, and I asked my old friend, Father O'Donovan, to stand in as my family," Rachel said. "It worked out well for Charles and Jessica to 'just happen' to be in town for the Fourth. Everyone kept our secret, so we ask you to do the same. Fred Becker will be the next to find out when we send him an announcement and photograph in a couple of weeks."

The rest of the visit flowed past like a swiftly moving river with splashes of laughter, quiet tide pools of conversation, and the surprising splats of water against hidden boulders of emotion. Alone in the guest apartment Monday night, Al and Joy went out on the lanai to enjoy the last shards of daylight. With feet propped up on the railing, they held hands and leaned back against the wicker love seat. "It's a beautiful evening," Al said, at last.

"Hmmm?" Joy didn't even turn toward him.

"I said, 'Elephants fly and pigs whistle.'"

"Hmmm." Joy nodded and squeezed his hand.

"What's going on in that pretty little head? Joy?" Al jiggled her hand until she looked his way.

"I'm sorry—what were you saying?"

"What's wrong?"

A cloud shifted and one last lavender blaze of evening sun shone through, illuminating Joy's face. "Almost anyone would have felt their troubles drift away after spending time with Doc and Rachel—even getting out of town helped. But now we're going back, and I'm scared, Al."

"It all scares me, too, Jinglebells. And that's what will keep us holding on to each other—knowing that we're in this together. This summer has shaped us, like wind sculpts a tree."

Joy released a sigh. "I was sort of feeling like how wind uproots a tree."

"Pretty hard to do when two trees grow together like we have. Look at that sunset—come here." He held out his hand and led her to the railing. His chin bumping against her head, he whispered, "Before God and His magnificent creation, I, Al Jenkins, do solemnly swear I will nurture our roots and protect our branches, 'til death do us part."

She responded tremulously, "I, Joy Jenkins, do solemnly swear before God and all He has made to water our roots deeply and prune our branches gently so our marriage can not only survive but provide shelter, 'til death do us part."

With glimmers of lavender haze lighting the way, Al led Joy inside. When night's purple robe swept over the horizon, they reached for each other and found solid ground.

After packing the car on Tuesday morning. Joy whispered to Alexander as said farewell, "We've got our bearings again. Thanks so much, Doc."

"Don't sell yourself short, Joy," he murmured. "You are a wise woman and a wonderful wife."

Behind them, Al talked with Rachel on the sidewalk. "I know you and Doc will have much happiness."

"As will you and Joy," Rachel said sagely. "It often takes a shake-up to make a good thing better."

A few blocks from downtown, Al stopped for a red light. "Look around us, Joy," he laughed.

"What's with all these RVs?"

"Must be an RV park nearby! Let's follow them and see."

Within minutes, they drove through the gates of a shaded and completely full park. All sizes and shapes of vehicles occupied the spaces. Some had towed cars or special trailers with motorcycles and even one golf cart. Each space showed individuality: a tabletop grill, or a dog on a leash, or a square of indoor-outdoor carpet beneath the steps, or a welcome sign stuck in the ground. Al drove slowly along each nubbin of road that formed a maze through the park.

"Do you believe this? It's a little town! Let's go see what the office is like."

They walked out half an hour later with their arms full of information. They had maps denoting other RV parks—but noticed very few anywhere near Prairie Rose. They had membership information for clubs they had had no idea even existed. They had a tri-fold brochure listing the Rochester park's amenities, rules and regulations.

Leaning against the car reading, Joy's mind hummed. *No clothesline allowed? Why can't each space have one provided? Pets can't run free? Why not fence in an area where pets could roam?* "Al," she said tentatively, "you know something? I think we could do this."

"What about all those wires tying you down?"

"No, I mean *this.*" She waved back at the office. "We could be managers at an RV park."

Al looked at the office, turned back to Joy's expectant face, looked around the park, back at the office, and finally pulled Joy, brochures and all, into a giant bear hug. "Jinglebells," he chortled, "you might just have the all-time winner of an idea. There's a big, wide world out there, just waiting for us!" He twirled her around.

"Al, stop it! We're dropping important stuff all over the ground!"

Whistling with a full accompaniment of finger snapping, Al scooped up all the papers and clutched them to his chest as he sang out, "*...king of the road!*" He repeated the beat with tongue clicks. "You know where our RV park could be, don't you?"

"Are you thinking about a certain deserted old farm, just under ten miles from town?"

"Yup!"

"Does that mean you're willing to stay in one place?"

"If you're willing to give up our home, I'm willing to do anything that gives me a new challenge, and this sounds like it fits the bill."

She flew into his arms and kissed him hungrily. Pulling away when she realized they were visible from several campsites, she said softly, "If you're happy, I'm happy. Doc said a true thing: you have many untapped skills. This idea gives them a chance to shine." Even with people looking on, they couldn't help it—they did a giddy dance right on the tarmac between a pop-up trailer from Texas and a full-blown Class A from Indiana. Holding hands, they walked slowly through the park, noting details they had missed earlier.

Between Rochester and home, they alternately drove and read aloud from their stash of information. In all, they pulled off to drive through four more RV parks, finding each unique and yet equally interesting.

Close to midnight, they arrived back home. "Thanks for such a perfect vacation, Joybells." Al kissed her knuckles as they drove along their quiet street. "Just when I was wondering what I do it all for—the postage stamps, the daily grind and all—suddenly there's a reason again."

"I'm glad you'll be able to just walk out those ol' Post Office doors someday and wander…all around the Lazy Meadows RV Park," she added impishly.

Al turned into their driveway. "The Lazy Meadows, huh?"

"What do you think?"

"I think it will make me grin…and want to spread a blanket on the ground every time I see the sign!"

Chapter 10

Throughout the next week, Main Street buzzed. Several commented around café tables about how Sadie seemed like the cat that swallowed the canary. Others pumped Milt for details about the vacant building next to the D CURL. He offered nothing informative, and seemed less enthusiastic about the SOLD sign in the window than one would expect of the realtor who had landed the unlikely sale of a building that had never had a prospective buyer.

Al called Joy one morning and insisted she drop everything and come down to the Post Office immediately. "Nothing bad, but it's so good I don't want anyone overhearing. And I sure can't wait until noon!"

"On my way," Joy assured him. She was at the Post Office in three minutes.

Al came out to the lobby. "Okay, here's the deal. You know how the best thing about this plan is that our family can work together?"

Joy nodded, unsure what was ahead, but certain she didn't want to quell Al's excitement.

"What's Dave's biggest concern?"

Edith Winthrop swooped through the door and Al warned, "Don't you dare start talking to her or she'll never leave!" He killed time straightening the fliers on the wall rack and Joy scanned the bulletin board while Edith methodically sorted her mail into two piles. Finally, she packed her bag, picked up her cane and left.

Al barely reached Joy's side before the door opened again and three people paraded into the lobby. Al threw up in his hands in disgust and pulled Joy into the office. Whispering in her ear, he blurted out his idea and pulled back to look into her face. "Pretty good one, huh? Almost on a par with yours about…*us*," he added.

She nodded thoughtfully. "I'll say! I'll swing by the café and invite Cate and Luke for dessert tonight."

Joy hummed happily for the rest of the day. The only wrinkle in the plan was having Dave around during the discussion but they could hardly banish him to his room. "Oh, well, it will work out," she said aloud as she set the pie on a cooling rack.

Luke and Cate pushed a baby stroller up the sidewalk at 7:00 o'clock that evening and Dave sprang off the porch where he waited with Al and Joy. "Can I take Juddie for a ride? I wouldn't push him over any potholes, or anything."

"Absolutely, Dave," Cate said. "Just be sure to pick up anything he throws away! He's pretty sneaky!"

"Perfect," Joy whispered to herself, hiding a grin.

With raspberry pie dished up, Al approached the subject from what seemed to be a back road. First, he introduced the point of his job change. When Luke and Cate had absorbed this shock, he filled them in on the developing plans for an RV park on the nearby farm. Finally, he brought up the most important topic of all. "Our family is looking forward to working together. That means Dave will be quitting at the grocery store in a few months."

"He's a great guy," Luke said, still reeling from all he'd heard. "I'll miss him," he added with simple sincerity. "Can I tell you something? The timing on this whole thing is mind-boggling. I've been struggling with how to talk to you about something I've been tossing around in my head for months—and then you come up with the solution. As Tori points out in almost every sermon, God really does have the big picture of our lives in mind!"

"What do you mean?" Al asked.

Luke said, "I've been trying to figure out how I could keep Dave on—and still follow through with a dream I've had."

"What's that?"

"I'd really like to hire Eric Carter to work with me in the store. And I can certainly carry both him and Dave for a few months."

Al and Joy looked at each other, back at their guests. Their smiles turned to chuckles and quickly transformed into outright howls of laughter. When he could talk again, Al said, "We really ought to stand up and belt out a quartet version of *He's Got the Whole World in His Hands* right here and now! That's precisely what this invitation for pie tonight is all about—we were going to suggest that you hire Eric!"

"You've got to be kidding!" Luke said. He and Cate joined in the laughter. Wiping tears from his eyes, Luke said, "Actually, one big delay in the store expansion has been getting the help. We're pretty small potatoes for the crews in Minot or Williston, but with Eric's skills, he could start working on the addition to the store and transition into grocery store employee as he completes other jobs he's promised to do."

Dave and Juddie returned at that point and joined them around the table. Al and Luke took turns talking about the idea of Eric coming on-board at the store and Dave took it all in stride. "I'll show him where stuff is in the supply room, but you'd better teach him how to use the cash register, Luke. You did a good job teaching me."

"Thanks, Dave," Luke said, and the evening ended without a single cloud marring the horizon.

Word soon leaked out that the Jenkins had plans, big plans. Once Al gave the okay, Dave could hardly quit talking about it all. Each conversation usually included extensive details about the riding mower. He eagerly awaited each trip to the farm, was itching to pack up and move, and all set to resign his job.

"Slow down, son! It's going to take us several months to get everything processed. We have to get all the licenses and permits required to put an RV park on that property, and we're still working out financial details. The guys in our family need to keep on going to our old jobs for a few more months so we can sock away more money for our big dream."

"But," Joy interjected, seeing Dave's face fall, "there are lots of things we can do while we wait for those pokey things to happen. We should draw out a big map of how we want the place to look. I want to put in a children's play area, and a fenced pet-run, and lots and lots of flowers. And we'll put up a permanent clothesline for each space. Plus, we'll need to get this house ready to sell. Once we move to the farm, we'll be busy fixing it up."

"And we've got to get the riding lawn mower," Dave added, joining in his parents' burst of laughter.

"How 'bout if we set a goal of opening the Lazy Meadows RV Park in time for the Fourth of July next year?" Dave raced to get a calendar, circled the date, and gave high-fives all around. Suddenly, the dream seemed real.

Frank continued to show up at the D CURL each morning. Clients sat in his chair, but conversation was sparse and formal. "It's like walking into a field of land mines," Ed told a customer at the garage. "If I talk to Frank, I feel like a traitor to Helen; if I talk to Helen, I'm afraid Frank will clip my ears!"

Helen canceled the interns and appeared to have accepted her lot in life, though she remained tight-lipped about the horrors of working beside her faithless husband every day. At five o'clock each day, she gathered up the money, divided out Frank's share—having kept a careful tally of his day's work—and disappeared into the apartment. Frank's mood darkened each time he heard the locks engage. First, a bar slid into place, then the knob button clicked. He always flinched as yet a third lock dropped. Helen's message was clear: *Keep out.*

Each night he walked home and disappeared into his house, leaving neighbors to wonder at his unseen activities. He lurched along behind the lawn mower each week, and other than haphazardly mown grass, nothing else seemed to change around the place. Frank never sat out on the steps, the picnic table collected bird droppings, the gutters filled with leaves and the birdbath sat empty except when it rained. Dave reported that the only things he bought at the grocery store were TV dinners. What he ate the rest of the time was a mystery because he rarely stopped by the café. Besides an occasional trip to see Doctor Alex, Frank was like a ghost who was only seen at work.

The day Sadie ripped July off her kitchen calendar, the phone rang. Mildred's voice was shrill with unrestrained excitement, "She's back!"

"Who is?" Sadie asked, miffed at being the recipient, rather than the relater, of any such news.

"Blyss Hathaway! You won't believe what she's doing!"

Ah ha! My moment has come. Sadie moistened her lips and said coolly, "I imagine she's moving into her store. Books, isn't it?"

Mildred gasped, "You knew? How on earth could you know? I just talked with her this morning, and she said she arrived during the night!"

In her kitchen, Sadie smiled smugly. "I have my ways." She sat down, waiting for her heart to cease its wild palpitations. *I'm the only one who learned about the building sale from Milt's clipboard. All this time, I've kept my own counsel.*

Mildred still had one card to play. "I want to tell you my news. Blyss has hired me for three days to help her unpack. I start today—goodness, I must get ready!"

Sadie's heart thumped like a drummer gone wild. It was all she could do to say coolly, "Thank you for calling, Mildred."

After a morning of pacing, Sadie knew she could not stay home another minute. It was one thing to *know* something, and quite another to *see* it. She needed to see. Choosing the straw hat with the widest brim to shade her inquisitive eyes, Sadie marched off toward Main Street, zeroing in on the freshly painted storefront with a sign above the door: BOOKS AND BLYSS.

Sadie peered in the window, memorizing all she saw: sparkling walls, floor-to-ceiling wooden shelves, good lighting. And Blyss busily opening boxes. She wore Capri pants with a leopard print and a matching blouse with its tails knotted at the waist. Her hair was tied atop her head with strands of white, black and yellow yarn, with ringlets escaping prettily all around her ears and neck. Sadie squinted. *Are those diamonds in her ears...and on her wrist...and on her fingers? Why, she's just begging to be robbed!*

Stacks of still-packed boxes towered beside Blyss. A stack of flattened empties filled a corner. Coming around a freestanding bookcase was none other than Mildred. *Happily employed Mildred. Smack-dab-in-the-middle-of-everything Mildred.* Mortally wounded, Sadie bemoaned every word and action that prevented her from being able to expect the welcome Mildred enjoyed.

Defeated, she backed away from the window and began a slow journey home. Just then, Petey rode by on his bicycle. "Petey!" she called out sharply.

The boy applied the brakes and looked back over his shoulder, uncertain as to what crime would be levied against him. "Yes, Widow O'Dell?" he asked, dread shadowing each syllable.

Sadie improvised on the spot. "Come to my house in fifteen minutes. I have an errand for you."

"Will I need my wagon?" Petey asked hopefully. "If I do, I charge an extra nickel because it's hard work to pull a wagon."

"Heavens, no!" Sadie's nostrils flared. "You charge quite enough as it is."

Bewildered, Petey watched her leave. Not having a watch, he decided the best bet was to follow the woman home and wait out of sight until it seemed enough time had passed. Eight long minutes later, Petey took a deep gulp of air and knocked timidly on Sadie's front door.

"So soon?" she said sternly through the screen door. "Just sit on the step and wait. I'm not ready yet. It's just as rude to be early as it is to be late, young man."

"Sorry, Ma'am," Petey sighed and sat back down.

Inside, Sadie petted her cat with such ferocity that the animal protested with mournful tones and leapt from her lap. Sadie had yet to decide precisely what it was she would ask Petey to do. She needed something to ensure Mildred would desert her coveted front-and-center position. Finally, she plucked a quarter from the sugar bowl and walked swiftly to the front door. Petey sprang into action.

"Go to the new store next to the D CURL. Ask Missus Windsor to come out to the sidewalk. Once she's outside, tell her I have somewhat of an emergency and I require her assistance immediately. Do not let Blyss Hathaway hear you. Mind you don't lose this quarter, because you won't get another one."

"Shall I whisper in Missus Windsor's ear so that other lady won't hear me?"

"Don't be ridiculous, Petey!" Sadie snapped. "The part I don't want spread around is about, uh, my emergency situation."

"Should I get Doctor Alex, too?" Petey asked helpfully. "I'd do it for the same quarter because the Clinic is right across the street."

"Mercy, no! Did I say anything about it being a medical emergency? Get along with you!"

While Sadie worked speedily to create a genuine emergency situation, Petey pedaled off and delivered the confusing message to Mildred Windsor. Sensing her skepticism, he added for good measure, "And don't tell Blyss Hathaway a single word I said. Widow O'Dell *pacifically* said that."

Torn between the enticement of being the sole member of Blyss Hathaway's temporary staff and the responsibilities accompanying a life-long friendship-of-sorts with Sadie, it was a flustered Mildred who scurried along the sidewalk. By the time she reached the house, she had conjured up the worst: Sadie attacked by a rabid squirrel, or Sadie scalded by a pot of boiling oatmeal, or Sadie pinned to the ground by a fallen tree. With such dramatic imagined scenarios, it was rather disconcerting to have Sadie calmly open the door and escort a flushed Mildred into the living room.

"What is it, Sadie? Petey said you're having an emergency, but you look fine," Mildred said crossly.

"It's an embarrassing situation. I've caught my underslip in my zipper and can't get out of my dress."

"Forevermore, Sadie. I declare; why are you changing clothes at this time of day, anyway?" Mildred scolded. "I don't consider this an emergency at all—certainly not enough of one to interrupt a busy person."

"Oh? You were busy?" Sadie queried guilelessly.

"I was helping Blyss Hathaway, which you must have known—you sent Petey to get me," she said shrewdly.

Sadie's heart sank. "I asked Petey to get you. He might have seen you through the store window," she said vaguely. "The boy does get around town on that bicycle of his," she added with a shallow laugh.

Luckily, Mildred's mind was occupied elsewhere. "I can't sit and gab. Let me see that zipper."

Panicked, Sadie plunged into murky waters. "I feel quite faint from all my attempts to get the zipper undone. Please just sit with me for a few minutes until I regain my energy. Tell me about the new store."

Mildred was happy to oblige. "It's more than just a store. Blyss will live upstairs. It's quite nice, the way she's fixing it up."

"Oh? She won't continue to live with Frank?"

"Not that she's said," Mildred admitted, woefully aware of how little she really knew. The only reason she knew Blyss even had an apartment upstairs was because she had been invited upstairs for a most interesting lunch—the oddest sandwiches, flavorful but totally foreign to Mildred's white-bread-and-tuna tastes.

"She plans to sell books, I believe," Sadie hinted broadly to prod Mildred along.

"Yes, she has thousands of books—she says they are like her family, but she's willing to sell them in hopes of elevating the social conscience of Prairie Rose. She plans to have several comfortable chairs and reading lamps and even a desk stocked with paper and pens if someone wishes to copy down a poem or some particularly meaningful quotation." Blithely, Mildred offered that direct quote from Blyss as if it sprang from her own thoughts. "By winter, she will have a wood-burning stove for a homey touch."

"I, for one, do not plan to darken the door to her store," Sadie said adamantly. "Imagine the germs lurking on those books—California is a veritable haven for germs. And who knows what, uh-hem," she leaned forward until she almost tipped out of her chair, "...*sexual diseases* can be communicated from the pages of a book."

Mildred gasped and examined the hands she had so recklessly plunged into dozens of boxes of germ-laden books directly from California.

"Come along," Sadie sniffed. "You can wash your hands with disinfectant soap."

It was a much-enlightened Mildred who walked slowly back to the perilous environment of BOOKS AND BLYSS. But working side-by-side with the enigmatic and possibly hazardous shopkeeper, Mildred found it hard to remember Sadie's warnings. There was lovely music playing, and not always music—sometimes soothing sounds like water babbling over stones, or the graceful calls of birds, or wind in the trees. And Blyss spoke of essays and poetry, epics and monographs, as if Mildred knew the works of those whose names flitted through the conversation as if they were neighbors or friends.

Then, there were the books—so enticing with their gold-lettered spines and shimmering covers. Richly bound hard-back classics, and slick paperbacks. Novels, mysteries, romances, adventures and tales of true crime emerged from the boxes, each more inviting than the last. Even the children's section intrigued Mildred with its assortment of shiny new books and plenty of gently read titles.

Never much of a reader, Mildred's entire collection of books could have fit into a shoebox. How she envied Blyss. To actually have such a business, to know so much about so many things, and to rattle off great chunks of poetic lines. When Blyss offered her employee a particularly appealing cookbook as a gift, Mildred cast off Sadie and her tales of doom like an old coat.

Blyss had hooked her first customer.

The next morning, the front door to BOOKS AND BLYSS opened at the same time as the D CURL. Fred Becker felt like a traitor walking past the warring Wilson duo on his way to interview the village's newest entrepreneur, but business is business and in the newspaper world, news is news.

Despite having chosen the work-out look that morning, complete with sweats, a T-shirt, tennis shoes and white socks, her ponytail swinging wildly and glasses dangling on a cord around her neck, Blyss proved be an engaging conversationalist, giving Fred the best interview he ever recalled. It didn't take any extra effort on his part to take a perfect picture of Blyss holding a stack of books—she had no bad side, apparently.

At her insistence, he carried home an armload of paperbacks, delighted with the selection and impressed by the quality of all he had seen. These details would figure prominently in his article, as would her previously unannounced service of ordering books. Not only did she offer best sellers—both new and used—and old favorites at reasonable prices, but she had a whole shelf of well-preserved Zane Gray books. *Oh, my!*

Granted, Fred could have buried the story on page three, but in a four-page paper, that hardly qualifies as interred. So, he ran the story front-and-center. Townsfolk read every word and drowned the pinpricks of interest with righteous indignation.

Helen gripped the newspaper until her nails sliced holes in it. With a low growl like a jungle beast, she flung the paper aside and stormed next door. She flung open the front door and balanced on the threshold. Blyss looked up and the two women faced off. Helen's upper lip curled; Blyss' eyes narrowed slowly. Helen opened her lips and worked her jaws. Blyss stepped forward. Helen held her ground.

"May I help you?" Blyss asked coolly.

Helen's mind recorded every detail. *So, now she's a cowgirl in red-framed glasses. All she needs is a horse. Brimmed straw hat with a feather, braids, jeans, western shirt and wide leather belt with a big fat buckle—and even a bandana sticking out of her back pocket. Enough silver-and-turquoise jewelry to weigh her down if a big wind blows through town. Louis L'Amour, where are you?*

Grasping the door to control her trembling, Helen demanded, "What is it you want? Do you want Frank? Take him—you've already branded him."

Blyss turned an icy gaze on Helen. "I don't want Frankie. Frankie wants me."

"So that's your game? Once you get something, you don't want it anymore?"

"Frankie's a fool. I don't endure fools."

"So why are you here? Why did you come back?"

"I didn't realize a person had to have an invitation to live here."

"Answer my question: why are you here? Who's next on your list of marriages to destroy?"

"There is no list. Frankie found me."

Helen's stomach lurched. She jerked back as if slapped. When she closed the door, the bottom scraped across her big toe, ripping at her toenail and grinding at the skin. By the time she reached the shop, her sandal was bloody and she was leaving a trail. Limping, she brushed past a flabbergasted Frank and walked across the shop to her apartment.

Sitting on the edge of the bathtub, she ran cold water over her foot and dropped her head to her knees. Tears ran down her leg and mingled with the pink-tinged water swirling around her feet. When she had cried herself dry of tears, she bandaged her toe and walked out to her car parked in the alley and drove out of town.

When she returned to the shop mid-afternoon, Frank waited for an explanation that never came. She simply picked up her scissors, looked around the room. "Who's next?"

* * * *

A few teens, intrigued by the music coming out the open door, wandered into BOOKS AND BLYSS during the days Blyss worked alone. They often stayed, snared by how Blyss treated them like adults who had interesting things to say. When she posted a list of required reading for freshman at NDSU and mentioned she simply adored discussing literature, they practically fought over copies of Dickens and Hemingway. It became difficult to spot a teenager without a paperback in hand.

Tiring of pointless conversations about strange words people had heard Blyss use, Cate brought a dictionary from home and propped it up next to the cash register. When someone pondered whether *sericeous* was insulting or merely descriptive, or under what conditions one could correctly accuse another of *chiasmus,* she merely handed over the dictionary. Some days it sounded more like a vocabulary drill at CATE'S CAFÉ than in Mister Garrett's sixth-grade classroom.

Feeding Juddie strained carrots one evening, Cate commented to Luke while he grilled chicken breasts, "I despise all that brought Blyss to town, but she's certainly rattled a few cages, which isn't a bad thing. She seems totally unconcerned with being an oddity. Insults, and worse, run off her like water off a duck. Justin got people thinking about new possibilities; she's got people taking a new look at themselves."

"How long do you think she'll survive without friends?"

"I don't know, but I admire her spunk."

"There's plenty of chicken. Shall we invite her for supper?" Luke asked.

Cate wrinkled her nose. "Ooo, that would really hurt Helen. Better not, Luke, but I love you for thinking of it. Ask Tori at your Leadership Meeting tonight how to solve this dilemma." She wiped Juddie's chin. "On second thought, don't. She's got the same problems we do with this whole thing. Whatever's right to do will surface."

Blyss seemed in no big hurry to officially open her store. She worked steadily, filling shelves, adding to the window display. One Monday, a poster on the store's bulletin board announced *Resumes—Secrets and Pitfalls. Thursday night. 7:00-9:00. Sign up here.* It seemed like Mecca to the teens, all longing for the day they would actually need a resume. The list filled in one morning.

Then, Blyss pulled out all the stops. Main Street was crowded with locals and out-of-towners all eager to shop at the SATURDAY STORE where the weekly business was a craft store. That's when Petey hit the streets. He distributed brochures announcing a children's story hour. From early morning until 10:00 o'clock, he pedaled around town, inviting all his friends to bring their siblings and accosting total strangers with young children in tow: "She's a real good storyteller." If he met with any hint of resistance, he added, apropos of nothing: "She looks goofy sometimes, but she doesn't live with Mister Wilson anymore."

So, while mothers learned how to appliqué, and fathers roamed the feed store or ate doughnuts at CATE'S CAFÉ, children filled every inch of floor space at BOOKS AND BLYSS and gave rapt attention to Blyss and her cast of teens who acted out stories. Laughter poured out the open front door. Each child received a bookmark listing books similar to the morning's stories. But most importantly of all—each child left bearing a coupon for a free used book for their parents.

Every parent—even the locals who would have loved to hate Blyss—cashed in that coupon by three o'clock. The prices being so reasonable, considering Blyss had essentially provided childcare for an hour, it seemed a shame to just grab a free book and run, so many lingered, humming along with the music, sampling shortbread cookies, and finally taking a stack of books to the library table Blyss used as her check-out counter.

When Blyss cashed out at the end of her first day of actual business, she smiled.

But next door, at the D CURL, things weren't quite as pleasant. Frank continued to entertain the notion that if he kept coming to work, eventually Helen would relent and they would live happily ever after. For her part, ever since her trip to BOOKS AND BLYSS, Helen had retreated into a zone of silence. She still directed no conversation to Frank, but now ceased acknowledging his arrival or departure with even so much as a glance. If their paths crossed outside of work, she looked right through him. When Tina and Robyn came to visit, they usually had dinner at Helen's apartment, drove to the house for unbelievably short visits with Frank, and left without seeing anyone else.

Not one of the Wilson clan could be considered happy.

As the days leaned toward Labor Day like dominoes ready to fall, Ed sat in the café and ran his hand over a fresh haircut and stared into space. Finally, a tablemate chided him, "You planning on talking today, Ed? Or are we supposed to play Twenty Questions to get a word out of you?"

Ed smiled vaguely at the jibing. "Frank's got himself in a real pickle, doesn't he? Helen's not budging an inch, Blyss has lost interest, and he's stuck in an empty house. Guy's gotta be miserable."

Charlie twirled his empty coffee cup in a circle on the table and drawled, "Appears to me, he's smack-dab in the middle between Blyss and Hiss." That got a brief laugh, most of those present having brushed up against the icy wall between Frank and Helen, but it felt uncomfortable to find humor in such distress.

"How can Blyss make a living selling books here?"

"Word is, she paid cash for the building. So, if she already had most of those books out in California, her only expense so far was getting them here. And Saturdays are good days for her. Who knows?"

"Strange, isn't it, how different it felt when Justin opened the SATURDAY STORE," Mitchell mused. "And I'm not saying that because Lewis and I are managers. I'd be just as happy if the store Blyss bought had stayed empty. But we've all spent our time moaning and groaning about the town dying off. And here someone opens a store and we sort of forget she's a taxpayer now."

"She's looking pretty contended these days," Floyd said. "I suppose she figures, come winter, we'll all get anxious to have something to read during the long winter nights and we'll come in with our wallets open."

"I think we ought to have a town meeting and set some guidelines for new businesses coming to town," groused Bernie.

"That's locking the barn door a bit too late. The only rule I can imagine we'd be able to come up with would be no more home-wreckers setting up shop. And how often will *that* happen again?"

"Maybe she's selling pornography," suggested Edith. "Then we could shut her down."

"She's not selling pornography," Cate interrupted in her well-known no-nonsense voice. "Those shelves are loaded with quality literature, best sellers, old-time favorites, and dozens of books for kids and teens. It would be very hard to run her out of town on any basis right now. After all, she's living alone over her store."

"So what you're saying, Cate, is we haven't got a leg to stand on."

"Bingo. I vote we give Blyss a chance, just like we would give every other visitor, especially since she appears to have turned over a new leaf." Never one to let harsh words settle in too deeply, she added in a kinder tone, "Who wants a fresh doughnut? Anyone who promises to buy a book at BOOKS AND BLYSS today gets it at half-price. Take the quarter you save here and put it towards a used book. Just don't tell Blyss how you saved that quarter!" She caught a few nervous glances and winked reassuringly.

Within the hour, Blyss sold a dozen paperbacks and never knew why.

*   *   *   *

Since their return from Rochester, Al and Joy had developed a new habit. Each evening they settled in on their porch swing with a three-ring notebook between them. They jotted down notes in any of the multiple sections, edited previous entries, and talked endlessly. Sometimes their conversation was sprinkled with laughter; sometimes they fell silent, each contemplating the other's ideas and concerns.

"I like it, because it will be a family business, it's something Dave could help us with, and we have good ideas that will improve on some places we've seen. Things are coming along so well, it's almost scary."

"So, instead of Al Jenkins, postmaster, and Joy Jenkins, retired schoolteacher, we'll soon be Al and Joy Jenkins, On-Site Owners of the Lazy Meadows RV Park."

"And don't forget, Dave Jenkins, groundskeeper."

"Absolutely. I'm glad he's excited about the idea, too. He'll be in charge of grass, shrubbery, trees—all that stuff." Joy pressed a finger against her lips thoughtfully.

"Oh, oh—I know that look! What's on your mind?"

"I'm trying to imagine what kind of an image would portray a lazy meadow. We need a logo for our signs and such."

"How about a rumpled blanket under a big old shade tree—with all sorts of field animals looking at it with their mouths hanging open and…" Al's voice faded as he looked beyond Joy.

She turned and felt a chill.

Frank stood outside their gate. "Is Helen here yet?" he asked.

"Helen?" Joy echoed.

"Yeah; she called and said to meet her here."

"When was that?" Al asked.

"About five minutes ago."

"She's not here." Al rose slowly from the swing. "Come in," he invited belatedly. The words were right, but the tone lacked the warmth of a true welcome.

The next few moments were awkward. Frank pulled a blade of grass and shredded it into thin strands, only to toss them aside. Joy bit her lip and watched for Helen. Al said a little too loudly, "I'll get lawn chairs from the back."

"No!" Joy said sharply, her color high. "Let's sit back there—it's, uh, cooler." *And out of prying neighbors' sight.*

Al caught her point and nodded. "So, how's it going, Frank?" he asked, at last.

"Could be better, could be worse, I guess," Frank said woodenly. "I'm working, you know."

"I know. You cut my hair last Saturday," Al reminded him.

"Yeah, right."

"So you're still on crutches," Al said, grasping at conversational straws. "How's your leg?"

"Fine." Frank's grip tightened on the handholds. Again, the awkward silence.

"How are the girls doing?" Joy asked a little too brightly.

"Fine, I guess," his voice trailed off sadly.

"Tell them to drop by next time they're in town. Oh, there's Helen!" Joy's relief was boundless. Helen swung the gate open and walked toward them.

"Come out back," Al said quickly and led the way before Helen could say a word.

They chose chairs and stared at each other. Helen took charge. "I'm sorry I didn't call, Jenks, before coming over…"

"No problem, Helen," Joy interrupted. "What's up?"

"I wanted witnesses for what I'm going to tell Frank."

Oh boy. Joy swallowed hard.

Is there going to be a fight? Al sighed.

At least she's talking. Frank sat up a little straighter.

Helen reached into her back pocket and pulled out an envelope. Frank automatically caught it when she tossed it in his direction. "That's the legal documents for a divorce. I'm leaving in the morning. I expect you to sell the house, Frank, and give me three-fourths of that money to cover my share of the shop, too. You can live in the apartment. Send the money to my lawyer and I'll get it from him."

A squirrel scolded them from overhead and they all jumped.

"Where are you going, Helen?" Joy asked, at last.

"I'd rather not say. If you need to reach me, contact my lawyer." She handed Joy a business card.

"I'm not living with Blyss anymore, Helen," Frank said pleadingly.

"No, you've got that wrong, Frank. It's Blyss who's not living with you anymore."

"I'd thought you and I could work things out."

"And I'd thought we would stay married until death do us part, Frank."

"I can't run the shop without you, Helen." His voice tottered between a whine and an entreaty.

"Then hire someone."

"I love you, Helen. I miss you. I'm sorry."

She held up one finger, "Love me? No, you don't." A second finger, "Miss me? No, you don't." A third finger. "*Sorry*? You're *sorry*? No, you're not. What you love is everything going your way; what you miss is anything going your way; what you're sorry about is that nothing's going your way. Guess what, Frank? You can live life however you want with no interference from me."

Frank's chin sank to his chest and he stared at the still unopened envelope in his hand.

"Jenks," Helen said, "I will miss you. This summer has been as dreadful for you as for me, and I'm sorry for that. I know you love me. Nothing you've done has forced this decision. Actually, Blyss helped me make it."

Three sets of startled eyes rose to meet Helen's forthright gaze. "Blyss did?" Joy stammered.

Helen merely nodded and stood up. "I'll be gone by noon." She walked several feet and halted. "Goodbye, Frank," she said without looking back. It sounded as final as a judge's gavel.

They heard the gate clank shut a minute later. Frank took in a shuddering gulp of air and leaned his head back against the chair. "I can't believe it's ending this way," he shook the envelope slowly. "Divorce."

"I think you need to go home now, Frank," Al said. "You've got a lot to think about, and Joy and I aren't in the mood to listen to you moan and groan about how rough you've got it. You're not the only walking wounded, you know."

Frank looked at them for a drawn-out moment and then eased himself into a standing position. "Just want you to know, I'm not proud of what I've done," he said and left, the personification of dejection.

Al held out his hand to Joy. They walked slowly back to the front porch. The basket with all its maps and notes seemed frivolous against the last hour. "I feel like Helen handed us divorce papers, too, Al," Joy said.

"In a way, she did. It's probably for the best—it will be easier for her to start a new life without old friends as constant reminders of what once was. Maybe someday it will be different. Right now, the greatest gift we can give her is to honor her wishes. We're moving on with our lives—and so is she."

"I want to take her something," Joy said resolutely.

"What?" Al asked.

"I don't know right now."

In the middle of a sleepless night, she sat up, crept out of bed, went downstairs and dug in her school boxes in the closet beneath the stairwell. After a few minutes, she found what she wanted. She went to the kitchen and selected a swan-shaped basket from the back of a cabinet and lined it with tissue paper, wrapped the two objects from her midnight search and tucked them into the basket.

Back upstairs, she crawled in next to Al and cried in his arms until she fell asleep.

The next morning, she called Petey. When he arrived, she paid him two quarters: one to give the basket directly to Helen, and the other to come back and tell her when the delivery was accomplished. The familiar basket would let Helen know the basket was from her, even without a note.

Within minutes, Petey returned to say, "She's got it, but I almost missed her. She was ready to drive away. Her car was loaded with tons of stuff. Oh, she said I'm supposed to tell you this." He screwed up his face and recited in a singsong voice, "*When my tears have come to an end.* That's all; she said you'd know the rest. But she wasn't crying or nothing, so that's a goofy thing to tell someone." He flung his hands in the air dramatically.

Joy promptly completed the lyrics from the old Chicago hit, "*…I will understand that I left behind part of me…*Oh, Petey, thank you." She leaned down and kissed the boy's cheek.

He wrinkled up his freckled nose and rubbed the back of one hand across his face. "You're welcome, Missus Jenkins. Now I've got to go take a pie from CATE'S CAFÉ to that new teacher, Missus Carter. If I don't drop it, I get to pick any cookie I want—plus, I get a quarter!"

*　　*　　*　　*

Helen kept her foot on the brake as she opened the first package, extracted a cassette tape, and inserted it in the car's tape deck. Closing her eyes, she leaned back against the seat's headrest for a moment, gripped the steering wheel and drove off. With the silhouetted images of Prairie Rose's grain elevators captured in the rear-view mirror, she turned on the tape deck. The song filling the car was what Petey sang as he sped through town:

I use my little compass to help me find my way.
If I get lost, I pull it out any time of day.

When I see where the needle goes,
That is where I'll point my nose…

Helen clutched the second package tightly in her hand until the children's voices faded into nothingness. Blindly, she pulled over to the side of the road, unwrapped and opened a small box. Pushing aside the paper, she lifted out the brass nautical compass that had graced Joy's school desk for twenty-two years and carefully placed in on the dashboard. Pulling back onto the road, she rewound the tape and played the song again. Her tear-laden voice joined the first graders on the final line: *Remember, north never moves.*

My Little Compass

0-595-24977-9

Printed in the United States
789400003B

9 780595 249770